Acclaim for Pat Barker's *Life* Class

"Pat Barker writes with clear, straightforward realism showing her debt to British writers such as D. H. Lawrence and George Orwell, and reserving a place for herself in English letters as the peacetime novelist who knows best how to write about war." —Alan Cheuse, NPR's *All Things Considered*

"Affecting. . . . *Life Class* contains confident echoes of Waugh and Forster." —*The Boston Globe*

"A complex page-turner." —*Time Out New York*

"Direct, unfussy, grounded, generous but never effusive." —*Financial Times*

"A testament to [Barker's] elegant style and psychological acuity. . . . The lessons in *Life Class* are deeply affecting and necessary." —*The Washington Post Book World*

"Few writers capture the debasing horror of what war does to men and women as well and as succinctly as Barker." —*San Jose Mercury News*

"This new work is masterful in conjuring a lost era. We smell and see these long-dead characters, once so young and quick." —*The Plain Dealer*

Pat Barker

Life Class

Pat Barker is the author of the highly acclaimed Regeneration trilogy: *Regeneration*; *The Eye in the Door*, winner of the Guardian Fiction Prize; and *The Ghost Road*, winner of the Booker Prize; as well as seven other novels. She lives in England.

ALSO BY PAT BARKER

Union Street
Blow Your House Down
Liza's England (*formerly* The Century's Daughter)
The Man Who Wasn't There

Regeneration
The Eye in the Door
The Ghost Road
(The Regeneration Trilogy)

Another World
Border Crossing
Double Vision

Life Class

Pat Barker

Anchor Books

A Division of Random House, Inc.

New York

FIRST ANCHOR BOOKS EDITION, JANUARY 2009

The Library of Congress has cataloged the Doubleday edition as follows:
Barker, Pat, 1943–
Life class / Pat Barker. —1st U.S. ed.
p. cm.
1. World War, 1914–1918—Hospitals—Fiction.
2. World War, 1914–1918—Psychological aspects—Fiction.
3. Human figure in art—Fiction.
4 Physicians as artists—Fiction. I. Title.
PR6052.A6488L54 2008
823'.914—dc22   2007040602

Anchor ISBN: 978-0-307-38780-6

Book design by Maria Carella

www.anchorbooks.com

Printed in the United States of America
10 9 8 7 6 5 4 3 2 1

For David

Part
One

1

THEY'D BEEN DRAWING FOR OVER HALF AN HOUR.
There was no sound except for the slurring of pencils on
Michelet paper or the barely perceptible squeak of charcoal. At
the center of the circle of students, close to the dais, a stove cast
a barred red light onto the floor. The smell of burning coke mingled with other smells: sweat, hot cloth, cigar and tobacco
smoke. Now and again you could hear the soft pop of lips inhal-
ing and another plume of blue smoke would rise to join the pall
that hung over the whole room.

Nobody spoke. You were not allowed to talk in the life class.
In the Antiques Room, where they spent the mornings copying
from casts of Classical and Renaissance sculpture, talking was permitted, and the students—a few of the women, in particular—
chattered nonstop. Here, apart from the naked woman on the dais,
the atmosphere was not unlike a men's club. The women students
had their own separate life class somewhere on the lower floor.
Even the Slade, scandalously modern in most respects, segregated
the sexes when the naked human body was on display.

Paul Tarrant, sitting on the back row, as far away from the
stove as he could get, coughed discreetly into his handkerchief.

He was still struggling to throw off the bronchitis that had plagued him all winter and the fumes irritated his lungs. He'd finished his drawing, or at least he'd reached the point where he knew that further work would only make matters worse. He leaned back and contemplated the page. Not one of his better efforts.

He knew, without turning to look, that Professor Tonks had entered the room. It was always like this with Tonks, the quiet entry. He seemed to insinuate himself into the room. You knew he'd arrived only when you saw the students sitting opposite straighten their shoulders or bend more anxiously over their drawings. Tonks was a dark planet whose presence could be deduced only by a deviation in the orbit of other bodies.

Paul risked a sidelong glance. Tonks, bent at the shoulders like a butcher's hook, was scrutinizing a student's drawing. He said something, too low to be heard. The student mumbled a reply and Tonks moved on. Another student, then another. He was working his way along the back row, passing quickly from drawing to drawing. Sugden brought him to a halt. Sugden was hopeless, among the worst in the class. Tonks always spent more time on the weaker students, which indicated a kindly disposition, perhaps, or would have done had he not left so many of them in tatters.

So far his progress had been quiet, but now suddenly he raised his voice.

"For God's sake, man, look at that arm. It's got no more bones in it than a sausage. Your pencil's blunt, your easel's wobbly, you're working in your own light, and you seem to have no grasp of human anatomy at all. What *is* the point?"

Many of Tonks's strictures related to the students' ignorance of anatomy. "Is it a blancmange?" had been one of his comments on Paul's early efforts. Tonks had trained as a surgeon and taught anatomy to medical students before Professor Browne invited him to join the staff at the Slade. His eye, honed in the dissecting room and the theater, detected every failure to convey what lay beneath the skin. "Look for the line," he would say again and again. "Drawing is an explication of the form." It was one of the catchphrases Slade students sometimes chanted to each other. Along with: "I thy God am a jealous God. Thou shalt have none other Tonks but me."

There was no getting round Tonks's opinion of your work. Tonks *was* the Slade.

Paul looked at his drawing. If he'd been dissatisfied before he was dismayed now. As Tonks drew closer, his drawing became mysteriously weaker. Not only had he failed to "explicate the form," but he'd also tried to cover up the failure with all the techniques he'd learned before coming to the Slade: shading, cross-hatching, variations in tone, even, now and then, a little discreet smudging of the line. In the process, he'd produced the kind of drawing that at school—and even, later, in night classes—had evoked oohs and ahs of admiration. Once, not so long ago, he'd have been pleased with this work; now, he saw its deficiencies only too clearly. Not only was the drawing bad, it was bad in exactly the way Tonks most despised. More than just a failure, it was a dishonest failure.

He took a deep breath. A second later Tonks's shadow fell across the page, though he immediately moved a little to one side so that the full awfulness could be revealed. A long pause. Then he said conversationally, as if he were really interested in the answer, "Is that really the best you can do?"

"Yes."

"Then why do it?"

Why indeed? Paul made no reply and after a moment Tonks moved on. At last, from somewhere, a rush of anger. "If I knew how to draw I wouldn't need to be here at all, would I?"

He'd shouted, though he hadn't meant to. All around people were turning to stare at him. Without giving Tonks a chance to reply, he threw down his pencil and walked out.

The corridor, empty between classes, stretched ahead of him. Its walls seemed to throb with his anger. The heat of it kept him going all the way to the main entrance and out into the quad. There he stopped and looked around him. What was he doing, storming out like that in the middle of a session? It was asking for trouble. And yet he knew he couldn't go back. Students were sitting in small circles on the grass, laughing and talking, but they were mainly medical students enjoying a break between lectures, and there was nobody he knew. He threaded his way between the groups and out through the iron gates into Gower Street. At first he started to walk towards Russell Square, the nearest green space, but that wasn't far enough. He needed to get right away, to think about his future in unfamiliar surroundings, because although, in one sense, his spat with Tonks had been relatively trivial, he felt that it marked a crisis in his career.

If you could call it a career.

He'd been walking round and round the lake for over an hour. His shadow, hardly visible when he first entered the park, now trotted at his heels like a stunted child. Round and round the problem went: no talent, wasting my time, better leave now and get a job. Or would it be more sensible to wait till the end of the year? He'd always intended to spend two years at the

Slade and it seemed a bit feeble to leave before the first year was over, but then what was the point of continuing when his work not only failed to improve but actually seemed to deteriorate from week to week? It wasn't as if he had unlimited money. He had a legacy from his grandmother, a slum landlord of quite astonishing rapacity who, by skimping on repairs and bringing up her large family on bread and scrape, had salted away a great deal of money in the box under her bed. What would her advice have been?

—*Have nowt to do with nancy-boy stuff like art, there's no money in that, and if you've got tangled up in it, lad, get out as fast as you can.*

She'd been horrified when he went to work as an orderly in a hospital; real men earned their living by their own sweat and blood.

This was getting him nowhere. He found a bench and sat down, feeling the heat heavy on his shoulder blades. Craning his neck, he looked up at the tops of the trees, dark against the pulsing sun. Everything was flooded in lemony light. After a while he straightened up and looked about him, and it was then that he became aware of the girl on the other side of the lake.

A young girl, still with the childish blondeness that rarely survives into adult life, was wandering along the waterside. She was about fifteen, dressed in the shabby, respectable clothes of a maid, her only ornament a bunch of purple velvet violets pinned to the crown of her black straw hat. Sent into service, he guessed, away from her own overcrowded home. Girls that age are not easily accommodated in two-bedroomed houses, parents needing privacy, adolescent brothers curious, younger children sleeping four to a bed. This would be her afternoon off.

He tracked her with his eyes. A few paces further on she stopped, standing at the water's edge looking down into the depths. Thinking they were going to be fed, swans, geese, and ducks set off towards her from all parts of the lake, so that the slim, gray figure quickly became the focal point of thirty or more converging lines. There was something odd about her and at first he couldn't think what it was, but then he noticed that the buttons on her blouse had been done up in the wrong sequence. There was a glimpse of what might have been bare flesh between the edge of her blouse and her skirt. He kept expecting her to pull her shawl more closely round her or turn away and put herself to rights. But she did neither. Instead she stumbled a few feet further along, then stopped again, the shadows of rippling water playing over her face and neck.

She was swaying on her feet. At first he thought nothing of it, but then it happened again, and again. It came to him in a flash. Incredibly, this fresh-faced, innocent-looking girl was drunk. He looked up and down the path to see if she was alone and there, about twenty yards behind, stood a portly, middle-aged man watching her. *Ah,* authority. Probably the man was her employer—he was too well-dressed to be her father—but then, if he had a legitimate reason to be interested in her, why did he not approach and take control of the situation? Instead of strolling along at that loitering, predatory pace, his eyes fixed on her back. No, he was nothing to do with her—unless of course he was the man responsible for her condition. That, or he'd noticed the state she was in and recognized easy pickings when he saw them.

Bastard. All Paul's long frustration in the life class—a frustration which could never be vented on Professor Tonks because he respected the man too much—boiled over into hatred of this man with his florid cheeks and his expensive suit and his silver-topped cane. He jumped up and began striding along the path, meaning to cut them off before they reached the gate.

The sun, past its height, had begun to throw long bluish shadows across the grass. Paul's heels rang out on the pavement as he half walked, half ran round the head of the lake. He felt vigorous, clear. All the disappointments and complexities of the past few months had dropped away. He drew level with the girl, who had once more paused and was gazing out over the lake. A few yards away from her the geese were beginning to come ashore. Big, webbed yellow feet made puddles of wet on the dusty path as they lurched towards her, open beaks hissing. Startled, she took off her shawl and flapped it at them until at last, honking and hissing, they flopped, one by one, into the water again.

Now that Paul was closer he could see that her hair had slipped loose from the pins at the nape of her neck and straggled down her back. The blouse was badly torn, it must have been ripped off her back. Looking down, he saw that only one foot had a stocking on; the other was thrust bare into a down-at-heel shoe. He looked at the slim, naked ankle and felt a tweak of lust that hardly broke the surface of his consciousness before it was transmuted into anger. Who had done this to her? She was such a child. He was afraid to startle her by speaking to her and, anyway, she might well misconstrue his intentions.

The middle-aged man had stopped a few yards away and was gazing at him with obvious resentment. Paul turned to stare at him. Medium height, heavily built, bulky about the shoulders and chest, but a lot of that was flab. His trouser buttons strained to accommodate his postprandial belly. His eyes kept sliding away from Paul to the girl and back again. At last he stepped to one side, ostentatiously allowing Paul plenty of room to pass. Paul held his ground.

Meanwhile, the girl tried to move on, but staggered and almost fell. She seemed disorientated now and after standing for a moment simply flopped down on the path. With a glance at Paul the man moved towards her. Paul stepped forward to cut him off.

"What do you want?" the man said.

A Yorkshire accent? "Are you responsible for this?"

"What?"

"This."

"I never saw her before in my life." Grayish-green eyes, the color of infected phlegm. "I was going to put her in a cab and send her back to her family."

" 'Course you were."

"Do you have a better idea?"

"We could take her to the police station."

"Oh, I doubt if she'd thank you for that."

"Let's ask her, shall we?"

The man leaned forward in a fug of port-wine breath. "Look, piss off, will you? I saw her first."

"I'm not going anywhere."

"It's not your business." A hiss the geese would have been proud of. "For God's sake, look at her. Don't you think you're closing the stable door after the horse's bolted?"

"And a slice off a cut cake won't be missed. What a fund of homely northern wisdom you are."

Gooseberry-green eyes swelled to bursting. A purpling of pendulous cheeks, then Paul caught a flash of silver from the upraised cane. He raised his arm to break the blow and pain jolted from his forearm into his shoulder. Now he had his excuse, his legitimate reason. He twisted the cane out of the other's hand and brought it crashing down onto his shoulders, once, twice, three times, and then he lost count. There was no reason ever to stop, he'd never felt such joy, strength seemed to flow into him from the sky. But a minute later, as the man turned away, presenting only his bowed shoulders to the blows, Paul started to recover himself. In a final burst of exhilaration, he sent the cane whirling in a broad arc over the lake, its silver knob flashing in the sun.

"Fetch!" he shouted, feeling his spit fly. "Go on, boy, fetch!"

The cane plopped and sank. Concentric rings of ripples laced with foam spread out over the surface of the water. Its owner turned to face Paul, goosegog eyes red veined with rage. "Do you know how much that cost?"

"More than the girl, I'll bet."

The man's neck seemed to swell over the rim of his starched collar. He's going to have a stroke, Paul thought with interest, but the moment passed. At that point the girl, whom they'd both forgotten, staggered off again, stumbling from side to side of the path. Paul followed her, glancing over his shoulder to make sure he wasn't being accompanied. No, the man merely stood and stared. Paul turned and went on walking. A second later, a blow between his shoulder blades sent him sprawling headlong. He was up and on his feet again in a second, fists raised, but the other man backed off, collected his bowler hat from the ground where it had fallen and, with several looks behind him to make sure he wasn't being followed, walked away. At first it was a brisk trot rather than a walk, but when Paul showed no sign of wanting to pursue him, his step became more nonchalant. A hundred yards further on, he might have been any prosperous businessman out for an afternoon stroll.

Paul was still shaking, as much with glee as anything else. Again and again he relived that moment when the cane had wheeled through the air and disappeared into the waters of the lake. The return of Excalibur. Except that made him Sir Bedivere and beer gut back there King Arthur.

By now, the damsel in distress was several hundred yards away, walking quickly in the direction of Lancaster Gate. He hurried to catch up, aware of a curious doubling, for now he was doing exactly what beer gut had been doing a few minutes before. With different motives, he reminded himself sharply. Nevertheless there was something disturbing about it and, half consciously, he slackened his pace. No, but this was stupid, he had to see it through. He'd call a cab, select the most respectable-looking driver he could find, and pay for the girl to be transported back to her own people. If she'd go. Suddenly the simple plan bristled with problems. She wouldn't be keen for her parents or her employer to see her in this state. And could he trust the driver not to take the money and tip her out of the cab as soon as they turned the corner? He'd have to go with her, that's all, but then, would she get into a cab with a strange man? He'd face that problem later.

Decided now, he quickened his pace, but just then a group of nursemaids pushing perambulators came bowling along towards him, taking up the full width of the path. By the time he'd made up the lost ground, the girl had turned through the gate. Panting as he reached the spot, he looked up and down the road, but the pavements were crowded and, among the hundreds of hurrying people, her unsteady gait was no longer so conspicuous. And then he saw her, far away now, on the other side of the road, but there was no pause in the traffic to let him cross. He stood on tiptoe, seeing the black straw hat with its little bunch of cloth violets bobbing along, until eventually it was lost to sight in the milling crowds.

■

He'd left all his things at the Slade, so he had to go back there. Jumping on a bus, he found a seat on the top deck and gazed out over the heads of the crowds. For the first few minutes he kept on searching for the girl, though he knew he wouldn't see her.

The exhilaration had gone now. He was back with his own problems. Should he admit defeat and leave the Slade? Was he wasting Nan's legacy?

—*'Course you bloody are. Art! It's not for people like us, such as that.*

What "people like us" did—or, more frequently, didn't do—had been a favorite topic of hers, the pincers used to nip off any green shoot of hope and ambition one or other of her children might have been cherishing. They'd learned not to, fast enough. She hadn't applied it to herself though, at least not towards the end of her long life. At eighty, she'd bought herself a motor car. The only motor car previously seen in their streets belonged to the local doctor. Every Friday afternoon and all day Saturday she'd been driven round to collect her rents, sitting up on the backseat, ramrod straight (though she was a martyr to her back), dismounting now and then to bang on the doors of one ramshackle house after another, wresting coppers from reluctant hands. She must have been the most hated woman in the city.

—*Aye, mebbe. But it put the clothes on your back, didn't it? And paid for you to go to that posh school.*

He got off near Russell Square and walked the rest of the way. Students were streaming away from the Slade as he approached, but he kept his head down, not wanting to speak to anybody. He hadn't reached a decision, though if anything all that pacing round the park had strengthened his feeling that he ought to leave as soon as possible.

The Antiques Room did nothing to change his mind. Plaster casts of Classical and Renaissance sculpture stood in a line along one wall.

—*Cartload of fellers showing their whatsits.*

He'd spent whole mornings copying them, whole days when he first started, except for an hour at the end of the afternoon session when they were allowed to troop down the corridor to join the life class. On benches at the far end were smaller pieces: decapitated heads, limbless torsos, amputated arms and legs. Like an abattoir without the blood.

Had all his time in this room been wasted?

No time to be asking that question now. He picked up his bag and was about to leave when he heard a noise and turned to find Elinor Brooke standing by the open door.

"I thought I heard somebody," she said.

She came towards him until she was close enough to touch. A stir of desire, almost indistinguishable from irritation. He wasn't in the mood for "the treatment"—by which he meant the air of intimacy Elinor created between herself and any man she spoke to, though to be fair it wasn't only men, he'd seen her adopt exactly the same approach to women. No, he wasn't in the mood for Miss Brooke, but then she raised her gigantic blue eyes to his . . . "Gig lamps," his father used to say. "Eyes like gig lamps." It had been one of the magic phrases of his childhood.

"Are you all right?" she asked.

"Why shouldn't I be?"

"Only I heard you'd walked out of the life class."

He wondered which of the men had told her. "I needed a bit of fresh air."

"Was it something Tonks said?"

"You know Tonks. He more or less said I was wasting my time."

"Ouch."

"Ye-es, *ouch*. Anyway, after that I thought I'd better go away and do some thinking. I couldn't just go on drawing."

"Where did you go?"

"Hyde Park." He smiled. "I didn't exactly run away to sea, did I? Do you mind if I smoke?"

"No, go ahead. I might even join you."

Her pupils shrank as the match flared between them. "What are you going to do?"

No advice, he noticed. She often asked for advice from men, but never gave it. "I don't know. I don't know if there's any point staying till the end of term. I mean, you could say, if I'm wasting my time the sooner I'm out of here the better." A dragging pause. "He likes your work."

"Yes," she said, simply. "I know."

They smoked in silence for a while. Then she said, "Life drawing isn't the be-all and end-all, you know."

"It is here."

"So perhaps here isn't the right place?"

He shook his head. It had taken so much determination to cut loose from his background and come to the Slade that he could hardly grapple with the idea that he'd made the wrong choice.

"Anyway," Elinor said, standing up, "I'd better be getting on." She turned towards the door, then looked back. "A few of us are going to the Café Royal tonight. Would you like to come?"

He hesitated but only for a second. What else was he going to do except sit in his lodgings and brood about his nonexistent future? "Yes, I'd like that. What time?"

"About eight."

"Good. I'll see you there. Are you going home now?"

"Soon."

He opened the door for her and watched her walk away down the corridor. With her cropped hair and straight shoulders she looked like a young soldier striding along, and for a moment he saw something in her, something of the person she might be when she was alone, not adapting in that sinuous way of hers to other people, not turning herself into a mirror to magnify whatever qualities he—it was generally he—fancied himself to possess. He'd have liked to know her, that secret person, but the mirror was also a shield and she'd be in no hurry to put it down.

2

THREE HOURS LATER PAUL WAS PUSHING OPEN THE door of the Café Royal. Lying in the bath at his lodgings, he'd almost changed his mind about going, but the moment he walked into the Domino Room his mood lifted. The tall mirrors in which the heads of smokers, drinkers, and talkers were endlessly and elaborately reflected, the laughter, the bare shoulders of the women, the pall of blue smoke above the clustered heads, the sense of witty, significant things being said by interesting people—it was a world away from his poky little rooms in St. Pancras. A world away from home, too.

People glanced up at him as he passed, their faces illuminated by the small candles that flickered on every table. Everywhere, moist lips, glimpses of red, wet tongues, gleaming white teeth. How sleek and glossy they all were compared to the creatures who lived in the streets around his lodgings, scurrying about in their soot-laden drizzle, the women so tightly wrapped they seemed to be bundles of clothes walking. This was another England and, passing between the two, he was aware of a moment's dislocation, not unlike vertigo.

At last he saw Elinor, sitting at a table directly underneath one of the mirrors. She had her back to him but then caught sight of his reflection in the glass and raised her hand. It was a moment out of time, their two reflections gazing at each other. Then noise, laughter, movement rushed back, as he threaded his way between the last few tables to greet her. "Elinor."

"Paul."

She raised her face to his and for one mad moment he thought he was expected to kiss her, but then she turned away. "Teresa, this is Paul Tarrant. Do you remember I said he might be coming? Paul, Teresa Halliday."

The girl held out her hand. She was dark, with short, shining hair, high cheekbones, and red, painted, pouting lips. That mouth still had the power to shock, though he'd noticed that many of the women here wore makeup. She was wearing a high-necked brocade jacket that made her look . . . Russian, Chinese? Anything but English. He was instantly attracted to her and thought she was aware of him, though once the introduction was over she said nothing further, merely leaned back against the plush seat waiting to have Elinor's full attention again.

"And this is Kit Neville."

He'd seen Neville once or twice at the Slade. He was starting to be famous, a circumstance that some people attributed to a talent for painting and others to a talent for self-promotion.

"Kit was at the Slade."

Neville looked uncomfortable. "I left two years ago."

"But you're always coming back."

"Oh, we all come back." It was said easily, but he was obviously nettled by the observation.

"Not everybody."

Paul was trying to recall the stories he'd heard about Neville at the Slade. Hadn't he been expelled?

"What'll you have?" Neville asked, raising his hand to summon the waiter.

"Whiskey, please."

"I think the ones who keep coming back are the ones it didn't work for," said Elinor. "It's like turning a key in a lock. If it turns you forget about it. If it doesn't, you go on rattling away."

"Or move onto something else." Neville was flushed and miserable looking. "So," he said, turning to Paul, "Elinor tells me you walked out on Tonks today."

"He said he thinks I'm wasting my time. I didn't see the point of sitting there after that."

"He can be wrong, you know."

"How long were you at the Slade?"

"Two years. And I didn't walk out." Neville's eyes were alight with a blue, dancing truculence. "Probably should have done, mind you, but I didn't. I stuck it out, and in the end he more or less said, *Go*." He grinned, adding in a mock Oirish accent, "Never resign, mister. Get yourself fired."

"Why?"

"Why what?"

"Why did he throw you out?"

"He didn't like my work. I didn't like it much either so I can't hold that against him. And"—with a sidelong glance at the girls he lowered his voice—"he disapproved of my relationship with one of the models. She got pregnant and I refused to be fathered."

Paul was startled and a little repelled by so much intimacy so early in their acquaintance. "Oh."

"I said, Why the hell should I pay? There's at least a dozen others who could be the father and if you believe everything you hear Tonks was one of them. But of course he got on his high horse. What was it? For a long time he'd believed that nothing could exceed his contempt for my work, but in the light of recent events he now realized his contempt for my moral character was infinitely greater."

What an extraordinary story to tell against yourself. It argued either unlimited egotism or a talent for self-destruction, or both perhaps. It was difficult to know what to say. Trying to lighten the tone, Paul said, "Are all the models like that?"

"Like what? Oh, loose, you mean? Yes, a lot of them are, thank God. But . . ." Nodding towards Teresa, he raised a finger to his lips.

"She's a model?"

She was so unlike the generally rather battered ladies who modeled for the life class he could scarcely believe it. At that moment she glanced across and met his eyes, smiled a slow, incommunicative smile, and immediately turned again to Elinor. The two girls were focused on each other in a way he found provocative.

"What are you two getting so intense about?" Neville asked.

That was clumsy, and he wasn't a clumsy man. Too sure of himself for that.

"Teresa's husband's been snooping round again."

Husband. Paul's eyes went to her left hand, but she wasn't wearing a ring.

"Caught him out the back last night trying to see through the window. Least, I thought it was him. You know, I pulled the curtain back and there was this face squashed against the glass, didn't look like anything on earth, but then he stepped back a bit and of course I could see it was him. Anyroad, there's me screaming blue murder and the chap upstairs ran down to see what was going on—only by that time he'd gone."

"He's left you alone quite a long time, hasn't he?" Neville said.

"Going on a year. But that's what he does." She flicked a glance at Paul. "He starts getting on with his own life, but then the minute things start to go wrong he decides it's all my fault and comes looking for me again. And it always does go wrong. He can't hold a job down. I don't think it's ever going to end."

"It will," said Elinor. "He'll drink himself to death."

"That's a slow process," Neville said, gazing down at his empty glass.

Paul took the hint and summoned the waiter. Elinor shook her head—she'd scarcely touched her glass—but Teresa nodded. With a stab of excitement, Paul realized she was tipsy.

As he gave the order, he heard Neville ask, in his blunt, authoritative way, "What are you going to do?"

"Move, I suppose."

"Oh, you *can't*," Elinor said. "Not *again* "

"Well, I can't stop there. Even if he's not outside spying on me I always think he is. And if he finds out I'm modeling . . ."

"How could he find out?" Neville said.

"He's only got to follow me. I thought I saw him the other day just as I was leaving Tonks."

So she modeled for Tonks. Paul saw her slipping off her robe, mounting the dais, Tonks's hand on her arm adjusting the pose. The image produced such a rush of desire and envy he missed part of the conversation.

"Look," Elinor was saying, when he was able to concentrate again, "he's got to eat, he's got to sleep, he can't be following you round all the time."

"What else has he got to do? Except drink."

"Doesn't he have a home to go to?" Paul said.

"Well, you know you're always welcome to stay with me," Elinor said. "There's a sofa in the living room."

"I know, and it's kind of you, but you wouldn't have anywhere to paint. I've got to get it sorted out."

Neville's gaze on Elinor's face had become even more intent. "You should go to the police," he said to Teresa roughly, not looking at her. "That'd frighten him off."

"I'm his wife. I could go in with a couple of black eyes and a broken nose and it wouldn't worry them."

"Has he hit you?" Paul said.

" 'Course he has." Incredibly, she laughed. "Blames me for that too—he was never a violent man till he met me."

"Then Neville's right. You should go to the police."

"They're not interested."

"You have finished with him, I suppose?" said Neville. "*Really* finished? There isn't a small part of you still feels sorry for him?"

She looked away, resenting the question or made uncomfortable by it. "You can't be indifferent to somebody you've—" She shook her head. "No, it's over. I couldn't go back to him now."

The conversation lapsed, though after a while the two girls started whispering to each other again. Paul sensed they were getting ready to part.

A few minutes later Elinor stood up. "I've got to go, I'm afraid."

Instantly, Neville was on his feet. He was going past her lodgings on his way home, perhaps he could drop her off? She seemed about to refuse but then nodded.

"Teresa, are you sure you don't want to come back with me?"

"No, I'm all right, really. Don't worry about me."

They kissed good-bye. Paul watched as Elinor and Neville left together. At the door Neville put his hand between her shoulder blades, guiding her. They'd said nothing all evening to suggest they were more than acquaintances, and yet now, suddenly, he saw they had a close, perhaps even intimate, relationship.

Teresa had gone quiet. There were purple shadows under her eyes and he found himself wanting to touch them. He moved closer. They chatted about this and that, the conversation sputtering like a cold engine—on, off—until a shadow fell across their table and Paul looked up to find no less a person than the great Augustus John towering over them.

"Teresa," he said. "Why don't you join us? And your friend, too, of course."

She looked across him to a noisy table at the far end of the room. "Thanks, Gus, but I was just leaving. I've got a bit of a headache coming on." She was reaching for her bag as she spoke.

Another few words and, with a nod to Paul, the great man moved on.

She'd chosen to stay with him. Perhaps. More likely the headache was genuine and she was longing to get home. But that didn't seem probable either with a potentially violent husband prowling round her backyard. He looked at her and saw how the purple shadows had changed the color of her eyes from pale to smoky gray. The blood was thickening in his neck. "Shall we go, then?"

She nodded at once and stood up.

3

A LIGHT RAIN HAD FALLEN. THE STREET WAS busy, people hurrying to restaurants and bars. Women's scents, as they walked past on the arms of husbands and lovers, mingled with the smell of leather and dung from the cab horses that stamped and jingled in a long row by the curb. For no better reason than the freshness of moist air on his skin, Paul felt suddenly full of hope.

Teresa was pulling on her gloves, pale gray cotton, pressing each finger into place. She barely reached his shoulder but was so slim and held herself so erect that she struck him as a tall woman, and how beautiful that dark, warm coloring, those cheekbones that caught and held the light.

"I suppose you've already had dinner?"

"No, I came straight from modeling." Her voice had an unexpected rasp to it, like fingernails dragged across the skin. "I'll have something when I get back."

As she spoke her pale gray eyes darkened, and he realized two things: she was hungry—that must be why the wine had affected her so much—and she was afraid.

"Perhaps we could eat together?"

She looked up at him. A cleft in her chin, he noticed, rare in women. He struggled not to touch it, the side of his thumb would rest there so sweetly.

"That would be nice."

"There's a place over there. Shall we try that?"

They ran across the street and pushed open the heavy door of the restaurant. Steamy heat, a smell of onions frying. The waiter showed them to a table by the window where they could look out at people walking past. Paul was delighted, particularly since the couple at the next table were engrossed in each other. They were virtually alone.

"Would you like some wine?"

"*More* wine?" She blushed. "Yes, go on, why not?"

Her accent was very strong when she said that. He'd kissed and cuddled girls like her, standing with his back to the factory gates, pausing and pulling them deeper into the shadows whenever anybody walked past. But then he looked at her again and thought, Who are you kidding? You've never had a girl remotely like this.

They ordered soup and roast beef and talked about their mutual acquaintances. Had she known Elinor long?

"Two years. She was only seventeen, you know, when she came to London. She's always saying what an old stick-in-the-mud her mother is, but when you think of it . . . letting a seventeen-year-old girl come to London, unchaperoned. Most mothers wouldn't do it."

"Would your mother?"

Her face hardened. "I was married at seventeen. No danger of that with Elinor. Though it's not as if she hasn't had offers. You must have seen how men react to her?"

"I saw how Neville did."

"She keeps trying to get him interested in other girls." She looked at him mischievously. "Do *you* think she's attractive?"

"In a boyish sort of way . . ."

"Isn't that what men go for?"

"Not all of us."

"Neville does."

Perhaps she felt she'd said too much, because she immediately raised her glass, using it as a shield against her mouth as she gazed round the room.

"Do you like Tonks?"

Her eyes widened. "Yes, I think I do. He's a very kind man. *Underneath*."

"Tell that to Neville."

"Henry didn't like his work. But I think he always thought he had talent."

"Not the way Neville tells it. Tonks told him he despised his work—and despised *him* even more."

"Oh? I didn't know that."

"Henry," he noticed, and she'd called Augustus John "Gus." She was no more than a girl from the back streets of some northern town, and yet she assumed equality with these men. A fragile sort of equality, based, ultimately, on sex.

—*Whore*.

—*Now, now, Nan. Rest in peace*.

"It's not done him much harm, has it?" she was saying. "He's doing rather well."

"Painting trains."

"Not just trains."

"He'd like the view from my window"

"Oh, where do you live?"

"St. Pancras."

"I live there. Victoria Street."

They looked at each other, registering that when they left the restaurant they would be going in the same direction.

Over coffee he asked about her husband. He was afraid she might think the question intrusive, but once she started the words streamed out.

"I was seventeen. I can't even say it was a mistake, I had to get away from home. Dad left when I was eleven and three years later Mam took up with somebody else."

"You didn't like him?"

"That wasn't the problem."

"He didn't like you?"

"Not that either. I couldn't tell Mam, I dropped one or two hints and she just——" Teresa hunched her shoulders and crossed her arms over her chest. "She wasn't well. That was half the trouble—she was always in bed with poultices on her chest—her skin was raw, you used to have to put mustard on them. I couldn't see they were doing her any good, I used to hate putting them on, she used to scream, but the doctor would have it. He was costing that much you couldn't disagree with him. So anyway I was downstairs making these bloody poultices and he used to come up behind me. What could I do? I couldn't shout. And he wouldn't take no for an answer. Oh, and I wasn't allowed out, he was always saying he didn't want me running round with any of the local lads, getting into trouble. It's laughable really, all the trouble I had was at home. So in the end I ran away." She pulled a face. "Not very far—I went to me auntie's in Redcar. She's a dressmaker, so I used to help her with that and then I got on with Jack. He was a mate of Dave's—that's Auntie Nancy's lad. He was in the army and, oh, he was smart. I couldn't see the drink was a problem, but even if I had seen it, I'd probably still have married him."

"Were you in love with him?"

"God knows."

For a while she sat in silence, looking down at her glass.

"You don't have to talk about it, you know."

"No, I want to. It lasted about six months. I mean, before things started to go wrong. I fell pregnant and he was over the moon. Came out of the army—big mistake, but it didn't seem like that at the time—and he got a job in the ironworks. Laborer, but he was making good money. And then I lost the baby. The horrible thing is, I was quite relieved."

"Because you knew it was a mistake? The marriage?"

"Yes, I knew. Soon as he come out of the army. He was like a bloody sergeant major. Least little thing, his shirts weren't ironed right, I used to get belted."

"You could have left him."

"You get cowed, you can't do anything. Always being told what an ugly, useless slut you are. And then I fell pregnant again and he totally changed. He even stopped drinking. Only I lost that one too, and he got it into his head I'd done summat to get rid of it. Me auntie used to help women out, you know, and I think he thought she'd told me what to do. I told him I never did anything, but he didn't believe me and that's when it got really bad. I ended up in casualty twice. The second time me auntie says, 'Don't be such a bloody fool, our Teresa, he's gunna kill you.' So I ran away again, this time to London. She lent me the money for the fare—every little bit she had put by, it cleaned her out—but it didn't last five minutes here. I hadn't anybody I could turn to. Then I got on with this artist and he

says, Why don't you try modeling? The lasses at home, you
know, they'd laugh their heads off, me being a model. I used to
get called Chinkyeyes and Flatface at school."

"But he followed you?"

"Yes, I don't know how he found me but he did. He needs
me. Always did, that was the problem. You know, he'd be eff-
ing and blinding one minute and the next he'd be sat on the
floor with his head in me lap."

"My heart bleeds."

"That's what me auntie said."

"And now he's back?"

"Yes, but he'll drift off again." She nodded towards the far
end of the room. "I think the waiters are wanting to be off."

Paul looked over his shoulder, realized they were indeed
the only two people left in the restaurant, and raised his hand
for the bill.

Pushing open the door of the restaurant, he was surprised
to see the world going on as usual. "Shall I get a cab?"

"No, let's walk, shall we? It's not raining."

That was a relief. He had just about enough money left to
pay for a cab, but it would have been a worry.

She took his arm and they set off. It was exciting just to be
walking down a street with her, to match his stride to hers, to
feel her hand nestling in the crook of his elbow. He asked who
she was modeling for at the moment.

"Saracen. I'm supposed to sit for him tomorrow, but I
don't know if I can."

"Why not?"

"Jack. He might follow me."

"Won't he just get fed up and go away? You say he drifts off again after a while."

"Yes, but there's generally a pretty big explosion first, and I can't afford to lose work."

"Has he hit you? I mean, since you left him?"

She lifted her face to his and he saw the light of the street-lamps in her eyes. "Yes. Once. I'd been out and he was waiting for me when I got back."

If Paul had been settled in life, if he'd even been successful as a student, she couldn't have moved him as deeply as she did at that moment, but he had nothing to dilute this, no busy humming core of purposeful activity to protect him. He was mesmerized by her. That flat northern accent, so familiar to him, coming out of that scandalous painted mouth. But it wasn't just her looks. In spite of her bitterness, her evident cynicism about men and their motives, he sensed a capacity for passion in her greater than anything he'd so far experienced.

The rustle of her skirt both soothed and disturbed him. He hardly knew what they talked about. As the streets became grayer and meaner and the air began to smell of smoke and oil, she fell silent, looking down at her feet swishing in and out under the hem of her skirt. He touched her arm to get her attention. "Whereabouts do you live?"

"Just along here."

Twenty yards further on she stopped outside a tall, narrow house with cracked and blistered paint on the front door and skimpy, no-color curtains drawn across the ground-floor windows.

"I'm in the basement."

He unlatched the gate and looked down the steps. In the small yard at the bottom were five dustbins overflowing with rubbish. Behind them, a low door led into some kind of storage space, perhaps intended to hold the bins. As far as he could tell it was empty, but the light from the streetlamp didn't reach all the way to the back.

He sensed Teresa was frightened. "Would you like me to open the door for you? Check everything's all right?"

"Please. If you wouldn't mind."

She gave him her keys and he went down the steps ahead of her, his nostrils assailed by a smell of rotting cabbage. A few leaves, thick veined and gross, their stalks yellow and flabby with decay, littered the ground. He turned the key in the lock, but the door, swollen with damp, resisted him. All the time he was aware of the dark cavity behind him. Anybody could hide in there after dark. No wonder she was frightened.

The door gave before a more determined shove.

"There we are."

She'd stopped halfway down the steps. Now only her head and shoulders were lit by the streetlamp. Gradually, as she edged further down the steps, her face fell into shadow. Then she was standing beside him. He caught her scent, sweet and dark, above the stench of rotting vegetables.

"He got inside once."

"I'll have a look around."

He went first, walking ahead of her down a long passage, which bent sharply to the right in the middle. The lino was black with gray blotches, perhaps intended to suggest pebbles but looking rather as if somebody had spattered paint across it. She had two main rooms—big, but dark. A tiny kitchen opened off the living room. The bathroom was squeezed in next door to the bedroom. He looked in the airing cupboard, inside the wardrobe, under the bed—feeling, as he pressed his cheek into the musty-smelling rug, like a ridiculous old maid—then returned to the hall. "All clear."

"Good." She laughed on a sharply exhaled breath. "Would you like a cup of coffee? After all that."

"I'd love one."

He had no idea what the offer implied and daren't think. He told himself there was no hurry. Most of his sexual experience so far had been kisses and cuddles and worming his way into the drawers of girls whose sights were firmly set on marriage, always feeling a bit of a bastard since he had no intention of marrying anybody. That, and a series of rather unsatisfactory commercial encounters. They should have been easier, since both sides knew where they stood, but they hadn't been. In fact, the memory of the first time could still make him cringe. The woman, beside whom any one of his aunties would have looked like a mere slip of a girl, pointed him towards a bowl of water and a bar of carbolic soap and towel on the dresser by the bed. Obediently he started to get washed. Hands. Face. Neck. Ears. Even now he felt a hot blush of shame prickle his chest, as he remembered her laughter.

"Are you all right in there?"

He roused himself. "Yes."

"You've gone very quiet."

"Just thinking."

While she finished making the coffee he looked around the room. Her taste was good. She'd used deep shades of red and blue and positioned small lamps to cast golden arcs of light over the walls, so the effect was of being in a dark, rich cave. The dustbins and squalor outside were easily forgotten.

She came back into the room carrying a tray.

"The trouble with this place is, everybody comes down

here to empty the rubbish, so if I hear somebody moving about I don't know if it's him or just somebody from upstairs." She put the tray down on a table. "Or a Peeping Tom. You get plenty of them."

"You shouldn't really be living in a basement."

"I know, but it's got a garden. And it's cheap."

Taking the cup from her, he sat down on one of the sofas, feeling the sharpness of worn springs under the velvet cover. "Are you getting a divorce?"

"I'm not sure I could. It's a lot harder for a woman. A man only has to prove adultery. A woman has to prove adultery *and* cruelty."

"Do you think he'd divorce you?"

"Never in a million years." She forced a smile. "Anyway, that's enough about me. I seem to have been talking about myself all evening. What about you?"

"Oh, what about me? I think we come from the same part of the world. Middlesbrough."

She shook her head. "Grangetown."

"It's only a few miles. Just think, we might have walked past each other in the street."

"So how did you get to the Slade? Scholarship?"

"No, my grandmother died and left me a small legacy. I was working as an orderly in the hospital at the time, but I decided to use the money doing this."

"Is that what she'd have wanted?"

"Good God, no. She wanted me to be a teacher, I think, or a solicitor's clerk, something like that. Good, steady money and a pension at the end of it."

"But you didn't fancy that?"

"I thought I had talent."

"Thought?"

"There's not been much sign of it recently."

"Do you think you might be trying too hard?"

"I've got to try. I'm not like Neville. If I make a mess of this there's no feather bed for me to fall back on."

They talked for a while longer, but she was obviously tired and after a few minutes he drained his cup and stood up.

As she was opening the door he said, "Would you like to go to a music hall?" When she hesitated he said quickly, "But I don't suppose you feel much like going out at the moment?"

"No, I think it would do me a power of good."

"Friday at seven? I'll pick you up."

As the door closed behind him, he was amazed by the bone-aching pain of the separation. He'd known her only a few hours, it oughtn't to be possible to feel like this. He lingered, hoping she'd part the curtains and look out, but they remained closed, with only a strip of light to show she was still inside. How totally his life had changed in the space of a few hours. Fizzing with excitement, he set off to walk home. As he turned the corner of the street, a man walking fast, head down, hands thrust into his pockets, slammed into him. No apology. No acknowledgment even. Paul turned to stare after him as he strode away, the streetlamps passing his shadow like a baton along the pavement. He half expected him to disappear down Teresa's basement stairs, but, no, he went straight past, his hunched figure dwindling rapidly into the dark. Relieved, Paul turned and walked on.

4

The following day, Paul went to see Professor Tonks to apologize for walking out of the life class. The incident loomed so large in his mind it was salutary to discover how little importance Tonks attached to it. As for leaving the Slade . . .

"What's the point of going now? You may as well wait till the end of term at least."

"But if I'm wasting my time?"

"Are you?"

"You seemed to be implying that."

"I told you your drawing was bad. I don't remember saying you were wasting your time."

"I don't seem to be getting any better."

"Technically you are. Only . . ."

"Only?"

"Most people who come here are bursting with something they want to say, and the trouble I have with some of them is that they can't be bothered to learn the language to say it in. Whereas with you it's almost the opposite."

Paul would have liked to defend himself but didn't know how. This wasn't the criticism he'd been expecting.

"I *do* have a problem with life drawing, I know that. But I thought my landscapes were . . . Well. A *bit* better."

"There's no feeling."

"Perhaps I'm not managing to express it, but—"

"I don't get any feeling that they're yours. You seem to have nothing to say."

"I see. No, yes, I do see."

"Well, then." Tonks spread both hands on his desk, preparatory to rising. "I wish I could tell you what to do about it, but I'm afraid you're going to have to thrash this one out on your own."

"I don't know what to do."

"Why don't you start by asking yourself: Do I want to paint? Or do I want 'to be an artist'? Because they're two very different things. And try to be honest with yourself. It's not an easy question."

Tonks had been kind, if not tactful, and Paul backed out of his room feeling that one day, when the sting had worn off, he'd be grateful. At the moment he felt he hadn't been given much to go on. If Tonks had told him to go and learn anatomy, he'd have done it, no question. Ground and sweated away till he could name every bone and nerve and muscle in the body. He'd never been afraid of work. But "nothing to say"? What was he supposed to do about that? And as for wanting "to be an artist" . . . Well, of course he wanted to be an artist. It was the opposite of the life he'd lived in the shadow of the ironworks that gobbled men up at the start of a shift and regurgitated them twelve hours later fit for nothing but booze and sleep. Too bloody right he wanted to be an artist. And that meant? God knows. He knew what it used to mean. Getting on a bike on Sunday morning and pedaling like hell as far away from Middlesbrough as his legs would carry him to set up his easel in a field somewhere to paint trees and hawthorn blossom. Behind him, columns of black smoke, steam, spurts of flame, flakes of soot on sheets hung out to dry, the acrid smell of coke, sparks struck from boots as workers coming off the afternoon shift slurred over the cobbles.

Perhaps that was the trouble. Art had always been Somewhere Else. There flashed into his mind a memory of the back room in the Vane Arms, blue smoke, the rumble of dominoes being shuffled, knobbly hands, liver spotted, necks like tortoises', blank, incommunicative faces, terse greetings: "Now then," "All right?" and the cold northern light coming in through frosted-glass windows. If he closed his eyes, he could hear the scraping of dominoes on the tables. Which was also, come to think of it, the sound of the Café Royal. He'd never painted those men or even thought of doing so till now.

Leave it. Too complicated to sort out now and, besides, he had other things on his mind. Teresa. He thought about her all the time. She came between him and the page.

As soon as the morning session was over, he ran downstairs to the women's Life Room. Most of the students had gone, but Elinor was still there, putting the finishing touches to her drawing. Seeing her like this through the open door, he was attracted to her all over again, as he had been the first time he saw her in the Antiques Room. He'd come very close to falling in love with her that day. Everything about her had attracted him, from the crown of her shockingly cropped head to the slightly pigeon toes peeping out beneath the hem of her paint-daubed overall. What can you do to resist a girl whose defects are perfections? She was so much more *alive* than anybody else.

Today she'd been working in charcoal and had black smudges round her mouth where she'd absentmindedly sucked the stick. Ruthie Wilson, a small dun-colored girl, like a wren, quick and secretive in every movement, was tapping the corner of her own mouth to point them out. At last, losing patience, she got out her handkerchief, gave it a lick, and rubbed the marks away. Elinor stood motionless, like a small child, letting herself be cleaned up. There was so much intimacy in that action, Paul caught his breath.

How they dawdled, the two of them. Shifting from foot to foot, he waited while they got their things together and drifted towards the door.

"Paul," Elinor said.

She looked delighted to see him.

"Oh, hello," said Ruthie.

"Elinor, can I talk to you for a minute?"

"Yes, all right. We're on our way to Lockhart's."

The café was crowded by the time they got there, the queue stretching from the counter to the door. As soon as he entered, Paul felt his face grow slick with steam and grease. Lockhart's was cheap. Everything about it said cheap, from the smears of grease on the badly wiped tables to the brown crusts in the sugar where people had dipped wet spoons. Standing directly behind Elinor, he noticed how the hairs at the nape of her neck, fairer than the rest, crept into the center, half covering the tender runnel of white flesh. When they first met, the nape of Elinor's neck had kept him awake at nights.

Ruthie went off to join some friends, while Paul and Elinor found a table near the kitchen door. Paul had to squeeze

himself close to the table to avoid being jolted by waitresses going in and out, but at least they were alone.

"So," said Elinor, "what did Tonks have to say?"

"I should stay to the end of term."

"Was that all?"

"More or less." He didn't want to tell her about having
nothing to say, it hurt too much. "Common sense, really. I've
paid the fees."

"Do you *want* to stay?"

"Now, yes."

"Hmm." Her face was alight with curiosity. "How did
you get on?"

"With Teresa? Very well." He hesitated. "In fact I saw her
home. She lives in a basement, did you know?"

"No, I've never been. She always comes to see me."

"Mad, really. Anybody could get in."

Elinor took a sip of her coffee and emerged with a line of
foam on her upper lip.

"Elinor." He patted his upper lip, aching to be allowed
to do what Ruthie had done a few minutes earlier. Instead,
he passed a white, folded handkerchief across the table. Elinor
wiped the foam off on the side of her hand and handed his handkerchief back to him, still virgin.

"Have you known Teresa long?"

He tried to keep the question casual, though just saying
her name excited him.

"Two years? She modeled for me when I was up for the
scholarship. Free. It was very good of her and, well, you know,
it makes all the difference." Her eyes darkened. "She's had a
rotten life."

"The husband seems to be an absolute brute."

"He put her in hospital twice."

"Didn't anybody do anything?"

"No, of course not. He got off scot-free. Surprise, sur-prise."

She sat back, withdrawing her warmth from him as if he too were tarnished by the universal male stain.

"I'm surprised she doesn't go home."

"He'd still find her."

"Yes, but at least she'd have family."

"An auntie. What's the point of that? She needs six hulk-ing big brothers. Besides, the work's here."

"Modeling."

"Well, there's not much call for it up north. I know it's not much of a living, but—"

"How much does it pay?"

"You really do like her, don't you?"

"Ye-es. Yes, I do—only I'm not sure she's actually finished with her husband. *Finished* finished."

" 'Course she has, the man's an absolute nightmare. No wonder she's suspicious of men. And being a model doesn't help." She stared at him. "A lot of men think models are fair game."

"Neville."

"For one."

He was remembering Neville's story about the baby with a dozen possible fathers, though it had suited Neville to say that. "He seems to be an interesting chap."

"Oh, he's that all right. Have you seen his latest paint-ings? They're on in the Grafton Gallery."

"No, I haven't. I'll have a look."

"I don't like the new stuff particularly, but there's no

denying it's powerful." She was making patterns with the coffee dregs in her cup. "He knows exactly what he wants to do."

"I wish I did."

"So do I. Wish I did."

"You're doing all right. Everybody seems to think you'll get the scholarship."

"Yes, but it's all schoolgirl stuff, isn't it? There's nothing there."

So perhaps they were all dissatisfied with their work? Perhaps that was an artist's normal state?

Elinor pushed her cup away. "Shall we get back, then?"

He said good-bye to her at the top of the basement stairs. She was a good friend. If he'd learned nothing else at the Slade he'd learned that men and women could be friends, even intimate friends, without sex intruding. But then, halfway down the stairs, she turned and looked back, and there he was again, a rabbit caught in the light of the gig lamps, unable to move or look away.

No, it was impossible. He couldn't still be attracted to Elinor, not now, when all his thoughts were focused on Teresa. What on earth had possessed him to say Friday? He could equally well have said today or tomorrow, at least asked if she was free. As it was, he'd condemned himself to three whole days without her. *Fool.*

5

HE DIDN'T HAVE TO LOOK AT THE LEAFLET TO
know which paintings were Neville's. They leapt off the wall.
He'd done three studies of the Underground: streaks of light,
advertisements, perpendicular lines that suggested straphangers,
blurred heads and faces of people, everything fragmented, ex-
plosions of noise and speed. The sensation of noise surprised
him, but it was the right word. These were very noisy paintings. Did he like them? He didn't know, but he saw at once that
this was fully mature work streets ahead of anything he could
produce. So far ahead and so different in its subject from anything he would ever want to paint that he was protected from
envy. He got Neville's address from Elinor and wrote a warm
note of appreciation.

After posting the letter, he tramped up and down the
streets around his lodgings, so absent that a scrap of paper blowing across the road startled him. Every time he thought of Teresa
little flickering flames ran along his veins. In the end, because
he couldn't help himself, he went to her street. All around him,
in the long mean terraces, was a sense of furtive, scurrying lives,
of people living in one room, alone, cooking their suppers on a

single gas ring. Walking down the street, he touched each rail-
ing as he passed, as a small child might have done, until he
stood gazing down the basement steps at her front door. There
was the familiar reek of rotting vegetables, but no red glow
from behind the curtains. She was out. He was shocked by that.
But then, why shouldn't she be out? She had a whole life that
he knew nothing about. He ought to go, but still he lingered,
hoping she might somehow, miraculously, come round the corner. He was behaving like one of the Peeping Toms she com-
plained about and saw, abruptly, that the chasm dividing him
from those pathetic little men was no bigger than a crack in the
pavement.

Back home, he wandered between the two rooms of his
small flat, pausing to gaze out onto the railway lines through net
curtains stiff with dirt. He sat on the edge of his bed, staring
down at his clasped hands, and wondered where she was and
who she was with. This obsession grew like a tumor. One of
those spongy excrescences that grow on the throat or the side of
the neck and choke the life out of you. He was living his whole
life, minute by minute, breath by breath, solely in the hope of
seeing her again.

By the time Friday evening came he was exhausted, but
kept going by the energy of his desire for her. They went to the
Coliseum and sat in the front row of the balcony. He sat as close
to her as he dared, aware of the curve of her shoulder and arm,
of the vibration of laughter in her chest, far more conscious of
her than of anything happening on stage, where a couple of
grotesquely made-up men teetered about on high heels warbling
like prima donnas. Normally he loved the music hall. What
he liked best were the "turns"—comedians, acrobats, and jug-
glers—but most of all he was fascinated by the men in wigs and

makeup and outlandish female costumes and by the young girls swaggering up and down, immaculately clad in white tie and tails. They seemed to turn the whole world upside down, to suggest anything was possible. In the music hall it was Twelfth Night every day of the year.

After the interval there was a one-act play with a complicated plot about spies. One-act plays always struck him as being rather pointless—you'd no sooner worked out who the characters were than the curtain came down—and tonight he was even less inclined to pay attention than usual. But Teresa seemed to enjoy it. As they were leaving, she chattered about the play, and he smiled and assented and expressed opinions, but really he had no clear idea of what it had been about. In his inside pocket, burning a hole, as they say, was a packet of sixpennies. As he stood on the curb trying to hail a cab he was remembering the first packet he'd bought. Three visits to three different barbers before he plucked up the courage to ask for what he'd wanted. By the time he'd managed to get some, he looked like an ex-convict. A cab pulled up at last and he gave Teresa's address.

They sat in silence most of the way. They might have been a middle-aged married couple returning from their weekly night out, though he was so intently aware of her he could have counted the blond hairs on her forearm where they caught the light. He paid the driver, and exactly like last time went down the steps first to check that it was safe. Nothing felt safe. His heart throbbed in his throat. Turning the key, he heard a rustle in the cavity behind him and spun round, fists clenched, only to see a naked tail trailing through rubbish before the creature whisked away into the dark.

"We get a lot of cats," Teresa said.

"*Cats*? That wasn't a cat."

Once inside the dingy hallway, he stood and stared at her. All his carefully prepared speeches deserted him. And then they were kissing, a long hard kiss that seemed to drain him. He pulled away, holding her at arm's length, searching her face. In the dim light her eyes were more violet than gray. They went into the bedroom hand in hand, like children. With other women, he'd always felt rushed, even as he'd checked and held himself back. This was different. A slow, peaceful progression. He helped her undress and she stood in the lamplight, rubbing the pink stripes the corset had left around her waist.

"I'm only allowed corsets on my days off. Saracen'd have a fit if I showed up looking like this."

She was a tall, pale lily rising from the dark foliage of her dress. He knelt before her, his lips moving over the gentle curve of her belly where a few silver stretch marks rose from the bush of hair. The imperfection reassured him because it seemed to bring her beauty within reach.

"Are you cold?"

His voice creaked as if he hadn't used it for a long time.

"A bit."

She got into bed and lay on her side, facing him, her eyes full of candlelight. He freed his cock from the cling and torment of his underpants and heard her laugh, but it was a triumphant, friendly, sensual chuckle that brought them closer together. He walked towards the bed, hoping she'd touch him, not wanting to ask for it. She cradled his balls in her hand, he felt them lift and tighten, and then she leaned forward and kissed him there, licking and mouthing the purple, glistening knob. He saw the creases in her neck. Oh, my God, careful. He eased her lips away. A lot of this was being done in an almost jokey way.

Only when he climbed into bed and leaned over her did her smile fade. She stared up at him, her pupils flaring as his body cut off the light. She seemed wary, as he was himself. He lay half beside her, half on top, nuzzling her neck, shoulders, breasts, smelling the bitter almond smell of her nipples, brushing his face from side to side on her belly. A hot, briny tang was perceptible under the sweetness. He lowered himself onto her; her back arched as she rose to meet him. As they twisted and writhed, a knot of white limbs on the jangling bed, he was aware of the darkness outside, the wet, the cold, the gritty streets. A goods train rumbled past. He thrust deeper, trying to shut the noise out, but the roar of trains was part of their love-making, and when at last he let her go, they lay listening as a whistle shrieked and faded into silence and the rattling at the window frame ceased.

"Do they wake you?"

"Only if they're late."

"Yes, that's right." He felt a moment's delighted recognition, out of proportion to the small, shared experience. "You get restless, don't you, and then you realize what's missing. The sleeper's late."

"When I first moved in here, I thought, I can't put up with this, but then after a bit you can't imagine living without it."

In the brief interval between trains, he heard the wind rising and a few small drops of rain hit the glass. He started to kiss and caress her again and this time they reached a sharper peak. There was bewilderment, even pain, in her final cry. He bit into the pillow, tossing his head, trying to tear the cloth, then with a final roar fell forward and lay still.

After a minute he rolled over, smiled, laughed, wiped

sweat from his face, laughed again, and then they were hauling themselves out of the stormy sea and onto the safety of the rocks. He pulled her out of bed and they ran, naked, into the kitchen, where they cut themselves big, thick slices of bread and butter—doorsteps, she called them—and washed them down with strong, sweet tea. They kept looking sideways at each other, grinning. She put a match to the fire and they sat on the sofa side by side, stretching out their bare toes to the heat.

"Like bairns waiting for Christmas," she said.

"I just had my present."

She was rubbing the pink corset marks again. "I hope they're gone by morning."

"Why? Are you modeling?"

"Yes." Her tone hardened. "It's what I do."

He pressed his thumb against her cheekbone. "You should try head modeling, you know. No, really. You'd be amazed how few models have good heads."

She smiled, but looked away. What did it matter if other men saw her naked. It wasn't worth arguing about and, anyway, what right did he have to interfere in her life? Only he wanted her to himself. He lay back and held out his arms for her to join him. Immediately she came and snuggled into his side. Soon her warmth and the heat of the fire began to make him drowsy. He'd drifted off to sleep when, jarringly, she jerked upright.

"What's the matter?"

"Ssh." She raised a hand. "Can you hear it?"

He listened. "No."

Perhaps he had heard something, but only the fire collapsing in on itself where it had burnt hollow. His mother had always said a hollow fire was a sure sign of disaster and would snatch up the poker and smash the coals into a more acceptable shape. Didn't help her much, poor woman. He sat up and shook himself awake.

"I'm sure I heard something," Teresa said.

"Could be somebody emptying the rubbish."

"No, out the back."

It was obvious what he had to do. Barefoot, wearing only his trousers, he let himself be led along the dogleg passage to the back door. There were two bolts fixed to the wall with rusty screws. For God's sake, you could kick it open. She pulled the bolts back and he stepped out into a small, dark basement court-yard. It smelled of damp and leaf mold. Steps led up to the main garden, where buddleia bushes with detumescent spikes loomed as tall as trees. Reluctantly, he stepped out into the yard, the raw, wet air on his skin shocking him into full wakeful-ness. The flags were slippery with rain and moss; snail shells crunched between his toes. As he went up the steps, he saw a stretch of wet lawn silvery in the moonlight and through the tangle of bushes a wire fence separating the garden from the railway line beyond. An intruder would have had to come in through one of the neighboring gardens, that, or risk crossing the main line. But nobody with any sense would do that. At the top of the steps he looked around: no sign of anybody, no sign that anybody had been there. A man crossing the lawn would have left footprints in the wet grass. Probably she'd imagined it, but he walked round long enough to convince her he was tak-ing it seriously, then went to stand by the wire fence. Beyond the slope of blond grass, the railway line had started to hum. He was aware of Teresa, at the top of the steps now, watching him. In a minute, a dozen or so rocking, swaying carriages hurtled past. A child with her face pressed against the glass waved to

him, but the small human gesture was lost in the grind of pistons. He felt a ripple across his naked skin as the displaced air
rushed back.

"Can you see anything?"

"No. If he was here he's gone."

"It'd be him all right."

"I didn't see anybody."

She gazed around her, the moonlight glittering in the
whites of her eyes. "Perhaps it's me. Perhaps I'm imagining
things."

But she didn't sound convinced.

Shivering, she pulled the edges of her wrap together and
went down the steps into the house, and with a last look at the
wet grass and the shining rails, he turned to follow her.

6

NEVILLE REPLIED TO PAUL'S NOTE OF CONGRATU-
lation with an invitation to lunch. *Just family,* he'd scribbled underneath his signature. *I thought we might go for a swim afterwards?*
Weather permitting, of course.

"I wonder what he wants," Teresa said.

"Does he have to want something?"

"No-o."

"Well, I'll know soon enough, won't I?"

Sunday found him in the Nevilles' dining room overlooking a balding lawn. The weather, after a few fitful weeks of
mixed sunshine and rain, was now definitely getting warmer.
The rhododendron leaves were limp in the midday glare.

Paul was sitting next to Mrs. Neville, a thin, energetic
woman who was an enthusiastic suffragist.

"Suffragist," she insisted. "Not *gette.*"

"No," Neville said. "But *gette*'s on the way, isn't it?"

"Well, if the moderates don't make progress, what do you

expect? Obviously people are going to be attracted to more extreme tactics."

"Don't start throwing bricks, my dear," Colonel Neville said. "You're a terrible shot."

Mrs. Neville seemed to be fond of her family, in an abstracted kind of way, though Neville, jokingly but with an edge to his voice, claimed she never listened to a word he said.

"Poof! What nonsense." She dropped a kiss on her husband's forehead, acknowledged her son and his guest with a vague, bright smile, and swept out of the room.

"It's true," Neville said, caught between amusement and self-pity. "Half the time she doesn't know I'm here."

Paul thought he detected a lot of tension beneath the surface in this family. Neville was in awe of his father, a war correspondent who'd faced danger in every corner of the world. Throughout his life the father had gravitated towards violent conflict, and the son was desperate to measure up. No easy matter if the worst danger you face is a collapsing easel. But it made sense of the younger man's preoccupation with virility in art. Paul had read a couple of Kit Neville's articles now, and both of them were full of the need to stamp out the effeminacy of the Oscar Wilde years. You'd think, the way Neville wrote about it, that the Wilde trials had taken place last year, not a generation ago. What a shadow it cast.

After coffee Colonel Neville retired to his study and the two young men went upstairs to Neville's quarters, a large studio right at the top of the house. The treetops were level with his windows.

There were several completed paintings to admire, one of them very fine indeed. Many were urban, industrial landscapes.

Paul was generous with his praise, though inwardly discouraged. In comparison with this his own work was immature, and he couldn't understand why. He wasn't particularly young for his age. His mother's long illness and early death had forced him to grow up and take on responsibility. So this maturity of vision in a man whom he found distinctly childish in many respects bewildered him. Living at home, spoiled, self-pitying, moaning on because his mother didn't pay him enough attention—for God's sake! The work and the man seemed to bear no relation to each other. And the contrast was all the more painful because Neville was painting the landscape of Paul's childhood. These paintings were the fruit of a trip up north to seek out the same smoking terraces and looming ironworks that Paul had turned his back on every Sunday, cycling off into the countryside in search of Art.

He glanced sideways at Neville. *One* of them was mad.

"They're very powerful."

"I managed to get inside one of the works and see a furnace being tapped. God, it's an amazing sight."

"You haven't tried to paint it yet?"

"No, I'm gearing myself up." He was pulling a bathing costume out of a drawer as he spoke. "Shall we go for a swim, then? It's too nice to stay inside."

Pausing on the landing to collect towels from the airing cupboard, he led the way downstairs. In the hall dust motes seethed in a shaft of sunlight. No sound anywhere, no voices, no traffic noise. Only the steady ticking of a clock.

"It's quiet, isn't it?"

Paul was referring to the absence of traffic noise, but Neville chose to take it more personally.

"Oh, it's always like this. Do you know, sometimes I don't talk to a living soul from one day's end to the next? Mother's got her blasted meetings, Father's never here. . . ."

"I suppose there's always the Café Royal."

"Can't stand the place."

He was there every night. "I thought you liked it."

"*Like* it? Of course I don't like it. It's vile."

They had turned out of Keats Grove now and were walking up the hill towards the Heath, the sun heavy on the backs of their necks.

"I've been meaning to ask," Neville said. "How did you get on with Tonks?"

"All right, I think. He doesn't seem to want to throw me out, and the fact is, I don't want to leave. There's too much going on."

Neville was too short of breath to reply and they climbed the rest of the hill in silence. When they reached the bathing area, he pushed the gate open to reveal an area of sparse grass covered in lobster-pink flesh. Paul stepped inside and took a deep breath. Smells of pond water, sopping towels, damp hair. The path ahead had wet footprints dabbled all over it.

"Reminds me of school, this," Neville said.

"I'm surprised you can stand it."

Neville looked a question.

"Well, you don't seem to have liked school much."

"Doesn't mean I don't remember it. Let's face it, Tarrant, it never really leaves you, does it?"

"Mine has."

"Where did you go?"

"Grammar school."

"Oh, well." He was tugging at his tie as he spoke. "I say, Tarrant, you're not chippy, are you?"

"I'm sorry?"

"Chippy. A bit, you know—"

"Not at all. I think it had a lot of advantages."

"Such as?"

"Not having to shower with your back to the wall."

"Oh."

Neville looked around him uneasily, but the men stretched out on the grass might have been asleep for all the interest they showed.

"Or perhaps you think that's an exaggeration?"

"Not where I was. The dormitory was a sewer."

My God. Paul hadn't expected either the frankness or the bitterness of Neville's response.

"Where do we leave our clothes?"

"C'mon, I'll show you."

Neville was obviously well known here. Several of the men lying on the grass looked up and greeted him as he walked past. Paul followed him reluctantly into a low brick building that housed the lockers. It was too soon after lunch to go swimming and he disliked padding about on other people's wet footprints. At one point he was holding on to the wall and shaking one foot like a disgruntled cat.

A few minutes later, walking along to the end of the jetty with his locker key on a string round his neck, he began to change his mind. The pond was a sheet of silver with concentric rings of turbulence around the dark sleek heads of the swimmers. He gazed out beyond the fringe of willows and hawthorn bushes to the sunlit hills beyond, then turned and started to climb down the steps, the icy water inching up his mottled thighs.

Neville came running along the jetty. "Jump, man. S'torture doing it like that."

A second later, he dived into the choppy water. Paul watched him resurface: eyes blind, slack mouth sucking air. Then he dived again. A gleaming back showed above the water and he was gone.

Challenged, Paul let himself fall backwards, through the warm skin of water into the murky depths. All around him now were white, struggling legs. Neville swam towards him, arms sheathed in silver bubbles, hair floating from side to side as he twisted and turned. They stared at each other. Absurdly, out of nowhere it became a contest. Who could stay down longest. Lungs bursting, Paul gave in and broke the surface on a screech of indrawn breath. He pushed the hair out of his eyes to see Neville, a few feet away, laughing into his face.

"It's bloody freezing," Paul said.

"You need to keep moving."

They swam off in opposite directions. Paul circled the boundary ropes twice, sometimes clinging to the rope to watch the other swimmers. The shock of the water on his skin had cleared his mind; that, or seeing Neville's work. The strength of it. In some mysterious way Neville had become his marker. It wasn't friendship, though a friendship might develop; it wasn't rivalry either. Neville was too far ahead of him for that. He didn't know what it was. Only that he'd had close friendships that were less important than this wary, sniffing-about-each-other acquaintanceship.

The banks were covered with the starfish shapes of men spread out to expose the maximum amount of skin. Deciding he'd had enough of the cold, Paul hauled himself out of the water, found a space, and lay down, shrugging away the scratching of coarse grass between his shoulder blades. Closing his eyes, he concentrated on the orange glare behind his lids. Purple blotches drifted across, fading to nothing. All his doubts about his painting, his envy of Neville's talent, his constant anxiety over Teresa's husband dissolved into the warm air. He was drifting off to sleep when the orange light behind his lids darkened to black and a shadow fell across his skin.

Paul opened his eyes, squinting between his spread fingers. Of course. Neville. Eyes gleaming bright and malicious beneath wet hanks of hair.

" *You* didn't last long."

"Bloody freezing, man."

"You should try it in winter."

Paul smiled. "You don't mean to tell me you come here in winter?"

"It's been known."

Extraordinary—when he seemed so fond of his comfort in every other respect. The man lying next to Paul stood up, scratched the grass marks on the backs of his thighs and wandered off. Neville took the vacant place.

Disliking the proximity of so much chilly wet flesh, Paul closed his eyes again. He could hear Neville's breathing, feel him wanting to talk.

"I've known Elinor a long time."

"Yes," Paul said, "I suppose you must have done."

"The thing is, I'm in love with her." He waited for a response. "And I think you are too."

Reluctantly Paul turned to face him. There was such an intensity of suffering on Neville's chubby features that Paul could hardly bear to meet his eyes. "*No*. We see a lot of each other, obviously, because we're in the same year, and I do like her. But I'm going out with Teresa."

"Teresa Halliday?"

"Yes."

"Ah." He took a moment to think about it. "That's all right, then."

What an inept, bumbling approach. He was a strange man. Talented, yes, but malicious, too tormented himself to feel much kindness for other people, and bitter. What did he have to be bitter about? Choking on his golden spoon. But since he was here, he might as well get some information out of him. "Have you known Teresa long?"

"Oh, yes," Neville said. "Way back. She used to model at the Slade when I was a student."

"Have you ever met her husband?"

"No—and neither has anybody else. Why?"

Paul could feel Neville's gaze on the side of his face. "I just wondered."

"You mean, you wonder if he really exists?"

Paul sat up. "You think she's making it all up?"

Neville shrugged. "I don't know. She likes drama. She likes to be at the center of the stage with everybody else revolving round her. You saw her, the first night we met. She wouldn't let Elinor talk to anybody else." He waited for Paul to say something. "You've got to admit it's a bit odd he never actually shows up. Look, all I'm saying is, *if* he's real, why has nobody ever seen him?" He rolled onto his back. "In two years."

"She does seem to be genuinely frightened."

"She's an actress. They all are."

They? Who were "they," for God's sake? Women? Models? None of it made any sense. And why should other people have seen Halliday? He was hardly likely to stroll into the Café Royal and drag her out into the street.

Abruptly, Paul got to his feet.

"It's getting a bit chilly."

He wanted to get away from Neville.

"If you don't mind, I think I'll get dressed."

He needed to be with Teresa, to reassure himself that none of this was true.

7

THAT CONVERSATION WITH NEVILLE CHANGED everything. He tried not to let it and, for a time, seemed to be succeeding, but the next time Teresa announced that she'd heard a noise and asked him to go outside and check, he refused. "I didn't hear anything."

They were lying in the bed after making love. For a moment there was silence. He felt the tension in the arm that lay alongside his.

"I'll go," she said, reaching for her wrap.

"No—"

Too late. He heard her bare feet slapping on the lino and then the creak of the front door opening. A current of colder air rippled across his skin. He waited. When she didn't return immediately he got up and followed her.

She was standing halfway up the basement stairs, peering out between the railings. "Look, do you see?"

He followed her pointing finger across the road to a house with a large porch. In the deep shadow he thought he could see a figure, but even as he watched, it split into two. A courting couple.

"It's nothing," he said, struggling to keep the impatience he felt out of his voice.

Teresa turned to look at him.

"Come back inside."

She followed him down the steps and back along the passage into the bedroom. "You don't believe me."

"I do. But there's never anybody there when I look."

"You think I'm making it up."

"No, I don't think that. But I do think you might be getting it out of proportion."

"I had another letter."

It was the first he'd heard of any letters.

"Saying what?"

"The usual."

"Can I see it?"

"I burnt it."

"*Why?*"

She turned away from him. "Because I couldn't bear to have it in the house."

"What did it say?"

"That he's going to kill me." She managed a smile. "They don't vary much."

"And you don't keep them?"

"Would you want something like that in your flat?"

"No, but I'd keep it. It's evidence, for God's sake."

She shook her head.

"If you took those letters to the police they'd have to take it seriously. Promise me you'll keep the next one."

"All right."

He sat down on the bed, his thoughts seething. He watched her carefully all evening. She didn't seem particularly worried. . . . Later, after they'd eaten, she got her dressmaking dummy out of the spare room and went on with a jacket she was making. She was actually humming under her breath as she draped cloth along its curved side. He lay on the sofa pretending to read, but then got his sketchbook out and started drawing her, because this gave him the excuse to do what he was compelled to do anyway: search her face. Her eyes. Her mouth, thinned suddenly to a hard line, bristling with pins. He didn't know what to think.

■

That was Sunday. On the Friday following, they got back to Teresa's flat from an evening at the music hall and found a letter on the doormat. No postage. Obviously delivered by hand. While Paul locked and bolted the door, Teresa carried the letter through into the living room.

He found her standing by the mantelpiece with a sheet of flimsy blue paper in her hand. Wordlessly, she handed it to him.

He read: I'LL KILL THE PAIR OF YOU—JACK

The capital letters exactly filled the space between the lines so the impression was of a child's handwriting exercise. "Are they all like this?"

"Pretty much."

She was waiting to see how he'd react. He'd have given anything, at that moment, to have believed her, but even as he took her in his arms his mind whirred with suspicion. Capital letters. Why go to the trouble of disguising your handwriting and then add your name? It seemed stupid, but then, for all he knew, Halliday *was* stupid. He knew nothing about him. No, this was madness. He had to believe her. If she was lying now she was . . . What? Manipulative? Insane?

She was smiling in triumph. "There, you see? I told you he was hanging round."

"Why do you think he sends them?"

"I don't know."

"Do you think he's drunk when he writes them?"

"I don't know. Probably."

"Did he always drink? I mean, when you first met him?"

"You mean, did I drive him to it?"

"No, of course not."

"Yes, he drank. Only it didn't seem to have the same effect on him then. He just got a bit . . ." A faint, unconscious smile. "Cuddly. But then after we married he started drinking more and . . . Well, if he was bad tempered when he started, it made him fifty times worse. Whatever he was feeling, it made it worse. I've seen him sometimes, on a Saturday night, he'd have offered his own granny out to fight."

"Where did he get the money?"

"He worked for it. He was a furnace man. They work bloody hard. And they do need the drink. You see them come off shift, it's straight across the road into the pub. They'll sink five, six pints, think nothing of it, and they're not drunk on it either. And if he was ever short of a few bob he only had to go bare-knuckle fighting. Take anybody on. The other lads used to lay bets on him."

The warmth faded from her face.

"Have you got a photograph of him?"

She looked puzzled. "Why?"

"If he's going to kill me I'd like to be able to recognize him. If you don't mind?"

She went to the sideboard, reached under a tablecloth in the top drawer, and brought out a photograph. It was a wedding portrait, the two of them together, standing outside a church. Teresa was plump, smiling, full of hope, pretty, but not beautiful as she was now. Halliday was tall, dark haired, not bad looking, though his head and neck were unusually long so that his shoulders seemed to be surmounted by a tower.

Teresa stared at the photograph and her expression softened. Oh, she'd loved him once. How on earth had they got from the moment outside the church to where they were now?

"I suppose he still loves you."

She waved the letter. "You call that love?"

Her face was white and shriveled. Coarse. For the first time she repelled him. Knowing it was the wrong thing to do, he began interrogating her. When had she left Halliday? How often did he turn up? When was the last time? She became restless under the questioning, and no wonder. He was being tedious, bad mannered. No, worse than that, he was behaving like a bully, but he kept on. It was a relief when she finally lost her temper and told him to get out. He went without argument. He'd got as far as the door when she came after him, holding on to his arm, begging him to stay.

He let himself be persuaded. As she led him along the corridor to the bedroom, he felt the same urgency of desire as he'd felt the first time. He knew he ought to break off the relationship now, but he couldn't. Beside these moments—the salty taste of oysters on her tongue, the fumbling with her dress, the smell of her skin, the rumbling of a train that shook the bed— besides these moments the threat from Halliday meant nothing.

After their lovemaking, he lay in the candlelight absentmindedly stroking her hand. She didn't wear a wedding ring, but worse—because it seemed to symbolize the power of the past more trenchantly—the flesh on her ring finger was permanently indented. Unconsciously, he began picking at the groove in her skin until she snatched her hand away.

Paul lay for a moment in silence. Then: "Was he a good lover?"

"Who?"

Who indeed. "Jack."

"No, not really. He only cared about himself."

He wondered what she'd say about him. After a while she turned away from him and he heard from her breathing that she was asleep, but it was a long time before he was able to follow her and even then he had long, confused dreams that were always threatening to turn into nightmares. In one of them he sat by his mother's grave drinking a cup of tea, with a plate of sandwiches and fancy cakes balanced on his knee. When he looked up, everybody he knew was there, eating and drinking, talking, laughing, their chairs turned in to face the headstone. And then, looking down, he saw the grave was open.

He came awake with a jump, staring around him, but gradually his breathing quietened. Nothing to be afraid of, he told himself, knowing all the time that he had every reason to be afraid. She'll never rest, his grandmother had said. And she never had. Night after night she walked the corridors of his dreams.

But he was used to her presence. He didn't mind. Pressing his cheek against Teresa's back, he breathed in the smell of her hair, and, after a while, drifted back to sleep.

Normally Paul left before breakfast, going back to his own flat to shave and change his clothes, but this morning he lingered. They ate toast and drank coffee lying in bed and then she went off to the bathroom to get ready for her day.

As soon as he heard the bathroom door close he was out of bed. He began searching through her drawers, the bottom of the wardrobe, the sideboard, anywhere, not even trying to justify his behavior. He needed to know—that was all. He didn't even admit to himself what he was looking for, until the last second, when he held it in his hand.

A cheap blue notepad. Going across to the window, pressing his shoulder against the glass to get as much light as the gray morning allowed, he saw that the paper was the same weight and color as the letter she'd received last night. He put the pad and the letter side by side, rubbed the bottom edge of the pages between his thumb and forefinger, held them up to the light to check the watermark. Identical. That, by itself, didn't mean much—notepads like this were sold in every corner shop and every branch of Woolworth's in England. But on the first page of the pad he could see the indentation of letters where the writer had pressed hard. The *K* in *KILL* was particularly sharp and deep, but if you looked closely you could make out the whole sentence.

I'LL KILL THE PAIR OF YOU—JACK

There could be no doubt. He saw no way round it. She'd written the letter herself.

8

HE WAS OUT OF HIS DEPTH: TOO INTELLIGENT NOT
to know it, too proud to admit it. He needed to talk to Elinor,
who knew Teresa better than anybody else, but it was difficult
to get hold of her. At last, though, he managed to corner her in
the Antiques Room and she invited him to tea at her lodgings after college.

Prompt at six o'clock, he knocked on her door. He heard
his name called and stepped back to see Elinor leaning out of a
window on the third floor, her heavy dark gold hair swinging
forward in two sharp points on her cheeks. "Hang on a sec. I'll
come down."

Footsteps, quick and light, and then the door was thrown
open and she looked out at him, smiling.

"Doesn't your landlady mind men calling?"

"*Men?*" She peered round him. "Oops, he's brought the
regiment. No, she's down in the basement. As long as there's
not too much noise, she lets us get on with it. She's even letting
us redecorate."

Elinor led the way up a broad staircase whose dark green

carpet had a beige strip in the center where the pile had worn through to the backing. She was clearly in the thick of decorating—he smelled distemper the moment she opened her door. Lolling tongues of rose-trellised wallpaper lay on the floor where she'd simply seized it and pulled it off the wall. A bucket of gray, glutinous sludge, a table, and a stepladder occupied the center of the room, but a sofa and two chairs had been pushed together at the far end so that some kind of normal life could continue.

"What color are you doing it?"

"Stone. I thought gray might be a bit too depressing."

"And you're doing it all yourself?"

"No, Ruthie comes round to help. She's on the floor above. We're doing mine first and then we'll do hers."

"It's a big job."

"Oh, I don't mind. I like it. Anyway, there's no choice. I can't work with that stuff on the wall. There's another room, if you'd like to see?"

The bedroom. Elinor's bed under a patchwork quilt, a chair, a wardrobe. Nothing else. Sunlight came in through the smeared window and crept in parallelograms of light across the faded carpet. From below came the hum and rumble of traffic.

"I'm leaving this till last."

He scarcely heard her. He was staring at a painting she'd propped against the wall: a female nude, facing away, rubbing a bath towel down her left arm. The ends of her glossy black hair stuck in wet coils to her white shoulders. "Teresa."

"She modeled for me. I said. Don't you remember?"

He did, now she mentioned it, but still it came as a shock. They gazed at the painting together. He felt a surge of desire, not for Teresa but for Elinor. He imagined kissing her, and the image was so vivid that for one crazy second he thought he'd done it, and was groping about in his mind for some way of repairing the damage.

"That's the one I won the scholarship for."

He realized she'd brought him here into her bedroom to show him this, but he didn't know why. A natural pride in a good piece of work? Or something more fundamental: a demand that he should recognize her as an equal? Well, if that was her motive, she needn't have bothered. There could be no question of *equality*. If he stayed at the Slade another ten years he'd never be able to paint sunlight on wet flesh like that.

"It's wonderful. I'm so glad I've seen it."

She smiled. "Come on, I'll put the kettle on."

"Can I do anything to help?"

"No, I don't think so. There's only room for one."

He stood in the kitchen doorway while she boiled water and made salmon-and-cucumber sandwiches. He wanted to say more about the painting, but he'd always found it difficult to praise an artist to his face, *her* face, or even to accept praise gracefully himself. Though that hadn't been much of a disability so far.

"Right, I think that's it," Elinor said, wiping her hands on her sides. "Here, you can carry the tray."

He set it down on a small table, which she cleared by sweeping piles of books onto the floor. They sat facing each other, the sofa and chairs so squashed together their knees were almost touching. She offered him a plate and a sandwich, but didn't immediately pour the tea. He noticed there were three cups.

"I got a note from Teresa saying her husband was prowling round."

"Ye-es."

"Poor Teresa. She must be terrified."

Her eyes had gone black with anger. Her sympathy reminded him how very much he liked her, and he was reaching out to touch her hand, when—

"Elinor."

Neville, gasping for breath after the long walk upstairs. He stopped in the doorway, registering the scene, and his face changed color—not a flush, but the most extraordinary darkening, like a male fish that finds itself unexpectedly confronted by a rival. "Oh, hello, Tarrant."

Why does she do it? Paul wondered. Obviously she'd invited them both to tea, at slightly staggered times, implying, though not promising—for when did Elinor ever promise anything?—that each was to enjoy a tête-à-tête. Now she avoided looking at either of them.

After an awkward pause, Neville produced a bottle of wine from the green bag he was carrying. "I thought you might like to celebrate the scholarship." He glanced at Paul. "You know about this?"

"I've just been admiring the painting."

"Oh, you've got it back?"

"Yes, this morning. Come through, I'll show you."

Paul listened to the murmur of voices from the bedroom. Neville loved her. It was unmistakable. He always spoke to her with a kind of clumsy, affable superiority, making the most of his extra years and his fame, but increasingly the mask of confidence slipped to reveal lust and pain and fear.

"I couldn't have done it without Teresa," Elinor was saying, as they came back into the room. "A model makes all the difference."

"Yes, and she's a good model too, isn't she?" Neville sat down next to Paul. "Are you painting her?"

"No."

"I'll get some glasses," Elinor said.

The two men were left alone. After a pause, Neville asked, "How's the life class going?"

"Oh, you know. I've more or less given up."

Elinor came back with three glasses and a bottle opener. Neville uncorked the bottle and poured. After they'd toasted Elinor's success, there was silence. Then Neville said, "Oh, I've got something to celebrate too. I've bought a motorbike."

He looked so pink and glowing, so insufferably pleased with himself, that of course they had to troop downstairs and admire the gleaming monster. Another craze, Paul thought, dismissively, another fad. That was the kind of reaction Neville provoked. Not contempt, exactly, but something close to it. The vanity of the man. The *wealth*. And yet you had to share his delight in his new toy. He was such a child.

"I don't suppose I can tempt either of you to have a ride?"

"No," Elinor said.

Paul raised his glass. "Not at the moment."

Back upstairs, flushed with wine and triumph, Neville became more expansive, reverting to the subject of Teresa's husband. He seemed to have forgotten Elinor was there. "Why does she live in that wretched little basement? There's no need. She's not that poor. And even if she was, some man or other would always fork out. If she was half as frightened as she says she is, she'd be only too glad to move. Look at it. No proper locks on the windows. Anybody could hide in that coal hole, the bolt on the back door doesn't work. . . . One screw—"

Too late, he stopped, stared into his glass, and emptied it in one gulp.

"She seems very happy there," Elinor said.

Nobody replied. Paul smiled and stood up. "I think I ought to be going."

Elinor was looking up at him with some concern. He shrugged, then bent and kissed her, rather enjoying the expression of pain that flickered across Neville's face. "Shall I see you in Lockhart's tomorrow?"

"Yes."

"One o'clock?"

"Yes."

"Right, then."

"No, wait, I'll see you out."

They walked downstairs together. "Are you and Teresa coming to the Café Royal tonight?" she asked, as he opened the front door.

"Yes, I'm meeting her there. Are you coming?"

"Don't know." She jerked her head towards the stairs. "I'll see how things are."

She was hugging her upper arms, though it wasn't cold. For the first time since he'd known her she seemed vulnerable, not dashing at all, a little half-starved cat. He put his arm round her. "I'm really pleased about the scholarship." He hesitated. "Elinor . . ."

"I know what you're going to ask and the answer is I don't know." She looked uncomfortable. "Yes, probably. But it was ages ago. Nev's a troublemaker, you know that."

He nodded. "Yes, I know. I'll see you later."

It was nothing to be miserable about, he told himself, walking off down the street, merely the confirmation of something he'd suspected since their first evening. What happened before they met didn't matter. It was far less important than the threat—if there was a threat—from Halliday.

9

THAT SATURDAY THERE WAS A FAIR ON HAMP-
stead Heath. He asked Teresa to go with him but he wasn't surprised when she refused. Instead, he arranged to go with Elinor
and Ruthie, and with Ruthie's friend Michael Abbott, a cheerful, sociable, self-confident young man who spent hardly any
time in classes and yet never seemed to doubt his ability as a
painter.

They met at Elinor's lodgings and went up together on the
bus, sitting on the top in the open air. This was the first day that
felt like summer. Paul managed to sit next to Elinor. As she
twisted round to speak to Ruthie, her knee pressed into his
thigh under the rain apron. He glanced at her sideways, but she
didn't seem to notice. She was full of life, carefree, and suddenly his affair with Teresa seemed limited, shadowed by the
bitterness of her marriage that he pretended to understand, but
couldn't. The cabbage leaves and the dark hole behind the dustbins seemed to epitomize everything he'd begun to dislike. But
then he remembered the sound of the trains, the vibration of the
bed as they roared past, the way Teresa's skin gleamed in the
candlelight.

"Hoy!" Elinor waved a hand in front of his face.

"Sorry, I was miles away."

"I know where you were. Couldn't she come?"

"She wanted to go to the Café Royal. I fancied a change." His words hung on the air, silence giving them a weight he hadn't intended. Say something. Anything. "How about Neville? I'd've thought a fairground was just the ticket."

"He's painting a factory in Leeds."

He sensed coolness, but whether directed at Neville or at him—perhaps she found the question intrusive—he didn't know. It didn't matter. It was a summer evening and warm and they were going to the fair together.

At the fairground they stood on muddy trampled grass, breathing in smells of candyfloss, roasting chestnuts, chips, beer from the beer tents where men queued and carried away bottles, two or three in each hand. On the boat swings girls hung on to their skirts, shrieks of laughter slicing the air. They went on the swings first. He handed Elinor in and sat opposite her as the chocks were pulled away. Hauling on the tasseled rope they rose higher and higher. He saw her open mouth and knew she was laughing but couldn't distinguish her laugh from the roar around them. At one point her skirt flew up. She squealed, like any shopgirl on an outing, and he caught the hem and pinned it down with his foot. By the time their go was over he'd had enough and so had she, jumping down and swaying against him, so that her nose bumped against his shoulder. He took hold of her arms to steady her, she looked up at him and for a second they might have kissed, but Abbott, waiting behind him, said, "Hey, get a move on. It's our turn."

They waited. All around overtired children whinged; mothers snapped and slapped; fathers took refuge in the beer

tents; gangs of youths roamed about, braying, jeering, contemp-
tuous, excluded. Paul wanted to get Elinor somewhere quiet
and alone, but she and Ruthie stuck together as they always did.
As soon as Ruthie got off the boat swing they were arm in arm
again, strolling towards the merry-go-round whose grinning,
blue-eyed horses rose and fell. When it stopped, Elinor said,
"Aren't you coming?" Her skin was orange in the light of the
naphtha torches, which cast shuddering shadows over the heav-
ing ground. "No, you go." You could only ride three abreast
and so Abbott was in his glory, with a girl on either side.

As the music started to play again, they laughed and
waved and set off, slowly at first as the man went from horse to
horse collecting fares, then faster, rising and falling, rising and
falling. They seemed at one point to ride him down, Elinor staring straight ahead, unseeing, as he slipped and fell under the
hooves. He was shivery, too hot and too cold at once, the awful warm gassy beer lying heavy on his stomach. He would
wait for them to get off, he decided, then find somewhere to sit
down. For a moment, he stopped looking at the horses and
gazed through them to the other side. A man stood there, a tall
man with a ginger mustache and a hat pulled down low over
his eyes. What little could be seen of his face was a beaten
bronze mask, expressionless in the light of the naphtha flares.
Paul stared. The man stared back at him. He was alone, which
seemed odd, but then perhaps he was waiting, as Paul was, for
somebody to get off the ride. Aware that his stare was becoming
confrontational, Paul made a deliberate effort to switch his gaze
away. A second later, unable to help himself, he looked back
and the man had gone, but so suddenly Paul was left wondering
whether there'd ever been anybody there at all. It was all this

nonsense with Teresa, he told himself. He'd spent so long staring at shadows, he was starting to imagine things.

By now he was feeling rather ill, but determined not to let it spoil the evening. The ride seemed to go on forever, but at last he felt Elinor's hand on his arm. He bought more beer because it was his turn, but the more he drank the worse he felt. They tried the Hall of Mirrors next, Elinor gazing at her reflection in the distorting glass, now tall, now short, now fat, now thin, all arms and legs one minute, all head the next. Like Alice in Wonderland. She even looked like Alice, with that short full skirt and her hair tied back with ribbon. Almost doll-like. He felt a spasm of dislike that came from nowhere and did nothing to lessen his desire.

Outside again, he said, "Do you mind if I sit down a bit? I'll just be over there by the bandstand."

"Are you all right?"

Elinor's face, looking up at him, seemed scarcely less distorted than her reflections had been. "I'll be fine. I'm just feeling a little bit sick, that's all."

"It's the beer," Abbott said, gloomily. "I've never tasted anything like it."

They went off to the Ghost Train, and Paul started pushing through the crowd towards the sound of a brass band. He felt adrift, disconnected from everybody and everything. Perhaps he should stop seeing Teresa. At the moment he seemed to be in a state where he was happy neither with her nor without her.

Despite the blaring music, the bandstand was a peaceful place. Many of the seats were empty. All around crowds of people surged from one attraction to the next. Sweaty faces under funny hats; fat men fanning themselves with handkerchiefs; children carried high above the crowds, their white, skinny legs clasped in their fathers' meaty fists. A stench of horse dung; leather; petrol fumes; raw, wet earth; trampled grass. Everywhere, couples, some of them now beginning to leave the fairground to look for peace and quiet, passion rather, under the trees. He felt a swell of yearning for Elinor or Teresa or . . . No, no, no, neither of them, for some anonymous girl he could pick up by the swings and take outside and never see again.

The band was playing a military march: "Men of Harlech." He sat down and listened and after a while he did start to feel better. Probably Abbott was right. It was the beer, and he hadn't had anything to eat. Perhaps he should get something. A bag of chips would do. When the band took a break, he stood up, intending to buy some food, but as he turned to go, his attention was caught by reflections in a tuba. Distorted figures, chairs, caravans. He shifted his weight from side to side and the images changed. A face loomed up behind his face in the shining metal, and, ashamed of the childish game he'd been caught playing, he turned away.

He sensed that he was being followed. Almost as if some menacing doppelgänger had jumped out of the tuba and was pursuing him. Paul slowed down, striving to appear unconcerned. He felt if he showed any sign of fear the other would feed on it. Out of the corner of his eye he could see that it was the tall man with the ginger mustache, the man he had not yet allowed himself to call Halliday. The other slowed too, marching in step. What a ridiculous situation. Paul wanted to get away, but he didn't want to go too far from the bandstand, since he'd arranged to meet Abbott and the girls here.

Oh, to hell with it. He turned on his pursuer. He wasn't

as tall as he'd seemed from a distance, but he was powerfully built. He wouldn't be easy to take on. If it came to that—at the moment he was grinning. A flush of anger prickled Paul's face and chest. "Do I know you?"

Eyes like polished black pebbles. "No, but we've got a fair bit in common. You're fucking my wife."

So this was it. Halliday. It was nothing like he'd expected. In the early days when he'd imagined meeting Teresa's husband, he'd envisaged a short, sharp, violent encounter in the basement or the street outside her flat. *Leave my wife alone, you bastard.* THUMP. Instead, here he was, not ten inches away, showing his teeth. Grinning. Paul walked away. He didn't want a fight—he needed to feel right was on his side before he could hit out, and it was difficult to feel that here. Teresa was married to this man. He strode along, weaving his way through the crowd, knowing Halliday was close behind. Without warning, he lunged forward and grasped Paul's arm. Paul stopped immediately, making no attempt to pull away. He was close enough to see the hairs in Halliday's nostrils. Close to, like this, close enough to smell the hot, beery fug of his breath, Paul could see how frayed and grubby his shirt was. His eyes were bloodshot, his speech slurred. The man was a wreck. Not just down on his luck but terribly, terminally stricken.

"You can't just walk off like that."

He sounded reasonable, even friendly.

They stared at each other. Paul said, "All right, spit it out. What do you want?"

"I want my wife back."

"That's up to her."

"Oh, I suppose you've nowt to do with it?"

"She was already separated when I met her."

"*I saw you.*"

"What do you mean, you saw me?"

"Fucking my wife."

The gap in the bloody curtains. "You can't blame me for the state of your marriage."

"I don't. I blame her."

For a moment Halliday's grin disappeared in a blaze of misery. Almost immediately, he was smirking again. Paul could have understood anger, but despite Halliday's words what he saw in his face was not anger but a kind of jeering complicity. He seemed more like a pimp than an outraged husband.

And, God, he was drunk. It hadn't been so apparent at first, but now he was swaying on his feet.

"You're one of a long line. Don't you go thinking there's owt special about you. She's had more men than I've had hot dinners."

"Aw, piss off. And if I catch you following me round again—"

"You'll do what?"

Suddenly Halliday's fists were clenched. Paul walked on again and this time he knew he wasn't being followed. When he looked back Halliday hadn't moved. He stood, shabby, burly, bereft, in front of the bandstand where now, under the conductor's raised baton, the band was tuning up again.

He had to tell Teresa. Tell her what? That Halliday was following him around, that he was angry, that he wanted her back; but she already knew all that. All the same he had to go to see her. Halliday was pathetic, with his swearing and his grinning and his melodrama and his filthy shirt, but he was angry and persistent, and he'd seen them making love. That would goad almost any man into action.

Why, with all her dressmaking skills, did she not run up a pair of curtains that met in the middle? It wouldn't have taken her more than an hour. Or get proper bolts fitted on the doors? Or live in a first-floor flat? At the moment he felt guilty for ever having doubted her, but when he stepped back a little he saw that her behavior was every bit as odd as Neville had said.

He would change the bolts on the doors. That was one practical thing he could do to help. And although his meeting with Halliday had left him more bewildered than ever, he didn't feel he could end the affair now.

In the distance he saw Elinor, with a bunch of pink candyfloss in her hand, standing a little to one side as Abbott and Ruthie talked. Waving, calling her name, he struggled through the crowd to join her.

10

THAT EVENING TERESA SAT AT A CORNER TABLE IN the Café Royal, staring all around her, noticing who was in tonight. She never seemed to get tired of the place, but Paul had begun to hate it. He felt all the time that, as Teresa's latest lover, he was being assessed, and he had no independent status to make the verdict a matter of indifference to him. A young man with a flushed, familiar, subtly jeering face came up and spoke to her, but she ignored him, and he rapidly withdrew. She had immense self-confidence with men, though with women she often seemed wary. She'd have said this was because she liked men better, that she preferred their company, but really it was all based on contempt. On long, hard experience of men as sexual predators. In Teresa's eyes, every man she met, from the waiter who served their drinks to the Archbishop of Canterbury, shuffled towards her with his trousers round his ankles and his dick pointing at the sky.

Paul kept his back to the room, leaning forward, trying to get her full attention. He wanted to talk to her, and he knew she was resisting him.

"Oh, look," she said, "there's Gus."

She raised a hand to wave, but Paul caught hold of her wrist. "No, don't do that."

She sat back sullenly. "You never want to meet anybody else. You only like being with me when we're on our own."

"That's not true. You could have come to the fair with us."

"The fair?"

He could see she wanted to pick a quarrel. Well, she could have one, but not about their social life. "I saw Jack this afternoon." He thought she changed color, though in this golden light it was hard to tell.

"Oh? Did he see you?"

"Yes, we bumped into each other at the fairground."

"By accident?"

"What do you think?"

She shrugged. "What happened?"

"What do you mean, what happened?"

"Did he try to start a fight?"

"No." He was watching her curiously. "He seemed a bit pathetic, actually."

"Did he?"

"Yes. Sort of a mangy-tiger feel about him." She winced and turned her head away. "For what it's worth, I think he's still very much in love with you."

"Then he's got a bloody funny way of showing it."

Tears, almost. Not quite.

"So you say. But he never actually does anything, does he?"

She stood up. "I'm going to say hello to Gus. Come if you want."

That was his last chance to speak to her. She was swallowed up in the crowd around the great Augustus, and soon he could see only her head and shoulders. He should have challenged her about the note, only he knew that if he did and she lied it would be the end of the affair. And he wasn't ready for it to end.

In the cab going back she hardly spoke. He went through the usual routine, going down the steps before her, looking in the coal hole, unlocking the door, going in first.

"I'll buy some bolts," he said. "It won't take me a minute to put them on."

He wondered why he hadn't thought of it before. She'd infected him with her passivity.

They undressed and got into bed. Their lovemaking had changed, become rougher, less nuanced, more abrupt. Every night, now, he seemed to be pushing at the boundaries of what was acceptable, waiting for a protest and then, when none came, moving still further away from tenderness. Was this what Halliday had done? After it was over he lay staring into the darkness, knowing he didn't want to spend the night with her. She'd lied to him; worse than that, she'd lied about something that mattered for reasons he couldn't understand.

He rolled over and kissed her upper arm. "I think I'll go back tonight, if you don't mind. I want an early start."

"Hmm? Oh, all right."

She was too sleepy to be surprised. He gathered his clothes together as best he could and went into the bathroom to dress. Letting himself out of the flat, he climbed the basement steps and paused for a moment, his face lifted to the light of the street-lamp, defying Halliday who might—*might*—be watching from the shadows but more probably was tucked up warm and drunk in bed. If he was going to do anything he'd have done it long since. Then Paul started to walk home. The gritty fumes from the railway line were mixed tonight with a fresher smell: the dawn smell, and as he walked he felt the wind quicken, flattening his trousers against his legs as he reached the corner of the street. He didn't look back.

Paul had never been a heavy drinker, but now he drank every night. He knew it was pointless looking for Halliday, he had to wait for Halliday to find him, and he felt it would happen. It wasn't over. On the last day of term he went with a crowd of students to the Crown. The evening was warm. All the doors and windows were open, the bar was crowded, drinkers spilling out onto the pavement. He drank four pints of tepid beer very quickly; argued passionately on subjects he didn't care about in the least; sang; swayed from side to side; vowed undying friendship to people he would never see again; became sentimental, demonstrative, then, abruptly, morose; and, deciding he wasn't fit company for anybody in his present state, plunged out into the night. He staggered and held on to the wall, while above his head pale London stars swam in shoals from roof to roof.

The city was brazen and clamorous. The crowded pavements exasperated him and so he turned into the side streets, letting his feet carry him forward, unthinking, until there was no sound except the echo of his footsteps and the stamping of horses at a cabstand. He turned left blindly, and found himself in a livery yard. The darkness now was full of tossing manes, snuffles, snorts, slurrings and scrapings of iron-shod hooves on stone. The horses were too intent on their hay to bother about him, though he caught a glint of eye white as a head turned. Was there a way through? He couldn't see, and didn't fancy slither-

ing all the way across the muddy yard to find out, so began to
retrace his steps. He'd almost reached the lighted pavement
when a shadow peeled itself off the wall.

"Sorry," he said, thinking it must be a groom or an off-
duty cabby. "Took the wrong turn."

"Too damn right you did." That voice. Genial, complici-
tous, dangerous, drunk. "Got you now, haven't I?"

The world shrank to a few yards of muddy ground. There
was no time except for the long second in which he turned to
face Halliday. He opened his mouth to speak and a fist smashed
into it, sending him staggering back against the wall. The next
two blows he dodged and then began to dance around, looking
for an opening. Nothing existed now except Halliday's eyes
and grinning mouth. Paul darted back, Halliday followed,
swinging his fist wide, unable to stop. As he lunged past, Paul
hit him on the mouth. The pain in his knuckles was pure joy.
Halliday shook his head. Anybody else would have been on the
ground. The punch seemed to sober him. He came for Paul,
who backed away, feeling the wall hard against his spine. The
next blow caught him on the side of the head and he went
down. Huddled against the wall, he felt Halliday's boot smash
into his ribs. And again. The sounds jerking out of him seemed
to come from the boot not his mouth. He tried to crawl away.
Halliday followed. In desperation Paul lunged forward and
grabbed Halliday round the knees. Halliday tried to kick himself free. When that failed, he pummeled Paul's head and shoulders, but Paul hung on. Hands came down, clawing, finding
the orbits of his eyes. He let go of Halliday's knees and pulled at
his wrists. Then a voice. Not Halliday's. Somebody else. He
seized his opportunity and crawled towards the light. Behind
him the voices went on. Then legs coming towards him. He

braced himself for another kicking, but, instead, a hand touched his shoulder. A face, not Halliday's, bent over him. He tried to speak, but his mouth wouldn't stretch. Everything hurt. Up to this moment, there'd been hardly any pain, but now, as the other man helped him to his feet, every move was agony. "I'm all right."

"Aye, you look it."

Paul was on his feet now, though only just. Halliday had gone.

"Can you walk?"

"I'll be all right."

As long as Halliday didn't come back. He looked around, tried to think. Get a cab. There was a stand not far away; he remembered that. He tried to walk, but after a few feet everything went black.

"Come on. I'll get you to a cab."

Every step sent a jolt of pain from his ankle to the top of his skull. Somewhere in all this he'd lost his hat. Dazed, he looked round and found it squashed flat into the mud. His suit was caked with mud and worse. Cab. Cab. He couldn't think further than that. They set off, Paul's arm across the groom's shoulder. He wondered if his mouth was bleeding, and pressed his lips to find out, but his hand was so filthy the blood—if there was blood—didn't show. At last, the cabstand. One cab waiting.

The driver took one look at him. "Sorry, mate. Can't do it. What you been doing? Rolling in it?"

Paul was too weak to argue, and the groom was going no further, he could see that. "Can't leave the yard. More than me job's worth," he said, though his breath stank of porter.

Paul struggled to get money out of his pocket and pressed it into his outstretched hand. "Thanks."

"Thank you, sir. Mind how you go."

Paul clung to the railings. There was a hospital half a mile away, or there was Elinor. Elinor was just round the corner. He could go there, clean up, then get a cab.

Shaking, though the night was hot, he staggered along, holding on to railings whenever he could. It was late, too late to knock on anybody's door, but he had no other way of getting home. He knocked and waited. Almost immediately the upstairs window opened. "Who is it?"

He stepped back into the light.

"Paul? What on earth—? Wait, I'll come down."

He swayed on his feet. The streetlamps blurred. Then the door opened and Elinor, still dressed, got hold of him. "What happened?"

"Halliday happened."

"Oh, my God."

He saw her hesitate, torn between loyalty to a friend and horror at the state he was in.

"Are you hurt?"

"I don't know. My ribs hurt."

She stepped back. "You'd better come in."

It took a long time getting up the stairs, hips jostling hard against each other. Her arm was round his waist. At last they reached her room and he collapsed onto the sofa. All he wanted to do now was sleep. Sleep or, preferably, die.

"Where does it hurt?"

No sympathy. She could smell the beer on his breath.

"Ribs. Mainly."

"Take your shirt off."

That was a struggle. When it was done, he fell back, hearing her make little tetching sounds of dismay or disapproval. She fetched hot water and soap from the kitchen and set to work to clean him up. "I daren't run a bath," she said. "It's too late. The boiler makes a terrible racket."

Ten painful minutes later: "You'll have to go to hospital, Paul. I can't cope with this."

"In the morning."

"Did he kick you?"

"Ouch!"

"It's got to be washed, Paul. It's filthy." She gently wiped the flannel across his side. "You should really have that stitched."

He was aware of her slim waist as she bent over him. The lace front of her blouse tickled his face.

"There," she said, at last, sitting back. "That's the best I can do. We'll get you to a doctor in the morning."

"I can't stay here."

"It'll be all right. You can't go home."

She made him toast and cocoa, fetched a pillow and bed-spread, and settled him down for the night.

"Call me if you need anything."

"I need to warn Teresa."

"Tomorrow. I'll go and see her, if you like?"

"He might be there now."

"There's nothing you can do. Try to get some sleep."

He lay down, dreading the long, sleepless night ahead, only to drift off almost at once. His sleep was full of confused, dark dreams. More than once he jerked awake to the sound of wheels clattering over cobbles, and hardly knew whether the cab was in the road outside or in his dream: the black, windowless vehicle that had taken his mother away. Glancing up at the curtains, he saw that dawn was mercifully close, and lay as still as he could, trying not to move his head.

Every breath hurt. Every thought hurt. Teresa had been telling the truth all along and he hadn't believed her, and now she too must be at risk. He ought to get up. He swung his legs onto the floor, and groaned. Enough of that. He had to get moving before people were about.

At the third attempt he got his right arm into his shirt-sleeve and then had to stop, wiping sweat away from his upper lip. All the while, in some separate corner of his brain, the fight with Halliday went on and on, every blow and kick constantly replayed. But it was merely background noise and still left him free to think about his future. There was no confusion now, only a dreadful clarity. The whole of the past year had been a complete waste of time. Hanging round the Café Royal with a beautiful model on his arm, spending too much, drinking too much, turning in work that would have disgraced a schoolboy. What did he think he was doing? His time at the Slade was ending in failure—and he deserved to fail.

It was time to go home, have one last try at painting something good—no, not good; honest. Honest would be a start. And if that didn't work, he'd look for a job—almost any job. Stop squandering his nan's legacy.

But meanwhile there was Teresa. That had to be finished properly. He had to make sure she was all right.

He was trying to get the left arm into his sleeve, but his muscles seemed to have stiffened overnight and he could hardly move. Bracing himself for another attempt, he looked up and saw Elinor, wearing a long white nightdress, watching him from her bedroom door.

"Are you all right?"

"Yes." Oh, God, that was a squeak. He took a deep, scaring breath. "Not bad at all."

"You look terrible."

"Ah, but you should see the other chap."

It hurt to laugh. Elinor came across and helped him into his shirt, then his socks and shoes.

"I'm sorry to be so useless."

He looked down at the burnished golden bell of her hair, and imagined stroking it. Get a hold of yourself, he told himself. You're no use to any woman in this state.

Once his laces were securely tied he stood up. The floor shelved away beneath him, the air turned black, but when the rush of blood subsided, he was still on his feet. She was brushing his jacket. Some of the dirt had dried and came off easily, but it was still a mess. Cautiously, with a lot of help from her, he managed to get into it and stood while she gave him a final brush down.

"You'll have to buy a new one. You can't go anywhere in this."

"No, I know."

"I'll make some tea. Have to be black, I'm afraid. I'm out of milk."

"No, I won't have any, thanks. I'd better be off."

"You need a doctor."

"I'll go to the hospital. Soon as I can. Promise."

"I'll come with you."

"No, better not."

He looked out of the window. The street was deserted. With any luck he might slip out unobserved.

"You're welcome to stay, you know."

"No. I shouldn't be here at all, really. It was selfish." He raised his hand and laid it against her cheek. "Dear Elinor. Thanks for putting up with me."

She blushed. "When shall I see you?"

"I don't know. Will you go to see Teresa?"

"Of course."

"I'll be over there as soon as I can. And then I think I might go home for a few days. I need to think."

"Good idea, let things calm down a bit. But don't think too long, will you? I'll miss you."

He bent and rested his cheek against hers. She let him out of the room and watched through a crack in the door as he tiptoed downstairs. The house was heavy with the breaths of sleepers. Opening the door, he peered out, and slipped into the street like a burglar.

The buildings he knew so well looked unfamiliar in the predawn light. Crossing the road, he limped along, stumbling once or twice where a tree root had raised the paving stones. At times he went dizzy, but steadied himself and went on again. Straight to the hospital to get his ribs bound up, then he'd go to see Teresa, to make sure she was all right. He owed her that at least.

11

Opening the door to let him in, Teresa kept her face averted, took him along to the living room, and left him there. He stood in the doorway and stared, struggling to take in the changes. She'd stripped the red and blue shawls from the furniture and taken all the paintings down. A beige sofa, so lumpy and ancient the springs bulged out of the seats, took up a huge amount of space. Cigarettes had burnt black holes in the arms. A greasy patch on the back showed where a previous tenant had rested his head. The pictures had left ghost squares on the wall. The rugs, rolled up, revealed the full horror of the carpet with its interminable, meaningless pattern.

The shock of this dismantling was very great. He went into the bedroom and found Teresa putting a folded skirt into the suitcase that lay open on the bed.

"What's going on?"

"I'm going away for a few days." Her voice was tight to bursting.

"Where? How long for?"

More than a few days. Two more suitcases, already packed, stood at the foot of the bed.

"My auntie's."

Her face was in shadow. He caught her arm and pulled her across to the lamp. She had a bruise on one cheekbone and a cut on her lower lip. "Jack?"

"Who else?" She laughed. It would have distressed him less if she'd screamed. "I might as well go home. I certainly can't model looking like this."

"When did this happen?"

He sounded overbearing, bullying. He was angry with her because he hadn't been there to protect her.

"The other night, after you'd gone. You left your ciga-rettes behind, I thought you'd come back for them."

"What did he want?"

"Oh, to tell me what a bitch I am. And how much he loves me. He was drunk, for God's sake."

"Did he . . . ?" He glanced at the bed. An old, brown bloodstain, the shape of Africa, took up the center of the mat-tress. He'd lain on that, night after night, and never known it was there. "Don't go."

"No choice."

"You're not going back to him?"

"What do you think?"

He sat down on the bed heavily. She tugged a blouse sleeve from underneath him, angry with him for being there and being useless. He didn't blame her. "When were you going to tell me?"

"Now. This evening." But she wouldn't meet his eye.

"Do you know where he's staying?"

"No." She was crumpling newspaper and stuffing it into shoes. "And I wouldn't tell you if I did." She squeezed a pair of shoes down the side of the case.

"What train are you catching?"

"The eight o'clock."

She closed the suitcase and snapped the locks shut.

"You were just going to leave, weren't you?"

"No, of course not. You know I wouldn't do that."

They stood and faced each other. She came into his arms and he held her, stroking her hair, but his thoughts were all of Halliday, the bright, black buttons of his eyes, the sweating bulk of him. "I'll find him."

"If you've got any sense you'll keep out of his way."

She made to lift the suitcase from the bed, but he got there first and did it for her.

"How are you getting to the station?"

"Elinor's coming for me in a cab."

"I'll come with you."

"No, better not. Honestly. Let's say good-bye here."

"You are coming back?"

"Of course, I always do. I just need to let him calm down a bit."

A knock on the door. Teresa went to answer it, slipping on the chain before she opened it. Elinor's voice. She came into the bedroom, wearing a small, rather elegant black hat, braced for conflict.

"Paul. I've been trying to find you all day."

"I've been at the hospital. Took ages."

"Are you all right?"

"Cracked ribs. Nothing that won't mend."

"I warned you," Teresa said. "I told you what he was like."

"I don't mind what he did to *me*."

They began a final search of the flat while he stood, helpless, watching them open and close drawers, check cupboards, peer under sofa and chairs. Both women were, at some level, enjoying this, Elinor more than Teresa. Finally, Teresa lay facedown and looked under the bed.

"Can't see anything."

The whole flat seemed to have been demolished, though in fact comparatively little had been taken away. The glow he remembered had always been an illusion, created by lamps and a few brightly colored shawls and rugs. All the time, underneath, there'd been this cold squalor. For the first time, he noticed a smell of rancid fat from the kitchen.

"You don't have to go on your own," he said. "We can go together."

"No, Paul. He mightn't bother tracking me down if he knows I'm not with you."

Elinor went to the door to see if the cab had arrived, leaving them alone for a few minutes. Teresa was looking in the wardrobe mirror, adjusting her hat. She paused, pin in hand, meeting his reflected gaze. "You'll get over it, you know. Quite quickly."

"I love you."

She turned to face him. "You don't love me. If you love anybody, you love Elinor, and you only love *her* because you know she won't have you."

He was starting to be angry, not just with Halliday but with her as well. How dare she tell him what he felt?

Elinor said from the hall, "The cab's here."

Paul could hear the cab horse stamping its feet, snorting, jingling its harness. The time they had left was measured in seconds; there was nothing he could do to stop her going. He lugged one of the three cases up the basement steps and went back for the other two, but the women were already carrying them. He brought the shawls and rugs. The cabman was strapping the suitcases onto the back. Elinor got into the cab.

Paul stood on the pavement with Teresa. Out of the corner of his eye he saw the cab rock as the driver climbed into his seat. "Well. Good-bye, then."

"Elinor's got the address."

"I'll come to see you, shall I? When you've settled in."

"No, I don't think that's a good idea." She was scanning the street, obviously still frightened. "Oh, God, the keys. I meant to take them back. Would you be an angel and drop them through the letter box?"

Somehow that phrase "be an angel" summed everything up. He kissed her dry mouth. She smiled and stroked the side of his face, then got into the cab. The cabby clicked his tongue, and the horse ambled forward. Paul watched them to the end of the street, the black, shiny cab lurching and swaying over the greasy cobbles. It was like the day they came and took his mother away, though he hadn't witnessed that. Auntie Ethel had made a great fuss about needing a particular brand of pickled onions and he'd been sent all the way into town to buy a jar. When he came back his mother was gone.

The cab turned the corner. He went and stood in the empty living room, looking around him at all the bare spaces. He said, "Teresa?"

The hum of silence answered him, broken by the persistent dripping of a tap. He walked from empty room to empty room, until at last he accepted defeat, closed and locked the door, and slipped the keys through the letter box. He heard a chink as they hit the lino and then he had to turn and walk away.

12

FLOATING ON HER BACK, ELINOR WATCHED THE treetops wave against the blue sky. Minnows darted all around her. When she closed her eyes she could feel thousands of tiny mouths rasping on her skin. This was the last hour of peace she'd have for some time. Kit Neville and Paul Tarrant were due to arrive on the ten o'clock train. She'd invited Kit first, weeks ago, but then he'd taken her home from the Café Royal and kissed her good night and she'd let him because she supposed she ought to want to, but immediately—the taste of his dinner on her tongue—she'd known it was a mistake. "Look—" she'd started to say, but he'd put his hand gently over her mouth. "Your eyes aren't for looking," he'd said solemnly. "They're for being looked at." She stared at him for a moment, then burst out laughing. She was an artist, for God's sake. If her eyes weren't for looking, what was she going to paint?

After she'd finally managed to persuade Kit to leave, she'd sat down and drawn a caricature of him on his motorbike, which made her feel better for a time. But the next day she'd got a letter from him containing a proposal of marriage. She'd expected another of his jokey, self-pitying apologies—and when she finally took in what the letter was saying she'd stuffed it in a drawer and tried to forget about it. She thought if she ignored it he'd soon realize what a fool he'd been and then it need never be mentioned again, but there was the weekend coming up. In a panic she'd invited Paul Tarrant as well. And then, knowing Mother would disapprove of her inviting two men, she'd asked Catherine to come along as well, only she'd had to cancel because her father was ill.

The whole thing was a mess. The thought of Kit and his constant, clumsy efforts to maneuver her into bed had spoiled the morning. Even before he arrived.

After swimming slowly to the rock, she clambered out, feeling the sun hot on the top of her head. A breeze ruffled the hairs at the nape of her neck. Raising her arm to her mouth she sucked her skin in sheer delight at her own taste. Why couldn't men leave you alone? Though this was her fault, really, not Kit's. She should have replied to his letter, said no, canceled the weekend. And that would have been the end of it. Instead she'd drifted, and now the confrontation she'd dreaded was inevitable, and it would be worse because she'd put it off.

Groaning at her own folly, she stood and started pulling on her clothes. Her stockings stuck to her wet knees and refused to rise higher. Bundling them under her arm, she walked back to the house, beech mast crunching under her feet. She was trudging along thinking of Kit and what she was going to say to him, but then suddenly she straightened her back and she was Rosalind in the forest of Arden, swaggering about in her doublet and hose. Really, she ought to stop going on like this. Any sane adult female ought to be able to walk through a wood without turning into Rosalind, but she never managed it. It was a sign of immaturity, this constant trying on of other identities. Fun, though.

She slipped across the hall without being seen and ran upstairs to her bedroom, where she wrung out her bathing dress and stockings and put them to dry on the windowsill. Her short hair was already starting to dry. "Oh, Elinor, you had such beautiful hair," Mother never failed to say on every visit home. "*Why* did you do it?"

I'll get it cut again next week, she thought. More than anything else, more than anything she'd ever said, the cutting of her hair had made Mother realize she was serious about painting. Like a nun setting sail for God.

"Yes, my girl. And a nun's the way you'll end up."

Elinor ran downstairs and along the hall to the breakfast room, where she found her mother talking to Toby and his friend Andrew Martin. It was unusual for Mother to be up as early as this. Was that a sign of trouble ahead? Toby and Andrew had huge plates of bacon, eggs, sausages, black pudding, and fried bread in front of them. Elinor teased them about getting up so late when she'd been for a swim already.

"Listen to her," Toby said. "I'll have you know we've done two hours' revision."

"Don't believe you."

"Andrew?"

"It's true, Miss Brooke."

"Good heavens, you must be desperate."

"Some of us *work*, sis. We can't all swan around all day with a sketchbook."

"If you think—"

"Elinor," Mother said.

Mother could never tell the difference between mock fights and the real thing.

Toby speared a sausage on the end of his fork. "So when are the beaux arriving?"

"They're not 'beaux.' "

Mother gazed at her with diluted blue eyes. "What a pity Catherine couldn't come."

"Perhaps Sis didn't fancy the competition."

"Her father's ill."

"We believe you. Thousands wouldn't."

Mother was rubbing her temples, a sure sign of a migraine on the way. Father had been meant to come home last night, but then a telephone call deferred his arrival till late this afternoon, and he was going back tomorrow. The minimum amount of time.

Elinor bowed her head over her scrambled eggs, pretending to an appetite she didn't feel. No man was ever going to entice *her* into a cage to mope and contemplate her moldy feed and peck at her own feathers till her chest was bald. You had that sense of Mother sometimes. She'd been a great beauty in her time. She must have hoped for more.

Men are April when they woo, December when they wed.

A trap driven by a dark-skinned, taciturn driver, with a fat chestnut pony ambling between the shafts, met them at the station. Neville heaved himself on board, swatting a fly that seemed determined to settle on his nose. Paul sat diagonally opposite. The driver flicked his whip and they lurched off. A slow shamble. The pony broke into a trot once, as they were leaving the village, then decided the effort was too much and lapsed back into a walk.

Neville was looking impatient, but Paul found it easy to settle into a slower pace. He was glad of this break. Since Teresa had left he'd been spending far too much time alone. He hadn't wanted to go home till the bruises had faded and was now thoroughly depressed and run down.

A hundred yards further on, the trap turned right into a narrow lane. So narrow it was like a tunnel running between the tall hedges, where bindweed, foxgloves, and cow parsley grew far above their heads. Leaves brushed the back of his neck; he felt the wetness of cuckoo spit on his skin. "I'm surprised Elinor comes to London at all when she's got this. I know I wouldn't."

"There is the little matter of stimulus, I suppose. The Café Royal, theaters, concerts, art galleries? Man cannot live on cowpats alone." Lowering his voice, he added, "Whatever you may like to think."

"Oh? I thought the Café Royal was 'vile'? And I seem to remember you were going to burn the National Gallery?"

Neville seemed very tense. He'd been argumentative on the train too, holding forth on the crisis in the Balkans as though he were an acknowledged expert, though Paul suspected his views were merely a rehash of his father's. Still, he sounded impressive.

The farmhouse was visible across the fields. Paul sat up and wiped the sweat from his forehead. Horseflies drunk on shit feasted on the men's upper lips. Neville kept trying to swat them, and they rose into the air buzzing angrily. The trap turned into another lane, narrower if possible, but here the trees met above their heads, so there was shade at least. Rounding a bend, they saw a long, low house set back from the lane with a gravel drive leading from the gate to the front door.

As soon as the trap stopped, Elinor appeared at the front door, greeted them boisterously, and led the way into the house. The porch was full of umbrellas, muddy boots, and mackintoshes. Smells of wet dog, leaf mold, saddle soap, and damp; but the hall, once they'd struggled into it, was impressive. Stone flags, rugs, a bowl of roses whose fallen petals lay like little gondolas on a lagoon of polished wood. Further along, a wide staircase led to the upper floors.

Mrs. Brooke came out of a door on the right and held out her hand to Paul. "Elinor's told me so much about you."

Paul felt Neville's gaze on the side of his face. He shook hands, uncomfortably aware that his palms were hot and damp. Elinor introduced Neville, then stepped back, awkward and gauche as she never was in London. When her mother left them, Paul saw her shoulders relax.

"Come through. I'll show you your rooms."

◼

Over lunch they met Elinor's brother, Toby, and a friend of his from medical school, Andrew Martin. Toby was a taller, masculine version of Elinor—the resemblance was astonishing. Andrew was a burly young man with small, shrewd eyes the same shade of reddish brown as his hair. Toby was helping Andrew revise for his exams. He'd failed anatomy and was having to resit.

"What are all you young people going to do?" Mrs. Brooke asked, as the coffee cups were cleared away.

"I thought we'd cycle to the church," Elinor said. "Have a look at the Doom."

"You'll have to count Andrew and me out, I'm afraid," Toby said. "We've got to stick at it."

"How long till the exam?" Neville asked.

"Three weeks," Andrew said.

"Oh, well, that's reasonable."

Andrew shook his head. "Depends how much you don't know, doesn't it?"

They fetched bicycles from one of the outhouses and set off for the church. The Doom had only recently been reclaimed from the limewash of centuries and was said to be very fine. Neville could dimly remember reading something about it in *The Times*. Left to himself he wouldn't have bothered going to see it, but Elinor loved it and that was good enough for him. He'd do anything for Elinor—even cycle two miles in this heat.

The sun had gained in strength while they were having lunch, burning away the last wisps of cloud. Neville wasn't dressed for the weather. His tweed jacket was far too thick, but it was the nearest thing he possessed to country wear. Elinor, looking trim and comfortable in a dark blue skirt and white blouse, led the way. Tarrant rode beside her; Neville brought up the rear. His joints had started to ache—they flared up from time to time for no apparent reason, and today they were bad— but even without that he wouldn't have been looking forward to the ride. It was ages since he'd ridden a bicycle, not since he was a boy, and he'd fallen off fairly frequently even then. His father had taught him, on the paths of Hampstead Heath. He could still remember the gritted teeth, the impatience. His father had always let go too soon, before he was ready. "You'll be all right," he'd called, as Kit, aged six, wobbled towards disaster.

Tarrant was pedaling like mad and still had enough breath left to talk to Elinor. She was pointing out a hill she used for sketching. "Miles and miles of grass. You know how the color changes when the wind blows over it?"

Oh, for God's sake. Grass is grass.

At last, they reached the top of the hill. He could relax a bit, even snatch glimpses of the hedgerows, which were covered all over with those pale starlike flowers. Bindweed. That was it. It was a triumph for him to be able to identify anything, but he remembered those flowers from holidays in his childhood, how they shriveled and puckered as darkness fell.

The lane smelled of tar. He remembered something else from childhood, how he'd been fascinated by tar bubbles, poking the dusty tops till they wrinkled like elephant's skin. You pushed them back and there were pools of inky black underneath. He'd got tar stains all over his shirt. Nanny had been furious, but Father seemed relieved, if anything. He was afraid I was turning into a sissy. Still is, for that matter. Oh, he'd die rather than admit it, but underneath that's what he thinks.

"Hey, watch it," Tarrant said.

Neville had nearly bumped his back wheel. "Sorry, old chap."

What a clown I am. No, that's not true. He was perpetually on the alert for disparaging remarks, even when they came from himself. Only there was something he did that other people didn't do. Like putting himself into situations where he showed to poor advantage and then, instead of learning from his mistake and avoiding those situations, doing it again and again and again.

"You're your own worst enemy." Those had been his headmaster's parting words. A bit rich, really, considering he was lying in bed with a fractured coccyx at the time and he certainly hadn't kicked himself in the arse. But there was a grain of

truth there, all the same. Only what people never seem to realize—his wet hands slithered on the handlebars, he was finding
it difficult to hold on—what people don't realize is that knowing that you're your own worst enemy doesn't automatically
turn you into your own best friend. Insight. The psychologist
Mother had insisted on sending him to, when he was fifteen,
had gone on and on about insight. Rubbish. He had insight by
the bucketful and it did him no good at all.

This was too bad. He couldn't breathe.

"Do you mind if we stop for a bit?"

Elinor braked at once. "Good idea. I'm feeling a bit
puffed."

She wasn't. She was only saying it to make him feel better; he hated her for that. He was boiling, eyes stinging with
sweat, upper lip prickling, temper and temperature sky-high.
They could have driven to the church in the pony and trap, for
God's sake. But no, no, they had to pedal along on these ridiculous contraptions. *Why?*

Once they'd stopped and were leaning against a fence
with their bikes pulled up onto the verge, he started to feel
better.

"Look, there it is," Elinor said, touching the back of his
hand. "Not much further."

"Are you sure you're all right?" Tarrant asked.

"Of course I'm all right."

As soon as he could breathe again, he remounted, wobbled, and set off down the lane. Tarrant. What was he doing
here? There wasn't much to recommend Tarrant, except his
looks of course. Certainly not his talent as a painter. Anemic
pastoral was the kindest description of what he produced. No
originality. No force.

At the top of the next hill they turned a corner, and there ahead of them was the church. It was isolated from the village, which lay in a valley half a mile further on. They propped their bicycles against the stone wall that surrounded the churchyard, pushed open the gate, and went in. Long grass, leaning headstones. Still gasping for breath, Neville pretended a great interest in the inscriptions. Dearly beloved wives, husbands, children, and fathers, all moldering away, their names half erased by wind and time.

Elinor was pushing her outrageously short hair out of her eyes. "Do you ever wonder what the real relationships were?"

"The real ones?" Tarrant said.

"Yes, you know, the lovers, the illegitimate children. It's all here." She swept her arm across the graveyard. "I bet there are plenty of people buried here with their husband or wife and their real love's in a grave a hundred yards away."

Neville found himself wondering about the parents' marriage. From what he could gather, Dr. Brooke spent Monday to Saturday in London. And his own parents, though they continued to share a house, lived entirely separate lives. He'd have liked to talk about it, but of course he couldn't because bloody Tarrant was there.

"Anyway, come on," Elinor said. "The Doom."

The porch, with its stone bench and handwritten notices about services and flower rotas and supplying Bibles to the heathen, struck cold after the heat of the sun. Neville was soon simmering with irritation again. He hated the way Elinor and Tarrant were approaching this. There was a smugness about it, a feeling of "Oh, well, you know, this is the *real* England." *Bollocks*. There was some excuse for Elinor, she'd grown up in the country, but what about Tarrant? If this was the real England, what did he think Middlesbrough was? A mirage? Neville wiped sweat from his chin. His scalp prickled. His toes swam inside his shoes, his knees ached, his ankles ached, his arse ached, and no, no, no, NO, this was not the real England. At that moment he'd have liked nothing better than to be back in London, in Charing Cross or Liverpool Street, flakes of soot on his skin, grit in his eyes, advertising everywhere, steam, people, pistons turning. Anything to escape from the clamorous boredom of trees.

Elinor turned the ring handle and they went inside. A shaft of sunshine, finding its way through stained glass into the chancel, revealed the myriad dust motes seething there. None of them was religious—nor exactly atheists either—and so, out of respect for something or other, their own capacity for aesthetic appreciation, perhaps, they spoke in whispers but did not kneel.

Elinor touched Neville's arm. "There, you see?"

He'd been looking straight at the east window, but now he raised his eyes to the chancel arch and saw that he was in the presence of greatness. The Doom, the figure of Christ in Majesty at its center, covered the whole arch. Below Christ's feet, St. Michael held the scales. A small, white, naked, squirming thing cowered in one pan; in the other, its sins, piled high, tilted the balance towards Hell. On the left, other wormlike people hid in holes in the ground or stared up at flashes of light in the sky. The women's drooping breasts and swollen bellies retained at least the sad dignity of their function, but the men . . . Albino tadpoles poured into the Abyss. On the right, the righteous were welcomed into Heaven by angels holding robes to cover them, as if the greater part of redemption consisted of getting dressed.

"It's amazing," Tarrant was saying, "the man who painted this wouldn't have had a clue what Tonks was on about. He wasn't interested in anatomy."

"Or beauty," Neville said.

Elinor said, "But you wouldn't want to put this on a bonfire in Trafalgar Square?"

"I don't know how I'd get it there."

"*Nev!*"

"Oh, all right, it's good. I'm just saying it's not relevant to the modern world. You can't *learn* anything from this."

"Do people change that much?" Tarrant said.

"Love would be the same, wouldn't it?" Elinor said.

"No, of course not. *Sex* might be the same, but not love. They didn't expect to love their wives."

"Then they were wiser than we are." She sat down in the front pew. "Anyway, I don't want to talk. That's the trouble with your crowd, Nev—talk talk talk. Nobody ever painted a better picture by talking about it."

"That's the Slade down the drain for a start."

"I don't want to talk about the Slade either."

All this while, above their heads, the Doom exerted its power, silencing them at last. Tarrant hadn't said much, Neville realized, or perhaps he had and been ignored. The man was an excrescence.

"I wonder how it happened," Elinor said. "Why they stopped believing the world was going to end?"

"Some people believe it now," Tarrant said. "There's a man marches up and down Oxford Street with a placard every Saturday morning." He deepened his voice. "*The End of the World Is at Hand.*"

"And everybody laughs at him," Neville said.

"They don't, actually. They don't see him."

"There must have been a moment, mustn't there?" Neville said. "I mean, obviously not a moment, a decade, a generation, when all this punishment stuff just didn't wash anymore?"

"Perhaps it was the Black Death," Tarrant said. "Perhaps they stopped believing then."

"You're explaining it away, both of you," Elinor said. "And you shouldn't, it's too good for that."

And he didn't even sign it. The painting disturbed Neville. He wanted to be out in the sunshine, to see Elinor's breasts under the thin blouse, to wipe away the memory of the maggotlike creatures emerging from holes in the ground. Gritting his teeth against the pain, he flexed his back. Every muscle in his body ached—and there was the ride back still to come. "Are we off, then?"

Elinor lingered. He and Tarrant were wheeling their bikes down the road before she caught them up. "Sorry, I couldn't tear myself away."

Neville was sweating before they'd gone a hundred yards. God, he hated this, and it was all so unnecessary. The pony and trap, for God's sake. Or they could have waited for Dr. Brooke's arrival and asked to borrow the car. Elinor drove, didn't she? Of course she drove. She did everything men did and generally better. She was standing up on her pedals now, toiling up the bank, but he noticed she still had enough breath left to talk to Tarrant. They shared so many interests. The same poets, the same artists, the same blasted countryside. Sit them down over a glass of wine and they'd chatter on for hours about cornfields and trees in a way he found completely incomprehensible. Though he and Elinor had a lot in common too. She loved music halls and cafés and dances and fancy-dress parties and nightclubs and street markets and Speakers' Corner on Sunday mornings and barrow boys selling hot chestnuts on winter evenings and the river—all of these things they shared. The one time he'd said something about how well she seemed to get on with Tarrant she'd just shrugged her shoulders. "Why not? We're friends. You share different things with different people."

Only it wasn't friendship Neville felt. Tarrant's affair with Teresa had ended badly, but he'd get over that fast enough, and then he'd be looking around. He was attracted to Elinor, that was obvious, always had been, and Neville thought he detected signs that she felt the same way about him. Tarrant was better looking than a man had any legitimate reason to be. And he could be charming, but really there was nothing to him.

They were nearing the crest of the hill. He hoped they'd stop and wait for him, but they didn't. By the time he'd sweated the last few yards, they were freewheeling down the other side. Elinor was squealing with pleasure. And suddenly he thought, to hell with it. Why can't I be like that?

He took a deep breath, gripped the handlebars, and pushed off, bumping down the hill, gathering speed, wobbling from side to side, afraid to steer because he knew if he changed direction he'd fall off. He had no hope of avoiding the pothole that swallowed his front wheel and sent him careering over the top of the handlebars. Sun and trees flashed, the world somersaulted, then shrank to an inch of tarmac level with his eyes.

Am I dead? Cautiously he moved his arms and legs and they seemed to be all right. He lifted his right hand to his face. The palm was scuffed and bleeding, the grazes coated in grit. That's going to hurt. His bike lay, twisted, a few feet away, but as soon as he tried to lift his head to assess the damage he knew it was a mistake. Black spots drifted between him and the light.

Trees and bushes rotated round his head and went on circling even after he lay back.

He heard Elinor call his name. "Nev, are you all right?"

He didn't know. He required advance notice of that question. Running footsteps. Two heads bent down to peer at him.

"What happened?" Tarrant asked.

Bloody obvious what happened. No breath for stupid questions.

Elinor said, "Can you sit up?"

He tried again, but something was wrong with his head; the slightest movement made him feel sick.

"Did you lose consciousness?" Tarrant asked.

"Don't know." His voice was moldy, like something kept in a cupboard for years.

"Can you move your legs?"

Yes—though they didn't seem to have much to do with him.

"Look," Elinor said, "I'll get the car. Dad'll be home by now."

"No, I'll go. I'll be quicker. Help me get him to the side of the road."

"Should we move him?"

"Can't leave him in the middle of the road. We're too close to the bend." Tarrant turned to Neville. "Do you think you can manage it?"

Somehow, with Tarrant supporting his head and shoulders, Neville shuffled to the side of the lane. The grass felt cool after the hot tar of the road. A smell of stagnant water rose from the ditch behind him. There was a whole succession of plops as frogs and toads leapt for cover.

They were talking together in low voices, Tarrant and Elinor. Like parents. He didn't like that.

"Are you feeling better?" Elinor asked.

"Yes." He made himself speak in a stronger voice. "But I don't think I can ride the bike."

"You certainly can't. You've buckled the front wheel." She turned to Tarrant. "You're right, you'd better go. If Dad isn't home, bring the trap."

Tarrant ran down the hill, then, obviously revising his ideas of what constituted an emergency, slowed to a walk. They watched him mount his bicycle and pedal away.

"He won't be long."

He could take forever as far as Neville was concerned. Elinor was kneeling beside him. He caught her smell—peppery, intimate—as she bent over him. The dark circle of a nipple pressed against the white lawn of her blouse. He detected, or imagined he could detect, that bitter almond smell—or was it taste? You could never be sure. Some people couldn't smell it at all.

"If you took your jacket off I could bundle it up and put it under your head. The grass is damp."

No, he didn't think he could manage that. Instead she lifted his head onto her lap and he lay back, feeling a bit of a fraud. The first shock was wearing off. He'd stopped feeling sick and was beginning to suspect there was nothing much wrong with him, except for a large bump on his forehead and the skinned palms of his hands. Possibly he could have walked back. But this was better. Elinor had avoided being alone with him ever since he'd sent that letter, three weeks ago now, suggesting marriage. Well, now was his chance. "Elinor, you know what I said in my letter?"

He felt her thigh muscles tense. Her hand, which had been resting on the side of his face, was abruptly withdrawn. "Ye-es?"

"Have you thought about it?"

"No, not really. I can't take it seriously."

"Why not?"

"I don't think you've thought it through."

"I have. No, listen." He tried to sit up, then, remembering her sympathy for his injuries was perhaps the only factor working in his favor, groaned, and fell back again. "We have a lot in common."

"That's why we're friends."

"Two can live as cheaply as one."

"Doubtful."

"You'd be able to get away from your mother."

"I already have."

"We could share a studio."

She was shaking her head. "It wouldn't be like that. You'd have to get a job, or accept commissions you didn't want, and I'd be in the kitchen cooking dinner and before we knew where we were there'd be babies crawling all over the floor."

"There doesn't have to be."

"Anyway, that's not the point, is it? I just don't want to." She turned away from him. "All the good things we *might* have if we got married we've already got as friends, so why change?"

SEX, he wanted to shout, but of course he couldn't. "I'm a man," he said, at last. "You can't blame me for wanting more."

"I don't. Blame you. But I *don't* want more." She shook her head, defeated, as he was, by the lack of a shared vocabulary. "I don't want that."

He pressed, because he had to. "That?"

"You know. Sexual intercourse."

She made it sound like a weird practice allegedly indulged

in by primitive tribes in the Amazon basin. "You only say that because you haven't experienced it."

"I say it because I've never wanted to."

"If you'd only let me try."

"No, and it doesn't matter how many times you ask, the answer's always going to be the same. I'm happy as I am."

"Are you? I don't think you are."

"All right then, I'm not." She started picking at her finger-nails. "But I'm not going to pretend I feel something when I don't."

If only she'd let him try. He'd take care of her, he'd make sure there wasn't a baby, and if she didn't want marriage, all right, they'd have a different kind of relationship. And all the better, a sly, self-regarding voice inside him whispered. Was he really ready to forsake all others and cleave him only unto her? He wasn't trying to fool her when he talked about marriage, but he sometimes thought he might be trying to fool himself.

Exasperated by the complexity of his feelings, he clasped her hand, only to release it with a cry of pain as the pressure forced grit deeper into his raw skin.

"I think you'd better lie down," she said, dry, sensible.

"I won't give up," he said.

"And I won't change my mind."

Neville closed his eyes and concentrated on feeling the warmth of her thighs through the nape of his neck. Somewhere close at hand a frog croaked.

13

Elinor escaped upstairs to her room for the last hour before dinner, leaving Paul and Kit talking to Father on the terrace. He'd brought a stack of newspapers back with him from London and they were deep in discussion about the European crisis, which seemed to be getting worse every day. Nobody bothered to mention Ireland anymore.

Pouring water into the bowl, she splashed her face and neck. Behind the drawn curtains, the room was full of syrupy light. A floorboard creaked in the passage outside her door, but it was only the old house flexing its joints. Mother wouldn't appear again till dinner. She'd been tired for as long as Elinor could remember, rousing herself to give instructions to the housekeeper after breakfast, then slowly sinking into inertia. Sometimes she got a headache and took to her bed for days at a time. "Be thankful you don't suffer from migraines, my girl," she'd say on these occasions. "They're a real problem." But to Elinor it had always been obvious that migraines were not a problem but a solution. Generally one would strike whenever Father rang from London to say he wouldn't be home for the weekend. In addition to his post at the London hospital he had a large private practice, and one set of patients or the other could usually be relied upon to supply a weekend emergency. Once, speaking to Toby, Elinor had referred to their parents' separation and he'd gaped at her. That was how skillfully they'd managed it. Their own son didn't know.

And against this background she was supposed to believe in marriage.

She pulled the curtain aside and saw Father and Paul talking on the terrace. The bumble and rumble of male voices reached her but only a few distinct words. Germany, Serbia, Austria-Hungary, Russia, mobilization, ultimatum, alliance, triple alliance—on and on it went. She was so bored with it.

Letting the curtain drop, she caught sight of herself in the dressing table mirror and was startled by her fugitive expression.

—*I'm happy as I am.*

—*Are you? I don't think you are.*

No, all right, I'm not. She hadn't been happy for weeks. That night in the Café Royal, seeing the expression on Paul's face as he stared at Teresa, she'd felt herself diminished. Neutered. Waiting for marriage was all very well, but suppose you didn't intend to marry? What were you waiting for then?

. . . then worms shall try

That long preserved virginity,

And your quaint honour turn to dust,

And into ashes all my lust.

More to the point, what was she going to wear tonight? She had one evening dress left over from her pre-Slade past— white satin with a bow across the chest. Fetching it from the wardrobe, she held it up against herself. No, it reminded her too much of herself as a chubby, giggling teenager. There was nothing else, except her dark blue dress and they'd all seen that fifty times already. Rachel had left some of her dresses behind when she got married. Quickly Elinor slipped across the corridor into what had been her sister's bedroom.

The wardrobe released a smell of faded roses: the ghost of corsages past. Elinor ran her finger along the rail, selected a black dress, and, standing in front of the cheval mirror, held it against her. Another girl stared back at her: alert, aroused, apprehensive, excited. She undressed, fetched a pair of Rachel's stays from the drawer, and squeezed herself into them. Now the dress. A black waterfall of satin fell heavy and cool over her face. She looked in the glass again, afraid of seeing a child dressed up in her big sister's clothes—though she was older now than Rachel had been when she first wore this dress. Instead, she saw that the dress had transformed her. Her breasts were hoisted up by the stays. She looked down at them, feeling her breath hot on her skin, excited, though more by the imagined reaction of men than by any desire of her own. *Yes*— smoothing the skirt down, admiring the shape the stays gave her—*yes*. The effect was too formal, for what was, after all, little more than a family party, but that didn't matter. She'd make a joke of it, explain her mother was always complaining she made no effort, so look, here I am, she'd say, making an effort.

Halfway down the stairs she saw herself endlessly replicated in the tall mirrors that faced each other across the landing. She realized she was dressed entirely in black. Perhaps she should go back and get a stole, or a necklace, anything to make her appearance less uncompromising. In this light even her eyes looked black. She didn't feel particularly well—she had a pain in her stomach on the left side, low down—and yet she looked better than she'd done in weeks. Earrings, that would do it. But then the study door opened and Father came out. He looked up and she saw the flare of pride in his face. So, altering her posture and movement to suit the dress, she glided downstairs and into his arms.

"What's all this then?"

His breath tickled her ear. "Nothing. Just thought I'd make an effort for once."

"Well, you look wonderful. I think I'd better go and spruce myself up."

"Where's Toby?"

"Conservatory. Helping Andrew with his revision."

"I'm surprised he hasn't got you giving a tutorial."

"Oh, no. I'm off duty."

The conservatory blinds were pulled down and the whole room glowed orange-gold. The two young men seemed to hang suspended in the viscous air. Elinor stood quietly in the doorway, blinking in the changed light. Toby had taken off his shirt and was standing motionless, arms outstretched, like a crucifixion—though the effect was rather spoiled by the loops of his braces dangling round his hips. His trousers had been pushed down: she saw a glint of dark gold hair pointing up towards the navel, matching the meager twist between his breasts. Andrew was leaning towards him with something, a pencil, or pen, in his hand. She realized the network of dark lines that covered Toby's skin were not, as she'd thought at first, shadows cast by the baskets of big ferns that hung from the ceiling, but writing or drawing of some kind. A pattern? A map? Then she understood. Toby's nerves had been drawn on his skin.

"Keep still," Andrew was saying. "Hard enough without you wriggling."

And then they saw her. Andrew straightened up at once and took a step back. Toby gave a brief, hard laugh. "C'mon in, Sis."

"What on earth are you doing?"

"Living anatomy," Toby said.

"Will it wash off?"

"Oh, yes," Andrew said. "We do it all the time in college."

Toby was taking in every detail of her dress. "You're looking good, Sis."

"It's Rachel's."

"I thought it wasn't your usual style. No, you look good."

Andrew was staring from her to Toby and back again. He looked as if he couldn't believe his eyes. She felt herself blush. "Don't you find it hot in here? I'm surprised you can work."

Toby reached for his shirt. "It's a scorcher, isn't it? I think I'll have a cold bath, try to cool down."

"I'm going to sit outside." She wanted to be away from the undercurrent of tension in this room, which she could neither understand nor persuade herself she was imagining. "Have you seen Kit?"

"I think he's upstairs," said Andrew.

"Nursing his concussion," said Toby.

"Headache." She giggled, only to feel immediately disloyal. "Actually, it was a very nasty fall."

As soon as she stepped across the threshold, the colors changed again. The ooze of sticky golden light that seemed to clog your movements was gone. The sky was a clear translucent blue, fading to mauve above the horizon, with small, flossy orange clouds dotted here and there—that outrageously improbable orange that never seems real even when you're staring straight at it. The trees loomed tall against the glow of light, casting long blue-black shadows over the lawn.

A faint breeze blew, pimpling her skin. Chafing her upper arms, she looked down towards the wood, wondering whether there was time for a walk. Rachel and Timothy would be here soon, and she needed time to think. Somehow mulling over a problem in her bedroom never seemed to work; the familiar walls and curtains merely repeated her thoughts back to her. She was sorry for Kit, of course she was, but angry too. All very well for him to talk about the months and years he'd loved her, but he'd had two other women in that time. Two *that she knew about*. Kit was very successful with a certain kind of woman. Here, she pulled herself up short, repelled by the snobbishness of the phrase, which seemed to go somehow with the dress, as if by changing her clothes she'd also changed her attitudes. Disliking herself more by the minute, she walked across the lawn and into the wood. Dry beech mast crunched under her thin shoes. She remembered the feel of it under her bare feet, walking back from her morning swim. She'd been Rosalind then, and it hadn't been an escape; she'd been happy. Now, only twelve hours later, she wasn't happy and would have welcomed a way out, but she was stuck with being herself. High time too, Kit would have said. Kit, Mother, Rachel. She didn't want to listen to them, though. Her head was full of other people's voices. What she needed was to get her own mind clear.

The pool. She and Toby had swum there as children; she'd followed him in—she remembered this clearly—she'd followed him, though she wasn't supposed to; don't go in, she'd been told, it's too deep. Stepping gingerly, she'd clung to the reeds, her toes curling with disgust in the cold ooze. Sun on her back, white, thin legs angling into the water. Why did they seem to bend like that? She'd stared down at them and tried to understand. Minnows would appear from nowhere and graze her toes. There, if anywhere, she might recover some sense of herself. At the moment her life at the Slade, the life she'd struggled so hard to achieve, seemed meaningless. Oh, she'd get over it, back in London, painting again. . . . Only tonight the sense of . . . exclusion? Was that it? Something like that. She felt sidelined, a spectator at the feast, while all around her other people stuffed food into their mouths. I don't like being sexless. If that's what I am. The pool glinted between the trees, catching the last of the evening light, reflecting it back at the sky. Drawing a deep breath, or as deep as the stays would allow, she ran towards it.

Neville was lying on the bed in his room watching a square of sunlight retreat across the carpet. He had both windows wide open, but the air was hot and still and he couldn't splash cold water over his face because he'd get the bandages on his hands wet. All he could do was sweat and fume.

He hadn't enjoyed the afternoon much. Sitting in the car, the backs of his thighs damp against the hot leather, he'd felt a complete ass. It was a relief to be back in the house, in the cool shade. Dr. Brooke examined the bump on his head, peered at his pupils, made him close his eyes and touch his nose with his index finger. Did he feel sick? Not now. Drowsy? He did, a bit, but he wasn't going to admit it. He was too afraid of being packed off to bed, leaving Elinor and Tarrant together. No, bugger that for a lark. He didn't feel drowsy. As a matter of

fact, he'd never felt more awake in his life. Dr. Brooke washed
his hands carefully while Neville watched, breathing audibly
through his nose. But even as he gritted his teeth, he was remembering how Elinor had bent over him, how the dark circle
of her nipple had pressed against the white cloth. He wanted to
groan and, since the impulse coincided with Dr. Brooke's ex-
tracting a particularly large piece of gravel from his palm, groan
he did. Twenty minutes later he was free to sit outside on the
terrace reading the newspapers, waiting for the pain in his
hands to subside.

Only when Tarrant announced he was going for a walk
did Neville feel able to go upstairs and lie down. He took off his
outer clothes and stretched out on the bed, but he didn't feel
like sleep. Whenever he closed his eyes Elinor's slim body ca-
vorted on the inside of his lids. Images spawned other images.
He lay and watched like somebody in a picture palace who has
no control over what he sees. The orgy of voyeurism filled him
with shame, but he didn't know how to make it stop. She could
stop it, Elinor. If only she'd learn to behave like a woman. This
was more like being in love with a brilliant, egotistical boy
than a girl. Except a boy would have slept with him by now.
She was so utterly self-centered. Nothing mattered except her
talent and whether she was fulfilling it or not. What made him
really angry was that she asked the impossible, and she didn't
seem to know it was impossible. She expected him to stifle his
desire for her and treat her exactly as he would Tarrant, or any
other male friend—not that Tarrant was a friend exactly—and
she didn't seem to see how unreasonable she was being. Better
end the friendship than go on like this. Perhaps he should say
that? It might shock her into seeing their situation from his point
of view. Nothing else worked.

Exasperated, he forced himself off the bed and into his dinner jacket. Every muscle in his legs and back ached. As he stared at himself in the glass, fingering the bump on his head, he was briefly freed from desire and saw instead the small, sad figures of the Doom tumbling into Hell. Then, pulling himself together, he straightened his tie, smoothed his hair back, and went downstairs.

Finding nobody around, he let himself out onto the terrace and walked diagonally across the lawn into the wood. Once inside, his eyes adjusting to the shafts of sunlight that slanted down between the trees, he made his way along the path. He caught a glint of water between the trees and was tempted to explore further, but perhaps he ought to remain within earshot of the house. Lighting a cigarette, he leaned against the nearest trunk and looked up at the sky. All he wanted was a few minutes' peace before he had to go back and face people. Sitting at the dinner table with Elinor a few feet away, saying virtually nothing—he'd noticed at lunch how subdued she was in her own home, how many irritated glances her mother cast in her direction. Only on the trip to see the church had she been anything like her normal self, and he'd ruined that.

And then he heard rustling, twenty or so yards ahead of him, near the pool. At first he could make nothing out, just a dark shape that seemed at first to be merely a thickening of the shadows, but then she moved again and he saw her pale face, bare shoulders, thin arms. She was walking towards him, the hem of her dress lifted well above the ground. And what a dress. He had never seen her wear anything like that before. She looked, for almost the first time in all the years he'd known her, like a woman. And yet there was something childish in the gesture—a little girl taking care of her best frock—that made his heart contract; but then she saw him, and immediately became her usual smiling, teasing, confident self.

"How're your hands?"

"Stings a bit, not too bad."

"Do you think you'll be able to paint?"

"Oh, yes."

He wished she hadn't mentioned painting. It was what they had in common, the foundation of their friendship, but it was useless to him now. He wanted to make love to her, but he didn't know where to start. And so, though he was furious with himself for giving in, he ended up nattering on about painting. Had she ever painted the pool? Yes, she'd painted Toby swimming. He threw his cigarette away, a bright arc falling through the blue air.

"I suppose we ought to be getting back," she said.

No. He drew her to him, feeling the winged collarbones alien against the palms of his hands. Her skin felt cool, his hands hot and heavy. Thick, raw hands—he brushed the image away. She was looking up at him nervously, as he lowered his mouth to hers. He kissed her lightly, his lips barely brushing hers, then clasped her more tightly and began to probe. As he tasted the salt of her dry mouth, he thought of the right word for her expression. *Experimental.* He was aware of a coldness, no more than virginity perhaps, but it was a barrier he had to break through. He shut his eyes. Nothing now except his strong muscular tongue threshing against hers, though she was pulling away. He felt her neck muscles go rigid as she tried to pull her head away. He hollowed out his body so she wouldn't feel his hardness pressing into her. His fingers twined around the short hair at the nape of her neck. She pushed her hand between them, round his throat, and he felt his blood pulse against her thumb. He was thudding, contused, breath thick in his throat, praying for her to respond, but she was all the time trying to break away, and at last the pressure of her fingers on his wind-pipe forced him back.

She stared at him, her eyes black. "We've got to go in now. That's the gong."

Reluctantly, even angrily, he stepped back, hearing the dinner gong sound for the second time. From where they stood he could just make out lighted windows between the trees. "Af-ter dinner," he said. "Tonight."

She was already moving away. He could see the sharpness of her shoulder blades. "I don't know."

"No, you've got to promise."

She turned on him. "No, I don't have to promise. I don't have to do anything I don't want."

They left the wood and walked across the lawn, their feet leaving dark trails in the wet grass. She pushed open the door of the conservatory. Half a dozen colorless moths came in with them and immediately began to flutter around the single lighted lamp. In the hall, he caught a glimpse of her reflection in the mirror. White-faced, her eyes huge. She looked shocked, but she couldn't be. She'd wanted that kiss as much as he did, *and* wanted more. Neither of them looked normal. They were night creatures, like the moths, as endangered as they were by the light.

"Perhaps I'd better go in first," she said. "Do I look all right?"

Lichen clung to the back of her dress. He brushed it off, then stood while she dusted the crumbly gray-green scurf from his shoulders. Tarrant came down the stairs and stared at them

curiously. Neville turned to greet him and by the time he
looked round again, Elinor had walked into the drawing room.
He followed her into the bright lights and the buzz of conversation, feeling naked, vulnerable, skinned, but almost at once
Toby came across and offered him a drink, and he talked to
Toby and Andrew, and then to a tall, etiolated man with a sad
mustache who turned out to be Elinor's brother-in-law, and
then it was time to go in.

Elinor was at the other end of the table opposite Tarrant.
I have to see her, Neville thought. I have to make something
happen.

14

THE HEAT IN THE DINING ROOM WAS STIFLING.
The windows couldn't be opened because of the danger of attracting insects into the room, though a daddy longlegs had got in somehow and batted noisily from wall to wall, casting huge shadows over the table and the heads and shoulders of the people gathered round it.

"Why *daddy* longlegs?" Toby wondered.

Nobody seemed inclined to speculate.

"Anyway it isn't," Elinor said, a moment later. "It's a harvestman."

Daddy longlegs. Harvestman. What did it matter? Why didn't somebody just get up and swat the bloody thing? Neville was fidgety, miserable, bad tempered. All he wanted was to be alone with Elinor. Instead he had the prospect of an hour, perhaps more like two, talking to people who didn't interest him in the least.

What was keeping Dr. Brooke? Five minutes after the rest of them had sat down the chair at the head of the table was still empty, but then, smiling, apologizing, he appeared and sat down. Immediately Mrs. Blackstone wheeled in her trolley and started dishing out soup.

Soup?

Cold, thank God.

Dr. Brooke was saying the call had come from the hospital.

"We've been asked to clear the beds. Postpone nonurgent operations."

Nobody spoke for a while. Then Andrew said, "Do you think there's going to be a war, sir?"

"I hope not."

"If there is I'll enlist."

Toby looked across at him. "You'd do anything, wouldn't you, rather than revise?"

"Oh, come on. If it was a choice between enlisting and stuffing your head full of boring anatomy, which would *you* choose?"

"Enlisting, of course."

Dr. Brooke straightened his knife and fork. "I think you'll find the army can manage quite well without help from either of you. That's what professional armies are for."

"It's the not knowing I can't stand," Elinor said. "It's like a thunderstorm hanging over you and it just won't break."

It occurred to Neville that his father, by this time in the evening, would know what was in tomorrow's paper. He'd have started work on Monday morning's article by now. After dinner, he'd give him a ring, see what he could come up with. It pleased him to be in the know, to have access to more up-to-date information than anybody else.

Tarrant was sitting opposite Elinor. She still looked very pale. Her bare shoulders were really not appropriate for such an

informal gathering, and the black satin, settling in oily, glistening folds around her hips, seemed to eat light rather than reflect
it. There couldn't have been a greater contrast between the two
sisters. Rachel was a great, blowsy, overblown rose, beginning
to droop. Her expression had hardened when she saw Elinor
coming towards her in the black dress.

"I hope you don't mind," Elinor had said.

"Of course not. Suits you."

Her sister's dress. Well, yes, of course, it had to be. Could
anyone seriously imagine Elinor enduring long hours of pinning
and fitting to possess such a thing? Though it was a bit tactless,
in view of Rachel's matronly bosom and slipping hair, to con-
front her with a younger, slimmer version of herself. Certainly
Mrs. Brooke seemed to think so. Whenever she glanced at her
younger daughter there was a tightening of the lips that suggested she didn't find her an altogether pleasing sight. Once,
Elinor caught the glance and lifted her chin defiantly. He understood Elinor better for having met her mother. He could see
what she was reacting against.

After a gloomy start, nobody mentioned the European crisis again. Toby and Andrew laughed a lot and Rachel joined in,
becoming more boisterous, even a little tipsy perhaps, as the
evening progressed. For the past year, Paul gathered, her baby
had absorbed the whole of her attention. Now she was almost dis-
abled for adult company, shrieking away like a much younger
girl, observed, a little anxiously at times, by her husband, from
behind his pebble glasses.

Neville talked mainly to Dr. Brooke, while shooting fre-
quent glances along the table at Elinor. He listened to Dr.
Brooke, asked and answered questions, even launched into a

vigorous defense of modern art, all without engaging more than a tiny fraction of his mind. Dr. Brooke seemed to be knowledge-able about the London art scene, at any rate about Tonks and that Slade crowd, though he was inclined to underestimate his daughter's achievement in winning the scholarship. It was a pleasure to put him right about that. He only wished Elinor had been close enough to hear him do it.

After a stodgy rhubarb pie had been served and valiantly consumed, Mrs. Brooke stood up. Neville leapt to his feet to hold the door, but although Elinor's arm brushed against his sleeve in passing, she didn't meet his eye. She seemed furious. With him? Or perhaps she disliked the custom of ladies with-drawing after dinner? His mother would have none of it.

Over port, politics was inescapable. Tim Henderson, Eli-nor's brother-in-law, spoke with a dry well-informed passion about the impossibility of avoiding war if France was attacked. Andrew, who seemed to have only one thought in his head, again insisted he'd enlist on Tuesday morning if he got the chance.

"What about you?" he asked, suddenly, addressing Ne-ville.

"Enlist, of course." No bloody choice. He looked up to find Tarrant on the other side of the table laughing at him. "What's amusing you?"

"You don't sound very keen. What happened to 'War is the only health giver of mankind'?"

Dr. Brooke looked puzzled.

"*The Futurist Manifesto*, sir," Tarrant explained.

"Oh, I see. Well, I suppose it's an interesting point of view, though if war's such a health giver I do wonder why we need to clear quite so many beds." He was standing up as he spoke. "Shall we join the ladies?"

Elinor, sitting by the open French windows in the drawing room, had been having a hard time. Rachel started the moment they entered the room. What on earth possessed her to wear that dress? Not that Rachel minded of course, she was welcome to borrow any of her old dresses, but why that one? It was far too low cut. And, anyway, it was a ball gown not a dinner dress. At the very least she should have worn a stole with it. And, besides, she was too thin to carry it, she looked positively scrawny round the collarbones. Why was she so thin? How many proper cooked meals did she eat in a week? In vain Elinor tried to insist that she did eat. It was just that she walked everywhere.

"I walk miles."

"Ye-es. Through London streets after dark."

"With other girls. I don't go on my own."

"Other girls aren't chaperones. If anything, they egg each other on. And as for inviting *two* young men for the weekend . . . For heaven's sake."

"I did invite another girl. She had to cancel."

"Then you should have called it off."

"At the last minute?"

"What *do* you think it looks like? You and four unattached young men."

"Four? Toby's my brother."

"A lot of families wouldn't let you invite one."

"*I* didn't invite Andrew."

"No, but he's unattached, isn't he? It's the same thing."

"Is he? I don't get that impression."

"Well, we don't know if he's attached, do we?"

Elinor laughed. "Oh, I think we do."

Mother was looking puzzled. "He hasn't mentioned anybody."

"Anyway," Elinor said, quickly changing the subject, "I'm not interested in Andrew."

"So which of them is it, then?"

"It's not like that. We're just friends."

"You're sailing very close to the wind. You know, you can only flout convention so far before you start to get a reputation. You might wake up one morning and find nobody wants to know you."

"The people I respect—"

The door opened and Mrs. Blackstone came in with the coffee. The two sisters sat in silence, fuming, until she withdrew.

"I don't have to sit and listen to lectures from you, Rachel. I've got my life, you've got yours; let's just leave it at that, shall we?"

"Shall I pour our coffee now?" Mother said. "How long do you think they're likely to be?"

"Not long," Rachel said. "I think Dad's hoping for an early night."

Elinor retreated to the terrace, where the night air on her skin felt like a hot bath. She was hurt, it had been such an onslaught. All the things she'd achieved in the past four years, the independent life she'd built for herself, seemed to count for nothing here. The only thing that mattered to her mother was finding a husband. As for painting, well, nice little hobby, very suitable, but you won't have much time for that when the children arrive.

What hurt more than anything was that she hadn't hit back. She could have done. Rachel had been piling on weight ever since she got married, she was fat by any standards, but did Elinor say so? No, not a single snide remark, not an unkind word, but, my God, it was open season on her when Rachel got going. Of course, if she did retaliate there'd be a breach. Well, perhaps it was time, perhaps there ought to be a breach. It wouldn't be easy to live with, though. All their childhood she and Rachel had been friends, allies, coconspirators in this not particularly happy household. If she quarreled with Rachel now she'd feel utterly alone. The warmth withdrawn, the chill along one side . . .

God, this heat. It was actually cooler inside the house; she was baking out here. She found a newspaper on the table and tried to use it as a fan, but it was damp and flaccid with dew and the newsprint came off on her hand. Times like this you need your friends. If only Catherine were here. Instead of that there was Paul, still mooning over Teresa, or so she supposed—she'd hardly had a chance to talk to him yet—and Nev. Who seemed determined not to be a friend at all.

Nobody had been kinder to her or more encouraging. He seemed to understand, better than most men, the problems a woman encountered in being taken seriously as an artist. And yet, in the next breath, he was holding forth about the need for virility in art. Virility was the essence of great art; effeminacy had to be extirpated at all costs. Where did that leave her? Counting the hairs on her chest? The glorification of war, "the beautiful ideas that kill, the contempt for women," the whole Futurist baggage. She didn't understand how he could believe all that—*if* he believed it—and still profess faith in her talent as a painter. Perhaps it was a mistake to take him seriously—he wasn't an intellectual by any means, though he'd have liked to be—but then, wasn't it patronizing not to take him seriously? And his ideas were rooted in his character. He was a bully. If she knew anything about him at all, she knew that. A bullied boy, a bullying man, it was too commonplace to be worth re-marking on. And it wasn't the whole truth; he could be very kind. And they had a lot in common. If only he could be content with friendship.

Though she couldn't blame him for trying it on tonight. Somehow, in this ridiculous dress, she'd sent out the wrong signals. She'd thought she was doing something rather clever, turning herself into a parody of a young lady dressed for the marriage market, but it hadn't turned out like that. She'd slipped into being the person the dress dictated, and now she was going to have to pay, in hours and hours of embarrassment. She *had* wanted him. Briefly. Or she'd wanted *something*—to be different. Rachel would say she'd led him on, but that wasn't true. She didn't want to marry him, or anybody. She only had to turn round and look at Rachel, nodding off in the armchair. Rachel, who before her marriage had been a promising pianist, and now sat with the baby on her knee, picking out nursery tunes with one finger. Nev said it wouldn't be like that, and she believed him—or at least she believed he meant it—but it would, because marriage changed everything. It had its own logic, its own laws, and they were independent of the desires and intentions of those who entered into it. She felt a moment's pleasure in the cynicism of this perception, though God knows it was depressing enough.

She heard Father's voice in the room behind her, then Kit, talking about the crisis of course, what else? Everybody was getting so excited, it repelled her. Particularly Kit. Look at him now, holding forth, puffed up like a toad in the mating season. He'd telephoned his father. Things were worse, far worse, than they'd thought. Germany had declared war on Russia and was advancing on France. If she invaded . . .

At last the buzz died down. Kit detached himself from the group and came to join her on the terrace.

"That's it, then," he said.

"Is it?"

"Seems to be."

"Do you think we'll fight?"

"Got to. We'll lose all credibility if we don't."

She turned away. "What will you do?"

"Well, I've got to get out there."

"Enlist?"

"Not sure. They mightn't have me. And anyway I need to be there now, not in six months' time."

"I don't see why you have to do anything. Let the army do it."

"I've no choice. Don't you see? You can't go around saying, 'War's the only health giver of mankind'—not that I ever did say that, incidentally—and then when one breaks out say, 'Sorry, I'm not going, I don't feel well enough.' "

"No, I do see." She was laughing.

"It's not funny. Father's going out next week. He asked if I wanted to go with him."

"And do you?"

"How can I refuse? It means I'll have to leave a bit early, I'm afraid."

She turned away to hide her relief.

"I do love you, you know. Can't we at least talk about it?"

"I don't see how."

"I could come to your room."

"You could not."

"Down here then, after they've gone to bed."

"There's nothing to say. I won't marry you, I don't want an affair. I'm happy as we are." She looked straight into his eyes. "I'm sorry if you're not, but there's nothing I can do about that."

He took a step back. "Perhaps it would be better if we didn't see each other for a while."

"If that's what you want."

"You don't care."

"I do. Just not in the way you want."

"This is torture. You've no idea."

"No, probably not."

"It's like being in love with a mermaid."

She understood what he meant and it hurt. "I think we'd better go in."

15

Paul to Elinor

Thank you for your very kind letter. I'm sorry to have been so
long replying, but the fact is I've been laid low with a feverish cold
that brought on a bout of pneumonia. As a result I feel a bit flattened,
though I'm downstairs now, sitting in the front room with a blanket
over my knees like a little old man. The blanket's not really necessary.
The weather's still warm, though not as unbearably hot as it was last
week when I was ill, but somehow if you're feeling weak it helps to be
covered up. I've been watching cabbage white and tortoiseshell
butterflies playing around the buddleia bushes in the front garden. I
counted eighteen this morning, then I had a nap. Exhausting work,
counting butterflies.

But I'm getting stronger every day. Have you heard from Teresa?
I still haven't, and don't expect to now. I mind a lot less than I
thought I would. Somehow the war and this illness between them have
clanged down like a great steel shutter between me and my previous
life. When I look back on my time at the Slade you're the only person
who seems real. And Neville, oddly enough. Now he has written, and
at length, which surprises me a bit. He's volunteered to drive an

ambulance for the Belgian Red Cross, but I expect you know that
already. He says it's the fastest way out there. Meanwhile, it all seems
very far removed, though my stepmother's bandaging class meets in the
room behind me so I hear all the chatter, and Dad brings the papers
home. Half a dozen sometimes. Everybody's very excited. I suppose
because they all feel they're caught up in history. I just cough and
count butterflies. I'm sure you're much more actively and usefully
employed.

Elinor to Paul

Well, it's active all right—I don't know about useful. We—
Ruthie and me—spent the first few days wandering round from place
to place, sitting in cafés, reading newspapers, jabbering till our jaws
ached, me increasingly fed up but somehow not able to pull myself out
of it. Still can't. London's full of heat and dust, the air's got that burnt
smell you get in August even in the parks.

We went to see the regiments mustering in Green Park and the
crowds cheering them, thousands, there were three girls in front of me,
shopgirls or housemaids and they were screaming and waving flags and
one of them jumped up and down so much she wet herself and hobbled
off with her skirt bunched up between her legs, shrieking and giggling.
In the evenings people gather outside Buckingham Palace or one or
other of the embassies, or the Café Royal of course for our crowd. You
know how glamorous it used to seem? Well I thought so, anyway. Now
it's full of frightened old men who think their day is over (and they're
probably right) and overexcited young men who jabber till the spit
flies, though it's only stuff they've read in the papers. The women have
gone very quiet. It's like the Iliad, you know, when Achilles insults
Agamemnon and Agamemnon says he's got to have Achilles' girl and

Achilles goes off and sulks by the long ships and the girls they're quarreling over say nothing, not a word, it's a bit like that. I don't suppose men *ever* hear that silence.

Nobody's doing anything. I mean nobody's doing any work. My teaching's dried up, the young ladies of Kensington are all learning first aid instead. And I can't paint. Everything you think of seems so trivial in comparison with the war—but I don't accept that. I just don't seem to have the energy to act on what I believe. Only Neville keeps going, but then he's painting the war, the regiments, the searchlights, the guns on Hampstead Heath—he can hear them from his studio he says. I bump into him from time to time in the Café Royal and he always speaks, though on the personal level we haven't been seeing much of each other recently. He has to do a first aid course and some kind of vehicle repair course before he goes out, but that only takes up the mornings and he paints like mad the rest of the time.

It's worse for Catherine than it is for me. Do you remember her? Catherine Stein. Tall and fair with goggly eyes? Before the war nobody ever thought of her as German, though we all knew she was, now suddenly it's the only thing that matters. And there's talk of interning German men which makes her worry about her father who's not in very good health.

I suppose there is a sense of being caught up in history, but in Catherine's case she's caught up like a mouse in a trap. I wish you were here—God, now I sound like a seaside postcard—it would be lovely to talk to you. Catherine's got her own problems and Ruthie's all very well but she knows what she thinks about everything and I never do, which makes her exhausting company. Please, please, Paul, come back to London soon.

What an extremely forward letter! Mother and Rachel would certainly not approve.

Paul to Elinor

I'm surprised you find the women in the Café Royal have gone quiet. The women in Beryl's bandaging class certainly haven't, I can hear them behind me as I write. Not entirely pleasant either. Women whose sons haven't enlisted are given quite a hard time by the other ladies. Beryl tucks the rug around me with great assiduity whenever they're here.

When I'm better I'll have to enlist. I thought at first I'd be able to stay out of it, but now I don't think I can, and I don't want to. I'm not sophisticated like Neville. To me it all seems simple. If your mother's attacked, you defend her. You don't waste time weighing up the rights and wrongs of the matter or wondering if a confrontation could have been avoided if only the batty old dear had been a bit more sensible. Only I can't, honestly can't, see what untrained volunteers are going to do. The last two wars in Europe have been fought by professional armies and they only lasted a few months. What I don't want is to spend a wet, cold winter in a tent on Salisbury Plain while proper, professional soldiers get on and finish the job.

Paul to Elinor

Today I tried to enlist. It wasn't anything like I expected. No open arms and welcome to the army, my boy, well done. Quite the contrary, in fact.

You spend an awfully long time sitting around with no clothes on waiting to have some part of your anatomy poked, prodded and assessed. We kept glancing along the bench, sizing each other up. Prime-quality male horseflesh; medium-quality ditto; skinny, knock-kneed, wheezy old nag fit only for the knacker's yard—me. Actually I did all right till they got to my chest, by, I must say, a somewhat circuitous route. (Details not fit for your maiden ears.) I was asked to cough—that wasn't a problem, I do a lot of that—only I couldn't stop. The MOs conferred, waited for me to stop coughing, and then asked me to cough again. I kept trying to explain I'd been ill, but by the time I got my breath back, they had stethoscopes in their ears and couldn't hear a word I said. Then the chief MO, who looked rather like a cynical sheep, shook his head. He was quite decent really, though he couldn't resist his little joke. He said the best thing I could do to serve my country was join the German army and cough a lot.

As I was getting dressed I managed to catch a glimpse of what he'd written on the form. A whole paragraph of stuff, and then at the bottom: Query TB.

The thing is I know it's not true. I'm coughing a lot, I do have night sweats, and yes there is family history, but I also know it's the aftermath of pneumonia. A few weeks' fresh air (admittedly in short supply round here), plenty of good food, and all this coughing and wheezing will clear away.

I don't know what to do. I have tried. I know I have—but that's no use, you see. I walk into town and there are newly enlisted men going to the railway station, men I went to school with, some of them, and I can't help thinking everybody's looking at me, wondering why I haven't volunteered. Perhaps I'm being oversensitive, but I seem to see that question now on every face.

Meanwhile, I'm attending a first aid class, a six-week course, and frankly a bit of a waste of time because I covered all this ground and more while I worked in the hospital, but at least it makes me feel I'm doing something. Or do I mean, makes me look as if I'm doing something? It's something for Beryl to tell her bandaging class at any rate.

I've written to Neville, to ask who he contacted to get into the

Belgian Red Cross. It's not what I wanted to do but it's better than nothing and I do have experience of working in a hospital. Fingers crossed.

I haven't asked if you're getting any painting done. I'd started drawing, in a rather pathetic, tentative way, but being turned down seems to have driven it out of my head.

Elinor to Paul

I'm sorry to hear you were turned down, since it's what you wanted, though selfishly of course I'm pleased. Father and Toby are rowing all the time about Toby enlisting. I've never seen Father so angry. Last night after dinner I heard them shouting. I keep out of it. Father thinks he should go on with his medical training, says he'll be far more use to his country as a doctor than he ever would be as a half-trained, cack-handed soldier, but of course Toby doesn't want to miss the fun—he's got the rest of his life to be a doctor.

We have first aid classes in the town too. Mother tries to drag me off to them, but so far I've managed to resist. I do sympathize with your sense of being stared at and questioned all the time. I feel it too— though in a milder way, there isn't the same pressure on girls, but it's still made perfectly clear that painting's a trivial occupation and ought to be set aside in favor of bandaging Mrs. Dalton-Smith's fat ankles— though what doing that contributes to the war effort God only knows.

I am painting again, though not with much conviction, it's more a feeling of defiance. I won't let Mrs. Dalton-Smith's ankles win.

Paul to Elinor

I was sorry to hear of Toby's battle with your father. Of course, your father's right. It would be more sensible to stay at medical school,

*but Toby wants the adventure. So do I, to be honest—or part of me
does. Another part knows perfectly well I'd hate every minute of it.
I'm not in the least militaristic, I've no desire to kill or injure anybody,
but if I could wave a magic wand and be out there now, I wouldn't
hesitate.*

*I'm glad you're painting again. It's more than I've managed to
do. I can't keep still. Twice a day sometimes I walk into town to buy
newspapers or look at the mobilization order on the Town Hall door—
in case it says something different from what it said last time. But I see
the doctor again tomorrow, and I think he'll say I'm fit enough to come
to London. If not I think I might come anyway. I've applied to the
Belgian Red Cross and Neville seems to think I stand a good chance. So
perhaps I'll see you again soon.*

Elinor to Paul

*Ruthie forwarded your letter. I'm staying in this tiny cottage
with Catherine. I'm so tired of the war, Paul. Rows at home and then
you go to London and there's no escaping it there either. At least here
you can forget it some of the time.*

*It was quite a last-minute decision. We just packed our bags and
walked out on it all and here we are. Free. In a tiny cottage down a
long narrow lane which starts off by the church. You can see the spire
over the trees. In fact, the Vicar's our landlord. I don't know how long
we'll stay but it's very cheap and quite tucked away. One bedroom,
with two little dormer windows. As you look up at the cottage from the
front they peer out under the eaves like the eyes of a Shetland pony. Do
you agree that houses have expressions? Some houses look quite mad;
this one looks interested and friendly and a bit wild.*

*Downstairs there's one big room flooded with light because it's
got windows on both sides. Hollyhocks and sunflowers in the garden.*

As sunflowers die they look more and more like old men: the stalks develop a hunched back and the seeds fold in on themselves the way old people's mouths do when they haven't any teeth. Look at one, you'll see what I mean. I've got two on the kitchen table where I'm writing and I draw them all the time.

I want to try to give you a flavor of our lives here because I'm happier than I've ever been before. On the other side of the garden fence there's lovely countryside and everything's fresh, not like London. Every possible shade of green and blue and gold and in the afternoons when the birds stop singing there's total silence. Just the hum of bees in the foxgloves, they start at the top and tumble down from flower to flower. Last night we had a picnic, cheese and bread and apples and a big bottle of cider, and when it was dark we went out onto the lawn in our nightdresses and danced. I can still turn cartwheels, Paul, so you see I'm not an old woman yet, though sometimes I feel like one. On the other side of the wall there's a cornfield with cornflowers and poppies. We walked all the way round the edge in the moonlight and the poppies looked black and the corn was silver. It made me shiver to look at it. We keep the cider cool by putting it in a bucket of water under the sink. I'm full of cider now and my lips are swollen, I think I must look like a fish. I am so happy, but Catherine keeps yawning and saying it's time for bed, so I must close.

The atmosphere at home is terrible, Toby said Father can't stop him serving his country in any way he damn well chooses, but the fact is, he does want and need Father's approval, and so far Dad simply won't budge. He says war should be left to professional soldiers and all these half-trained boys running about all over the place are more trouble than they're worth. I don't know. I side with Toby because he's my brother and we've always stuck together, but the fact is, I don't want him to go either. More than anything I resent the way the war takes over all our lives. It's like a single bullying voice shouting all the other voices down.

I wish you could come here, Paul. It would be lovely to see you, I do miss you, but now I'm just about to start writing real nonsense so it's high time I went to bed.

Love, Elinor.

Elinor to Paul

Yes, I know, two letters in one day! I expect they'll arrive in the same post, but I simply have to write again because something really awful has happened. We've been thrown out! The Vicar turned up, walking across the fields in his long black hassock (cassock?)—don't know, doesn't matter—his black gown, binding with briars my joys and desires. He said the Parish Council had brought it to his attention, etc. Oh, he was squirming, he didn't know where to look. But the upshot of it is, they want us out. Can't rent the cottage to a German. Catherine signed the rental agreement. Stein, of course. I nearly suggested she call herself Stone, but I didn't dare, it seems such an insult to ask somebody to change their name. Apparently I'm welcome to stay to the end of the month, but Catherine must go. Of course I'm going with her! And so here we are, suitcases packed, waiting for the cart to take us to the station.

Catherine's gone very quiet. I rant and rave and stomp up and down, but I know it's no use, really. I'm still quite shocked. It seems so . . . I don't know, un-English.

Anyway, there it is. We're coming back to London, so we shall be able to see each other after all.

I'm sending this to your home address though I suppose you may have already left by now. Oh dear, what a muddle it all is. I can't wait to see you, now more than ever. Elinor.

16

THE LAST THING PAUL HAD EXPECTED TO FEEL was nostalgia, but as he stood in the entrance to the Domino Room, taking in the crimson velvet, the gilt, the flickering candles, the caryatids, the cupids, the whole grandiose but cozy feel of the place, he did feel a ripple of affection. So many evenings spent here, most of them with Teresa. He waited for the pang of regret, but it didn't come. If anything he felt relieved.

Finding an empty table, he sat down, looking around, trying to work out what had changed. There was an edginess about the place now: excitement and fear. Not fear of disfigurement or death—most of the people in this room were at no risk of either—no, fear of being irrelevant. He looked from table to table, recognizing famous and not-so-famous faces, and what he sensed was a toxic mixture of excitement and paralysis. Though he only recognized it here because to a certain extent he'd felt exactly that himself, before he'd made himself start working again.

Neville was the first person to speak to him. "Hello," he said, coming over and shaking hands warmly, laying his free hand on Paul's shoulder in that domineering way of his. "Elinor says you've been ill. You all right now?"

"Fine. You?"

"Oh, you know, toddling on."

He was looking round the room as he spoke. Paul suspected he was searching for more important people to talk to, but he showed no inclination to move on.

"What'll you have?"

"Whiskey, please."

Neville gave the order. "I suppose you're up for the Red Cross interview?"

"Tomorrow morning."

"You'll be all right."

"When do you leave?"

"Two, three weeks." He seized his whiskey from the waiter's tray. "Did you try to enlist?"

"They wouldn't have me. What about you?"

"Went to see my own medical man. He told me not to waste my time. Anyway, the sooner I get started the better."

"Driving an ambulance?"

"Painting, you fool."

"Will you be close to the fighting?"

"As close as I can get." He was not so much drinking as throwing it back. "My father's been out there twice already. He went to one hospital where there were five hundred men lying on straw, covered in piss and shit—some of them hadn't had their wounds dressed in a fortnight. No anesthetics, no disinfectant, nothing. Whole place stank of gangrene. As far as I can make out the medical services have been completely overwhelmed."

"And that's what you're going to paint?"

"I'll paint whatever's there."

"You really do see it as a painting opportunity, don't you?"

"Too bloody right I do."

Paul caught a movement by the door. Elinor had come in, and, just behind her, Catherine. The girls hesitated, gazing nervously round the room. Elinor smiled when she saw Paul waving and came over at once, with none of the pauses to greet people that he remembered from the past. He leaned forward to embrace her. Her cheek was cool, even in this heat, and her scent reminded him of fresh linen sheets.

She kissed him, then held him at arm's length.

"You've lost a lot of weight."

"A stone and a half."

"You were thin to start with."

"I'm careful about cracks in the pavement."

Catherine shook hands, first with him, then with Neville. She was pale and wearing a black dress that drained her complexion of the little color it had. Neville hadn't spoken to Elinor, but now, at the last moment, he bowed and smiled.

"I called at your lodgings this afternoon," Paul said to Elinor, "but you were out."

"I thought you were still in the country," Neville said, almost simultaneously.

Catherine answered. "No, the Parish Council didn't like the idea of having a Church cottage rented by a German."

"A German—?" For a moment Neville looked puzzled. "Oh, yes, of course, I'm sorry, I forgot. And they threw you out because of that? But that's outrageous."

"Well, they did," Elinor said. "And they didn't even offer to refund the rent."

"Why don't you complain to the Bishop?"

"Because it wouldn't do any good."

"You can't let them get away with it."

She shook her head. "Catherine's got enough on her plate without that. I don't think you want the battle, do you, Cath?"

"Not that particular one." She turned to Neville, whose anger on her behalf, however misdirected, had obviously touched her. "You see, we may have to move house and if we do I've got to be there to help my parents, so I'm afraid painting in country cottages is a thing of the past."

"*Why* do you have to move?" Neville said. He was becoming more truculent by the minute.

"We live on the coast. Right on the front, in fact—the sea's about two hundred yards away—and people think we're signaling to German ships. It's ridiculous, but that's what they think." She tried a smile, but it wouldn't stay on her mouth. "If we close the living room curtains that's a signal. Open them, that's a signal. Flowers in the window: signal. And as for switching on a lamp . . . Well!"

"But that's insane."

"Oh, we're the lucky ones. A family we know—they're not even German, they're Polish—had bricks thrown through the windows."

Neville was breathing noisily, a dragon working up a head of steam. "Should you move? I mean, shouldn't you stay and face it out?"

"My father's lived there thirty years and last week . . ." She was fighting back the tears. "Last week somebody spat at him in the street."

"So, you see," Elinor said, "not being allowed to rent the cottage doesn't matter very much."

Neville was leaning towards Catherine. "Do you have people you can stay with?"

"My mother's sister. I'm staying with her at the moment."

Nobody came near them, though Neville and Elinor must have known everybody in the room. They were in quarantine, it seemed. Neville was aware of it, Paul could see that—he had that blue, dancing, truculent light in his eyes—he'd found a cause, and sooner or later everybody in this room would pay for ignoring Catherine tonight. Oh, he was a champion grudge bearer was Neville, but he was also on this occasion—and how distressing it was to admit it—right.

One way and another it was a relief when Elinor suggested they should leave.

"Good idea," said Neville, jumping up. "It's boring in here tonight."

It was raining, no more than a light drizzle but enough to make them decide to take a cab. Paul went to summon one, leaving Neville and the two girls standing in the shelter of the doorway. He'd just attracted a cabby's attention and was turning to call the others when an incident took place. A young man, rather foppishly dressed, carrying a silver-topped cane, stumbled against Catherine as he was leaving and knocked her to one side. It might have been an accident, but his grin suggested otherwise. Neville spun round and head butted him in the face. Blood spouted from the young man's nostrils and splashed on his shirt front.

Paul ran back to join Neville, whose fists were clenched in front of him. One of the young man's companions grabbed his arm and pulled him back. The other bent and picked up his cane. By this time the doorman and several waiters had appeared, obviously determined not to have a fight in the entrance. Gradually, with muttered threats of future reprisals, the young man allowed himself to be dragged away.

In silence, they walked to the cab. Catherine was white and seemed to be on the verge of tears. Elinor had an arm round her shoulders. Paul was stunned, less by Neville's anger, which he thought fully justified, than by the sheer backroom-brawl brutality of that head butt. He wouldn't have believed Neville had it in him.

They got into the cab. Gradually Neville's breathing returned to normal. None of the others could think of anything to say. Paul looked across at him—he was still shaking with anger but exhilarated too, you could see it in his eyes. He was like that all the time underneath.

The cabby was waiting for instructions.

"Café Eiffel Tower?" Elinor said.

Catherine shook her head. "I'm sorry, I just want to go home. You go."

"Why don't you and Tarrant go?" Neville said. "I'll see Catherine home."

"All right," said Paul, snatching the chance of time alone with Elinor, though amazed it had been offered. He shook hands with Neville. "Shall I see you again before you go?"

"Give me a ring tomorrow. We'll fix something up."

Paul got out and handed Elinor down.

"Well," said Elinor, as the cab drove away.

"He's found a cause."

"Hasn't he just? You know, he's always going on about his parents and their campaigning and how neglected he felt because of it, but my goodness the block chipped. Blocks."

"He likes Catherine."

"I hope he does."

"What do you mean?"

"I hope she's not *just* a cause."

"You don't mind him going off with her like that?"

"Good heavens, no. Lets me off the hook."

"Is it over? Between you and him?"

It seemed obvious that it was, but he needed to have it spelled out.

"It was never on." She walked a little further. "Did you see how he enjoyed hitting that man?"

"He deserved it."

"But Nev head-butted him."

"No, it wasn't exactly Queensberry Rules, was it?"

"You see, you're laughing. You're as bad as he is."

"I think that fellow deserved everything he got."

They were drifting aimlessly along. After a while she took his arm and that pleased him.

"Are we going to the Eiffel Tower?" he said.

"No, I've had enough of people for one night. Let's just walk."

London at night was more obviously changed than London by day. The lamps had been painted blue and cast a ghastly glow onto the faces of passersby. The darkened streets directed your attention to the sky, where searchlights stroked the underbelly of the clouds. All around was that burnt, used-up smell of late summer in the city.

"I hate August," Paul said.

"Well, this August isn't much fun."

"No, I've never liked it. My mother died in August."

"Oh, I'm sorry."

He smiled. "It was a long time ago."

Silence for a hundred yards or so. Then Elinor said, "What time's your interview?"

"Ten-thirty."

"Neville seems to think they'll jump at you."

"It's not fighting, but it's the best I can do."

"The best *you* could do is stay here and paint."

"Not an option. We can all go back to painting when it's over. Except Neville. Do you know, he told me he's going out there *to paint*?"

"I admire him, actually," she said. "He's the only person I know who kept going. Everybody else sat round and talked. Including me, I'm sorry to say." She glanced sidelong at him. "I suppose you've been too ill to do anything?"

"No, I did a bit."

"And are you pleased with it?"

Oh, that artist's question, both wanting and dreading to hear that another artist's work is going well.

"I am, quite."

"Oh, good."

This was the longest walk he'd done for quite a while, and he was pleased at the way his chest was holding up. It helped that the air was warm and slightly moist. They strolled on, leaning against each other now. The conversation flowed, but it was the conversation of friends and he wanted to change that. He needed to tell Elinor how he felt about her, even if it caused her to withdraw, and it probably would. Teresa had vanished almost without trace. Little remained of her now except a voice saying, "You don't love me. If you love anybody, you love Elinor, and you only love *her* because you know she won't have you." In his memory, even that remark had been pruned. "You don't love me. You love Elinor." That was what he remembered her saying because that was what he wished she'd said.

"Shall we have a walk round?" he said as they were passing Russell Square.

"I thought we were walking? Miles."

"Let's sit down, then."

Further in under the darkness of the trees he slipped his arm around her waist. He could feel the rise and fall of her breath. Their footsteps rang out on the path with that hollow sound of nighttime in the city. Veering to one side, he steered her onto the grass. Now there was only the rustling of leaves under their feet, the sharp smell of soil and decay. The searchlights were clearer now, sweeping from side to side above their heads.

"Nev's painted them, you know. The searchlights."

Bugger Neville. "I bet he has."

Before she could speak again he covered her mouth with his own. He could see hands, frozen in the air. At last, with a sigh, she let them settle on his shoulders. He stood with his back to a tree, holding her close, wanting to laugh and shout with triumph, simply because she hadn't pushed him away. Everything was possible now. He whispered in her ear, "I love you."

She was looking up at him. He saw the searchlights in her eyes, and pulled her deeper into the shade. He started to kiss her neck, then her throat, his hand closed around her breast, and then she was pushing him away. Breathing deeply, eyes closed, he heard a creaking sound. He looked up thinking it must be a

bough, but although the tree was in constant motion in the upper branches, the sound seemed to be coming from further
away.

"What is that?"

"I don't know."

Taking her hand, he led her towards it. Far from them being alone, as he'd thought at first, he realized the square was
full of couples, entwined together in the shadows of the trees or
stretched out full length on the ground. One couple were making love. As he walked past he glimpsed an elastic garter, a
stocking top, and a bulging white thigh.

The sound came from near the center of the square. He
could see what was causing it: a line of cylindrical black shapes
suspended from a metal frame, swaying in the wind and causing
the ropes they were suspended from to creak. Elinor walked up
to them and he followed.

"What are they?" he asked.

He caught the glint of her teeth as she smiled.

"It's the Kaiser."

She turned one of the bags round to face him and he saw
that a ferociously glaring mask had been pinned to the cloth.
They were just straw-filled sacks, used for bayonet practice,
weighted so they wouldn't move too easily. Pale gold straw
bled from rents in the material.

"I watched them practicing the other day. They're supposed to yell when they stick it in." She pulled a face. "Apparently nobody dies unless you yell."

She went along the line, setting them all in motion, one by
one. The snarling faces jiggled and turned.

He felt the evening start to slip away from him. As she

turned, he tried to kiss her again, but his kiss landed on her ear. "Can we go to your lodgings?"

Her hands had come up to form a barrier. "I don't think so."

"Can I see you tomorrow, then?"

"Yes, that would be nice."

He relaxed. She wasn't rejecting him. She just needed time. He guessed that glimpse of the girl with her skirt around her waist had frightened her as much as it had aroused him.

"Where would you like to go?"

"Anywhere," she said. "As long as it's not the Café Royal."

They laughed, and their laughter restored a kind of normality. Turning their backs on the straw men dangling from their gibbet, they began to walk towards Gower Street.

His hand settled on her waist. Till now he'd intended to stay in London only till the day after tomorrow, but now he thought he'd stay longer, make it a full week.

A lot could happen in a week.

Part

Two

17

EVERYTHING STINKS: CREOSOTE, BLEACH, DISINFEC-tant, soil, blood, gangrene.

The military authorities say uniforms must be preserved at all costs, but that means manhandling patients who are in agony. Cut them off, says Sister Byrd, and she's the voice of authority here, in the Salle d'Attente, not some gold-braid-encrusted crustacean miles away from blood and pain, so cut they do, snip, snip, snip, snip, as close to the skin as they dare.

On either side of Paul as he cuts are two long rows of feet: yellow, strong, calloused, scarred where blisters have formed and burst repeatedly. Since August they've done a lot of march-ing, these feet, and all their marching has brought them to this one place.

Sister Byrd's tough, tougher even than she looks. Auburn hair tarnished with silver; fine, pale skin mottled red on the cheeks; harebell-blue eyes—she must have been pretty once but now she's barrel shaped and dour, and amazingly good at her job.

Every few minutes the door's pushed open and the stretcher bearers shuffle in with their load, standing like cart horses between the shafts, waiting to be told where to set it down. They're there now, waiting. Sister Byrd pulls the blanket over the face of a man who's just died and his yellow ankles seem to get longer. Strong calves appear, fuzzed with black hairs, the muscles prominent from all the marching he's done in the last few weeks. She bows her head, but only for a second. "All right," she says, in French. "You can put him here."

In bad weather, as now, the rain pelts down on the corrugated-iron roof with the rattle of machine-gun fire. At the moment it's a real downpour. Waking from their half sleep, the bundles in the blankets begin to stir and cry out in fear. One of the head wounds throws off his blanket, clambers to his feet, and, naked, runs between the rows of beds. Two of the orderlies give chase and eventually grab hold of him, one by each arm, and hold him like that, his arms outstretched, a blood-soaked bandage slipping down across one eye. They soothe him, stroke his arms, tell him there's nothing to be frightened of, it's the rain, only the rain, no guns here, and perhaps he believes them, but more probably he doesn't understand a word, only the tone of voice and the touch. But he lets himself be led along, the strength that terror gave him ebbing with every step, until, by the time they reach his bed, he's walking with the slow, shuffling steps of a very old man.

At last Sister Byrd signals that it's Paul's turn for a break. They drink their cocoa in the sterilizing room, all of them, dressers, orderlies, nurses, surgeons, surrounded by hissing and bursts of steam. The cocoa's hot. It delineates his gullet as it goes down. Only his hands around the mug and the hot fluid in his mouth and stomach are real. The light over the dressing table blurs; he makes an effort to straighten up and focus on his surroundings. Swaying on his feet, and still four more hours to do. Sister Roper's saying something to him. He has to strain to hear her quiet voice above the roar and hiss of the boiler. Somebody new, a volunteer, arriving on the eight o'clock train. Will he go and meet him? "Take him to the huts first—he'll have luggage with him, I expect."

"Which hut?"

"Yours. It's the only spare bed."

Paul wants to point out that the bed in his hut isn't exactly spare, that the ambulance drivers sometimes use it, but it's already too late for that. They're all moving off again, back to the scrubbing room and from there into theater. He understands, or at least nobody contradicts the idea, that he's to leave what he's doing now and go to the station—a ten, fifteen minutes' walk away—and meet the eight o'clock train. It's a break, at least. He has no quarrel with that.

Outside, in the darkness of the yard, there's an ambulance crew, also drinking cocoa, leaning against the canvas side of their vehicle. He passes close by, grunts in acknowledgment of a raised arm, and heads off to the station. It's muddy underfoot, and cold, but fresh after the hot, steamy air of the sterilizing room. Rain falls on his face. He shivers, and a cold sweat starts up. Within minutes his armpits and groin are drenched, his feet swimming inside his boots. Nothing to do with illness or even change of temperature, this sweat; everything to do with being plunged into the normal world. He stumbles, nearly falls. Every step now brings him further out of the trance. He pauses. Lets his shoulders relax. He's waking out of his trance into the real time of the outside world.

On his left, there's a goods train—its doors gaping open—

and that shields him from the worst of the wind and rain. He walks along beside it, until, straight ahead, he sees the station and hears a man's voice making announcements. All the time he's coming back to himself.

The blue-painted lights of the railway station loom out of the dusk. He remembers the streets of London, walking through them that night with Elinor. All Europe now, he supposes, exists in this indigo twilight. Going into the station, he finds the platform crowded. Men, women, children—all waiting for the train. Eight hours he's been on duty. Long enough for the sound of a child's voice to be shocking.

Five to eight. If the train is on time, he won't have long to wait. He stands near the ticket barrier, stamping his feet to restore the circulation. A little girl stares at him and he smiles at her, but she clasps her mother's hand tighter and walks on, looking back at him over her shoulder. Perhaps pain, even other people's pain, becomes a smell you carry round with you?

A rumble in the distance, the light on the line shivers and a single blue eye appears, advancing towards them. Mothers pull their children back from the edge. A belch of smoke and steam and then the engine roars past, snorts, sighs several times, subsides into silence.

All along the train's length doors open and people spill out. Passengers greet friends, kiss, shake hands, ask and answer questions, pick up bags, begin to drift towards the exit. Soon the platform is almost clear and still no sign of the man he'd come to meet. Then, out of the darkness and the drifting smoke, a figure emerges and strides towards him.

Paul's first thought was, he won't last five minutes. He was looking at a gangly boy, all arms and legs. A sprinkle of freckles all over his face gave him a slightly surprised look, like somebody caught in a shower. Close to, there was something about his expression—not just youth and inexperience, something else—that made Paul uneasy. He felt irritated. He'd become rather good at coping with the work, but having a hut to himself had been an important part of that process. Now, he'd have to share it with this freckly-faced schoolboy—deal with his questions, his incomprehension, his shock. Everything that Paul had felt when he first started, and no longer permitted himself to feel.

He held out his hand. "Hello, I'm Paul Tarrant. Sister Roper asked me to meet you."

"Hello. I'm Richard Lewis."

A deep baritone—surprising, it didn't go with his appearance. Lewis was staring at him. Paul looked down at his tunic, which had bits of blood-stained gauze stuck to it. He picked off the bits and let them drop.

"Good journey?"

"Not bad."

Lewis was pink and excited, not at all tired from the journey, swinging a big, heavy bag from hand to hand.

"I expect you'll want to get rid of that."

"How close are we to the hospital?"

If Paul had been capable of smiling he'd have smiled then. "Not far."

They walked along beside the track, in silence. The path was thronged with weeds. Their boots swished through the long stalks, shaking off raindrops that flashed silver in the moonlight. Even with the moon it was hard to see the way ahead.

"I hope you've brought a torch?"

"Yes, in here." Lewis swung the bag to his other hand. "How long have you been here?"

"A month."

"Oh. So you know the ropes, then?"

Paul didn't bother to reply.

Five minutes later they were approaching a row of huts. He stopped at the third one along. "Here we are."

The door opened straight into the only room. Inside there was a puddle of wet footprints where somebody, one of the ambulance drivers probably, had come in and gone out again. Because he was showing the hut to Lewis he was forced to see it again himself. Two iron beds covered in brown blankets, a table with an oil lamp, two chairs. Nothing else, except a candle on the floor between the beds.

The huts had been assembled quickly, not intended to last more than a couple of months. Like everything else around here, they reeked of creosote.

Paul groped his way across to the table and lit the lamp. The flame fattened. Walls, chairs, table, beds seemed to take a leap upwards, as if the hut was startled by its own squalor.

Lewis, looking puzzled, stared around him.

"You'd best take that bed."

Paul pointed to the bed nearest the door. The draftiest and least comfortable of the two. Nothing like round-the-clock attendance on wounded and dying men to expunge the last traces of altruism. The bed was tightly made up in the hospital style, the ends of the coarse, brown blanket neatly mitered and tucked in.

Lewis swung his case up onto the bed. "It must have been rather nice having it to yourself."

"I don't mind. It's not as if I spend a lot of time here anyway. Do you want to have a rest now, before you go over?"

"No, I'd rather get stuck in."

"Right, then. Off we go. Your first sight of the Shambles."

Lewis looked blank.

"The hospital."

"Oh, I see. Sorry."

He thought it was a joke. Despite his eagerness to get going, he lingered for a moment by the door, staring from table to chair to bed and back again, willing it all to go away, so he could start again and have the experience he'd been expecting. He looked lost, standing there in his smart uniform.

Again the wave of irritation.

"You didn't think of enlisting, then?"

"I'm a Quaker."

"Sorry, I didn't realize."

"Why should you? We don't wear uniform. What about you?"

"Tried, wouldn't have me."

"Were you very disappointed?"

"At the time, yes. Not now. I mean, everybody I know who's enlisted is still in England." He turned the lamp out. "Strange, isn't it? The only reason we've got this close to the front is because I can't fight and you won't."

That came out hostile, though he hadn't meant it to.

"How close are we?"

"About two miles."

"I thought I heard the guns."

"Probably. It's a bit like the trains, after a while you don't notice them." For a moment he was back in bed with Teresa, listening to a goods train rumble past. "You can tell if it's really bad, the lamp jumps up and down."

"So it's quiet now?"

"So-so."

"I volunteered for ambulance driving."

"Me too. I think they must be short of ambulances. I don't really know, nobody tells you anything." He moved towards the door. "Let's talk later, shall we? I ought to be getting back."

"Wait, I'll get my torch." Lewis was almost stammering in his eagerness. "Oh, where's the . . . ?"

"Behind the hut."

Paul waited again, none too patiently, while Lewis disappeared round the side of the hut, no doubt expecting to find another similar hut containing the bathroom facilities.

A minute or so later he was back, head down, fumbling with buttons.

"If you get desperate for a bit of civilization, there's a hotel in town where you can get a bath."

"I don't understand."

"What don't you understand?"

"*This*." He looked around at the gulf of darkness, the dull blue lights of the station quavering as they always did on windy nights. "Where's the hospital?"

"There isn't a hospital." Paul felt weighed down, resenting the need to explain. "Look, there's a lot of huts built round a covered goods yard. I suppose the wounded were dumped there initially because it was the end of the line. I can't think of any other reason. When the Red Cross took over there were over a thousand men lying on straw in their own shit. Half a dozen orderlies, no medicine, no bedpans, no anesthetics. You name it, they hadn't got it. They weren't even being fed. They hadn't had their wounds dressed, some of them, for a fortnight. So however primitive you think this is, remember it's been a hell of a lot worse."

Lewis nodded, soaking it in.

"And you did volunteer."

His head went up immediately. "I'm not complaining."

They walked on in silence. When they reached the ambulances' turning circle, Lewis stopped and stared longingly at the three parked vehicles. In the moonlight, the red crosses stood out black against their pale canvas sides. No sign of the drivers, who'd be over in the canteen having coffee, waiting for the next call.

"Come on," Paul said. "You can look at them later."

He pushed hard against the hut door. Warm air tainted with gangrene gushed out to meet them. Behind him, he felt Lewis take an involuntary step back.

"We're in a quiet patch," Paul said, glancing over his shoulder. "You're lucky."

18

Sister Byrd greeted Lewis briskly, then turned to Paul. "You'd better take him round with you. Show him the ropes." She pointed to a man a little way along the row. "Start with him."

After fetching scissors from the sterilizing room, Paul led Lewis across to the patient. Pulling back the blanket, he saw that the man was naked from the waist down, his groin padded with a heavily stained dressing that was stuck to the skin. He set to work with the scissors, aware of Lewis watching him. Lewis was breathing with his mouth open, his rather full lips cracked and dry. Easing the lower blade under the bandage, Paul snipped close to the skin, trying to disturb the area as little as possible. Inevitably the scissors tugged and, every time, the man twisted and writhed. Paul stopped for a moment. He noticed Lewis had put one hand on the man's wrist, a firm, steady pressure.

After a moment he began cutting again. A few minutes later he'd reached the point of pulling the dressing away. This had to be done slowly and carefully. Speed would have been more merciful but risked doing further damage. He clenched his teeth as if he were in pain, though the pain was not his and never could be. He eased the dressing off. Shrapnel had come through from the back and severed the penis at the base. As they watched, urine welled up from the hole in his groin, hot acid spreading over raw flesh. The man arched his back and groaned again. Morphine. "Stay with him," he said, standing up and looking around for Sister Byrd. She was quick. She was always quick. Lewis watched her filling the syringe, flicking it, preparing to inject, with as much eagerness as if the pain had been his.

When the patient had settled a little, she said, "It's gone through the intestines. He won't last."

"Will they operate tonight?" Lewis asked.

Sister Byrd looked at him consideringly. How much use are you going to be? was the question written on her face. "There's not much they can do. Once the morphine takes effect we'll clean him up and see what Mr. Burton says." She waited, watching Lewis closely. "Would *you* want to live?"

"If it was me?" For a second he stared into the abyss, then shook his head. "I don't know."

It was what passed for a quiet evening. Three men died but they'd been expected to, and did so quietly and without fuss. Mess tins full of gray stew were carried up and down the rows of stretchers. Lewis fed several patients who couldn't feed themselves. He kept yawning, more from shock than tiredness, but Sister Byrd chose to regard it as the effect of his long journey.

"Look, why don't you go across to the huts and get settled in? We can manage."

Lewis blinked, from surprise, probably, that this experience had an end. Paul knew the feeling. When you first started, a twelve-hour shift could last forever.

An hour later Paul followed him across to the hut, the weak, sickly circle of torchlight playing across thronging weeds and stacks of abandoned sleepers. There was no light under the door. Cupping his hand round the beam of the torch he opened the door on a smell of damp socks and unwashed blankets. Lewis was awake. Paul could see the whites of his eyes among the flickering shadows but then with a squeal of springs he turned away.

Paul undressed quickly and got under the blanket before the slight warmth of his clothes could evaporate. He lay with his arms clasped across his chest, fingertips tucked into his armpits, doing everything possible to conserve heat. Sleep would come anyway—he was worn out—but it would last longer and stand a better chance of being dreamless if he could keep warm. He was aware of Lewis, breathing quietly, awake in the darkness. The pressure of that other consciousness was intolerable. Resigned, he turned heavily onto his side and set the candle on the floor between them.

"How many of them die?" Lewis asked.

"Thirty percent."

"Percent?"

Paul was puzzled, then realized Lewis was questioning his coldblooded way of talking about it. "That's good. When the Red Cross first arrived it was much worse than that. Now seventy *percent* survive."

"You know the very young one who died?"

Paul frowned into the darkness. No, he couldn't remember any of the three who'd died. Not their faces. He could remember their positions in the hut, because he'd taken note of where the spaces were so that he could direct stretcher bearers to them as quickly as possible, when the next batch came in.

"Sister Byrd said he had gas gangrene, but I thought the Germans haven't used gas?"

"They haven't. It's when tiny organisms in the soil get into a wound, they produce gas."

"And that's the smell?"

"You get used to it." Paul was struggling to keep his eyes open. This was no time for a tutorial. "Look, there are three ways you can tell if it's gas gangrene. One, the smell. And then there's a kind of crackling under the skin. It's . . . it's quite hard to describe, but you'll know it once you've felt it. I'll show you tomorrow if I get a chance."

He was turning away as he spoke.

"And the third?"

"I'm sorry?"

"You said three things."

"Did I? The third thing is they die."

Despite his exhaustion, Paul couldn't sleep. He was too aware of Lewis, now lying on his back in the darkness with his arms folded behind his head, not even trying to sleep. Eventually Paul nodded off, then woke, and spent the next hour wandering along the edge of sleep, afraid of plunging in, in case the freshening-up process that Lewis had started should extend to the deeper layers of his mind and reawaken the nightmares. During his first fortnight on the wards every horror had followed him into sleep. During the day he managed to lower a safety curtain that protected him from the worst of it, but at night it failed him. Then gradually—he didn't know how because no conscious effort would have done it—he'd somehow extended that protection into his sleep. Now he was afraid that wounds and mutilations would start pursuing him again.

After a while he started to drift off again, but time after

time, found himself pulled back from the brink. Lewis was asleep now, but the quiet breathing from the next bed drove Paul into a kind of rage. Only now, when he'd lost it, did he begin to realize how much he'd valued the peace and solitude of this hut where, in his off-duty hours, he could read or write letters or draw. Whether he could do any of these things with Lewis around, he rather doubted. He'd never willingly shared a bedroom with anybody, except a lover. There was something about physical intimacy without passion that he found distasteful. Of course, this was a trivial matter in comparison with the great events of the war, but he'd already learned that the war was a compendium of trivial matters, and anyway, this wasn't trivial to him. He needed space and solitude to go on working. Perhaps it would be possible to rent a room in town? He was always on call, but it might still be worthwhile to get a room and go there on his days off. Just to have somewhere he could draw and think. A cupboard would do.

Meanwhile . . . Sighing, he turned over again, and finally, just as the threadbare light of dawn made itself felt through a crack in the door, he fell into a deep sleep.

19

Next morning, when Paul opened his eyes, the first thing he saw was Lewis sitting on the end of his bed, fully dressed, smoking a cigarette. Several butts lay scattered on the floor, suggesting he might have been awake for some time.

"What time do we have to be over there?"

Paul looked at his watch. "Forty minutes."

Lewis seemed almost feverish, tensed up to face the day. No sign of the enthusiasm of the previous night. It made Paul feel nervous and irritable to look at him. Reaching for his clothes, he started to get dressed. Lewis got up and paced up and down, though there was hardly enough room for it: three paces either way and you had to turn.

"You could do that outside."

Lewis stopped, but his tension was visible in every muscle. He was straining to start work.

"Breakfast?" Paul said.

"I can't eat."

"All right. Watch me."

Outside it was still dark, the furthest sheds just beginning to show through the thinning gray. Far away, a train whistled.

As they set off, Paul felt Lewis veering in the direction of the Salle d'Attente; his feet seemed to head in that direction even as he tried to keep pace with Paul. He kept stumbling. Under the weeds the ground was full of holes.

Paul touched his arm. "You'll feel better for a coffee."

The dining room was another hut. The food came in huge vats from somewhere off site and was almost inedible, but the coffee, made on site, was good and Paul drank three huge cups of it before forcing himself to eat. Lewis pushed his croissants to one side but drank the coffee, cupping his hands round the mug. In the strengthening daylight he looked odder: frizzy hair; eyes, that clear pale Viking blue that makes their owners look capable of anything; skin so freckled it was almost a deformity. You thought of leopards, snakes, toads. Lewis put down his cup. Mouth as always slightly open, he was staring at Paul, a question on his face. Paul looked quickly down and away.

Burton came over and introduced himself. In the chill morning air, his nose was pinched, his eyes red rimmed with tiredness. Lewis looked up at him, eager to be impressed. Burton welcomed him "on board," recommended several good restaurants, and then, exactly as Paul had done the previous night, told him where he could get a hot bath and a shave. We're a disappointment to him, Paul thought, watching Lewis's politely smiling face, with our talk of percentages and our concern for our own comfort. He's looking for somebody to hero-worship, and we're not it. But then he wondered what gave him the confidence, the arrogance, to think he could understand Lewis on the basis of such a slight acquaintance. He might be tougher than he appeared on the surface. He'd better be.

Burton, who'd been the last to arrive, was the first to leave, and his departure signaled a general move across to the sheds. As they walked over the open space, Paul took Lewis to one side and pointed to the road that led away from the station.

"There, you see?" A convoy of motor ambulances was churning up the hill. "That's the first of them."

Paul stared at the road, trying to see it through Lewis's eyes. Motor lorries, horse-drawn wagons coming back from delivering the rations, a column of men marching. All along the horizon, guns rumbled and flickered. Occasionally a flare went up, illuminating a bank of black cloud.

"Can you get up there?" Lewis asked.

"Not easily. I suppose an ambulance driver might give you a lift."

"I'd like to go."

"Drive an ambulance and you will. Meanwhile . . ." He put his hand on Lewis's shoulder. "There's work to be done."

An hour later the black clouds are overhead. The wind rocks and shakes the roof; rain pelts down, sending waves of turbulence around the room. Outside, ambulances roar, cough, hiccup, splutter, stop, unload the wounded, and drive off again, churning the mud in the turning circle to thick brownish-black cream. By mid-afternoon every available space in the hut's been filled. Paul, Lewis, and three other orderlies move up and down the rows of stretchers, cutting men out of their uniforms, washing them, ignoring their pleas for water if they're going to the operating theaters, letting them have it if they're slight wounds who can wait or beyond hope. The most severely wounded moan on the edge of consciousness or lie in ominous silence. Continually, throughout the day, the procession of wounded comes. Each time the leading stretcher bearer holds the door open, a current of cold air rushes in, damp and brackish smelling, as if even the outside world's underground. And the gust of wind flutters the papers in Sister Byrd's hand and lifts the edges of the blankets.

Lewis follows Paul round, watching and copying everything he does. Once his shadow falls across Paul's hands at a crucial moment and Paul swears at him and sees him flinch. He learns quickly though, his hands are strong and deft, he doesn't tire, or anyway shows no sign of it, though he must be suffering from backache now, as they all are, bending and lifting the stretchers hour after hour. No, Lewis's problems are all in his head. Some of the things Sister Byrd says—"Take that stomach in next, and then the head"—visibly shock him. "Look," Paul imagines saying to him, "leave your fucking compassion at the door, it's no use to anybody here."

He's roused from his trance by a commotion at the door. Another stretcher's just been brought in. Hearing raised voices, Sister Byrd goes to investigate. The man on the stretcher waits till she's leaning over him and spits a gob of blood into her face.

Paul's on his way over, before she calls for him. Lewis, as always, follows. Paul turns to tell him to go on washing the patient he's just left, but Sister Byrd says, "No, it'll take two." The man's bucking and rearing against the straps that bind him. "You've got a right one there," the front bearer says, jovial now he's succeeded in dumping the problem onto somebody else. Wiping the blood from her face, Sister Byrd turns to the driver, who, unusually, has come in with the bearers. "He tried to jump out of the back of the ambulance," the driver says. "We had to tie him down."

Blood wells from the man's mouth, great thick black gobbets of blood. As he turns his head in the direction of their voices, his left eyeball swings against his cheek.

"Will he live?" Paul asks.

She shrugs. They carry him through into theater, Sister Byrd hurrying ahead to warn the surgical team. Paul takes the front of the stretcher. Lewis the rear, though they have to keep stopping, because the man kicks and struggles so much he's in danger of tipping himself onto the floor. His eyeball swings with every jolt.

The hot air of the operating theater hits them, a solid wall Paul has to push against. There are three tables in operation. Burton, Mercer, and Browne, wearing red gowns, or so it seems, are chatting to their teams and flirting with the younger nurses, unconscious of the stench of blood. The door into the sterilizing room swings open, belching steamy air as a nurse carries a tray of instruments into the room.

"Oh, my God, what's this?" Mercer says, looking down.

"Shot himself," Sister Cope says.

Mercer purses his lips. "Why, for God's sake? A million Germans getting paid good money to do the job and he has to go and shoot himself. Oh, well. Get him on."

Easier said than done. He spits, curses, struggles, finally lands a kick on Sister Cope's breast that makes her go white. It takes six of them in the end to bind him to the table and two to force the mask down over his face. Even as the ether takes effect, he's still straining against the straps, a torrent of mangled words spewing from his mouth.

"All right," Mercer says. "I think we can start now."

He's standing well back, pulling irritably at the ties on his gown. He keeps glancing at the clock and pulling his mask down to wipe away the mustache of sweat that constantly forms on his upper lip. Paul doesn't like Mercer, not that liking or disliking matter much here. He doesn't like the pale, large, doughy face or the way his features, individually rather small and delicate, cluster together in the center as if for safety. Mercer notices an amputated leg that hasn't been cleared away fast enough and, in a sudden burst of fury, kicks it across the floor.

"I need this place kept clear!" he shouts.

Sister Cope, still white from the kick, scurries across and removes the offending limb.

Paul and Lewis watch from the back, ready to step in should the man come out of the anesthetic fighting, as patients often do. Between other people's shoulders, they catch glimpses of the operation. Mercer locates the bullet, extracts it, drops it, with a small, disgusted clink, into a kidney bowl, and then maneuvers the eyeball back into its socket.

"All right." He straightens up, presses one hand hard into the small of his back, leaving a red print on the white cloth. "What's next?"

He's marginally better tempered now because he feels he's done a good job, as no doubt he has. Paul and Lewis come forward, unbuckle the straps, and lift the man onto the stretcher.

"Through there," Paul says, nodding at the door behind Lewis.

Lewis backs out into the cold corridor. Immediately, they both begin to shiver. Within a few seconds Lewis is shaking uncontrollably, whether from cold or shock it's hard to tell. If it's shock, Paul doesn't want to know. Keep the patient warm, that's all that matters. "*Move,*" he says. Lewis backs away down the corridor.

They deliver their unconscious burden to the recovery

ward, his restored eye gazing sightlessly up at them, and leave him there.

"What'll happen to him?"

"He'll be shot."

Lewis gapes. "I don't believe it."

" 'Course he will, suicide counts as desertion."

"But that's mad. Why not just let him die?"

"*Pour encourager les autres.*"

They're standing in the weed-thronged yard, by the pile of railway sleepers.

Paul looks at Lewis with a mixture of pity and exaspera-tion. "I think you're allowed a cigarette before we go back."

Lewis shakes his head, then lights one anyway, remember-ing, a second later, to offer the packet.

"No, I won't, thanks." Paul waits, watching the dry, fleshy mouth drag on the cigarette. "Look, that was a bad busi-ness in there. But it's not typical."

"What I don't like is that we're part of it."

"Of what?"

"Sending him back to be shot."

"What's the alternative? Let him die?"

"It's what he wants."

"Well, if you're going to start letting them do what they want . . . Most of them want to go home."

"And I'd let them."

"Then it's just as well you're not in charge."

Lewis is already stubbing out his half-smoked cigarette. "Come on, we'd better be getting back."

He sets off at his loping pace across the waste ground, his boots flashing silver drops of rain. Paul follows at a slower pace. He hasn't had time to sort out his own reactions. He's been too busy coping with Lewis. Now he finds it difficult to tell which are Lewis's feelings and which his own. He feels as if he's been crowded out of his own mind.

But then, that's the question. Should you even pause to consider your own reactions? These men suffer so much more than he does, more than he can imagine. In the face of their suffering, isn't it self-indulgent to think about his own feelings? He has nobody to talk to about such things and blunders his way through as best he can. If you feel nothing—this is what he comes back to time and time again—you might just as well be a machine, and machines aren't very good at caring for people. There's something machinelike about a lot of the professional nurses here. Even Sister Byrd, whom he admires, he looks at her sometimes and sees a automaton. Well, lucky for her, perhaps. It's probably more efficient to be like that. Certainly less painful.

Taking a deep breath, he follows Lewis into the building.

20

Elinor to Paul

You say you don't want to burden me with the horrors but you must not hold back because of me. I want to know everything, and anyway, why should I be sheltered? I feel the same kind of guilt when I tell you about the Slade and painting and parties in Gordon Square. (Where I've been invited twice now.) You have so little time and probably by the end of the day so little energy and nobody to talk to about the things that really matter and I have so much of all these things. Are you managing to do any work at all? You know what I mean—your own work? If you've got the hut to yourself isn't it possible to do a bit in the evenings?

I carry your photograph around with me everywhere. At home—"home" meaning Gower Street—it's on the bedside table where I can see it when I wake up, but here I have to keep it in a drawer in case Mother comes in. She's always on the lookout for what she calls "the One." She wants me to go to her bandaging class with her this afternoon so I can witness her triumph over Mrs. Bradley. Toby has received his commission and been gazetted. I'm not sure I can face it. The thought of Mrs. Bradley in her camisole reclining on a chaise longue while the whole twittering first-aid class clusters round and tries to diagnose her! I've had enough of Mrs. Bradley to last me a lifetime. She's the one who kept making snide remarks to Mother because Toby hadn't enlisted yet, really made her life a misery. There was a lovely moment last week when Mother got flustered and attempted to apply a tourniquet to Mrs. Bradley's neck. "What a stupid, stupid mistake," she kept saying all the way home. "I can't think why I did it. I know perfectly well you don't apply a tourniquet to a neck wound." Mother's one of life's innocents, I'm afraid. She doesn't know "mistakes" sometimes have inverted commas round them.

Paul to Elinor

You should never be afraid of telling me about your work—or the parties. The thought that there are some people out there still painting and drawing, still thinking art matters more than anything else, is one of the few things that keeps me going. That and remembering the Slade. I close my eyes sometimes and see you and Catherine walking around the quad, Catherine with her arm around your waist. How I used to envy her. And I hear Tonks shouting: "I suppose you think you can draw?" That's not so good! How is Tonks? And yes, I do manage to do a bit of drawing when I'm off duty. Or rather, I did.

The trouble is, I've acquired a roommate. Hut mate, I suppose I should say. He's perfectly pleasant, young, enthusiastic, full of admirable qualities—and he's driving me mad. Partly it's that I don't take kindly to sharing a bedroom with anybody—only child, didn't go to boarding school, etc. I find the sound of somebody else's breathing intensely irritating. It stops me sleeping. Oh, and everything's new to him. Every impression of the hospital, the wounds, the gangrene, the amputated limbs stacked up outside—so of course I start seeing it all again through his eyes, whereas most of the time I go around in a kind of dream state. Like being inside a rubber glove that covers all of you, not just your hands.

I've been made more or less responsible for him, I think. And I can't complain because when I look back now I can see how kind people were to me when I first arrived, how patiently they answered idiotic questions and redid jobs I was supposed to have done.

But. But I can't draw with him in the room. He looks over my shoulder all the time—pretends not to, but he does. And I can't lie on my bed, in the evening after we've all come back from the café, and say good night to your photograph. Can't talk to it either. All such indulgences are at an end.

What all this has done is to bring forward a little plan I was hatching anyway, which is to hire a room in town. All the tourist trade's gone. The brass hats are accommodated in hotels or in posh houses overlooking the main square, but in the back streets there are plenty of rooms that used to be let out to summer visitors going very cheap indeed. I think I could get somewhere for about five shillings a week in English money, so that's my new project. It's what keeps me going.

I liked your story of your mother and Mrs. Bradley and the tourniquet.

Have to go now. I'm writing this early in the morning with Lewis snoring in the next bed—actually he doesn't snore, he whistles—and he's showing signs of stirring. It's time for breakfast anyway. I'm hungry!

Elinor to Paul
Things aren't good at home. Toby's gone off to officer training, Mother's taken to her bed, and everybody—by which I mean Father and Rachel and even Toby—thinks I should throw everything up and

go home to look after her. I'm the one who isn't doing anything important, you see. Rachel's pregnant, Toby's in the army, Dad's got his work. All I've got is painting, which doesn't matter and specifically doesn't matter now. You'd be amazed how many supposedly intelligent people think of art as some frivolrous (sorry, can't spell it!) distraction from things that really matter. By which of course they mean the war the war the war. Since I'm not involved in any way with that, why can't I go home and look after Mother?

How's Tonks? Thinner, gloomier, snappier—at the same time rather splendid, I think. You'd never get that art-doesn't-matter nonsense out of him. As for the rest, well, the Slade's almost deserted. Difficult not to speak in a whisper sometimes, you get such a strong sense of people who should be here and aren't. The men's life class limps on, but I don't see how it can keep going much longer. Even the women are beginning to drop away. Ruthie's nursing—she volunteered the same day as her three brothers enlisted—Marjorie's talking about leaving, Catherine's gone. Her father's been interned, but at least it's in London and not on the Isle of Man, where a lot of them are sent.

Doesn't summer seem a long time ago? When I try to think back all I can see is a huge blue-black cloud chasing its own shadow over the shining fields. And I see us on the lawn—Catherine and me—drinking disgusting warm cider from a bucket under the sink that never really kept it cool. All those lovely golden bubbles streaming to the surface and our thoughts flowing with them, though really when I think of the things we talked about. Why do angels wear clothes when they're free from original sin? Do they have private parts? What do they need them for? Do they even have to have wings? There's that strange bit in the Bible where two angels come to visit Lot and a crowd gathers outside shouting for them to be brought out so they can "know them." I didn't realize at first that means "have sexual intercourse with," but of course it does. So obviously they didn't have wings. They must have been just two extremely beautiful young men. If the Parish Council could have heard us talking about naked angels they'd have thought Catherine's being a German was the least of their worries. That still makes me angry.

Oh dear, this isn't a very good letter, I do try. I think what gets in the way is the sense that whatever we do here is so much less important than what you're doing over there. I can't imagine your world. You can pop your head back inside mine any time you like, it hasn't changed much, though now it must feel like a doll's house to you. Is she still going on about that? you think. But that was ages ago—decades.

There are changes. When I look down into the quad—where you say you remember Catherine and me walking up and down with our arms around each other's waists—I see wheelchairs. Men in blue, some with missing legs. Arms as well sometimes. They wheel them here from the hospital on fine days—it's still quite warm—though I think some of the men look cold. They can't move around to keep the circulation going and they're sometimes left out a long time. I walk past them on my way in and again on my way back, and either I walk quickly with my head down or extra slowly and give them a big cheery smile and say hello. I watch them watching me noticing the missing bits, looking at the empty trouser legs or, equally awful, not looking at them. And I feel ashamed. Just being what I am, a girl they might once have asked to dance, is dreadful. I feel I'm an instrument of mental torture through no fault of my own. And then I'm ashamed of feeling that because after all what do my feelings matter? I think the world's gone completely mad.

I'm looking out of the window now. If I narrow my eyes and make a rainbow with my lashes the men in wheelchairs disappear and

I see you as you were last winter in that long black coat of yours. I used to call it your cassock, do you remember? (That was before I knew you better!)

I hope you find a lovely room. It'll make all the difference to have somewhere quiet where you can draw or read. Paint even.

Write soon. Love, Elinor.

21

THE WOMAN WHO CAME TO THE DOOR LOOKED TO be in her early forties, with a clear brown complexion marked by two lines of force from the nose to the corners of her mouth. She kept her left arm folded at the waist, under her pinafore so it bulged out in front of her like a pregnancy.

"I've come about the room," he said.

She stood aside to let him in. "For you?"

"Yes, but I wouldn't be here all the time. I live at the hospital. I'm looking for somewhere to paint."

If she was surprised she didn't show it. Instead she led the way upstairs.

"A lot of steps," she said, unnecessarily, on the third floor. He was gasping for breath and they were still climbing. The stairs ended in a door, which opened to reveal a narrow corridor. The floor was covered in dingy brown linoleum and the row of small windows on his left gave hardly any light. He was getting ready to explain why the room was unsuitable when she threw open the door at the end of the corridor. The room was full of light.

As he followed her in, he realized why. They were above

the rooftops and there were two windows: one at either end of the room, which was long and narrow, running the width of the house. He went straight to the back window, admiring the sloping roofs, the angles, the sheen of light on gray tiles, the warmth of red brick. He opened the window and a moist green smell came rushing in. Far below was the garden, handkerchief sized from this height, with a row of outbuildings leaning against the far wall.

Madame Drouet directed his attention to the bed, the chair, the wardrobe, the washstand with its blue-and-white jug and bowl and matching chamber pot in the cupboard underneath. No running water—a major defect—and the privy was at the foot of the garden. But the room was beautiful: though the walls were limewashed, the rugs threadbare, no-colored, and the curtains so skimpy that even drawn they'd let in most of the light, none of it mattered.

"How much?"

In English money she was asking five shillings a week, half what he'd have had to pay for a studio in London. Though this wasn't exactly a studio.

"Yes," he said, at once. "I'll take it."

He walked away from the house excited, full of joy. He knew he could paint there, but it was more than that even, it was privacy, normality, his own mind back. He was almost hugging himself as he pushed open the door of a café, planning how he would go back to the hut after lunch and move a few clothes and books and his drawing equipment. He'd send for his paints, make it a proper studio, or as close as he could get. His happiness was almost painful, like circulation returning to a dead leg.

Over his coffee, he pulled out a writing pad and started to tell the one person who'd understand what the room meant.

It's nothing, really. The sort of room that would be given to a maid, very plain and bare, and the door has a stable latch, not a proper knob like the rooms downstairs. Curtains and rugs a bluish gray, though only because they've faded to that color, I don't think they started out that way. The bed takes up most of the space, which is rather a pity since I shan't be using it, but I can push it back against the wall. Even dismantle it, I suppose. I don't think the landlady minds what I do. She's only too glad she's got a taker.

The café overlooked the main square. It was market day, the busiest of the week. Paul loved this scene and often sat in the window to watch it. Most of the women of the town were out doing their shopping with bags or baskets over their arms, looking at the food on the stalls, still quite plentiful, their eyes shrewd, fingers shiny from long immersion in hot water, rubbing the coins before they parted with them. They enjoyed their marketing, the little haggles they had with stallholders, the small triumphs, the stopping for chats and gossip. The younger women had children hanging on to their hands, whining for things that couldn't be afforded. Now and then you saw an impatient tug or a slap, but mainly it was a happy scene.

At the edge of the square, ambulances roared past. Only a layer of thin canvas divided the men inside from the people in the square. The stallholders and the shoppers couldn't see the men inside, but surely they must be able to hear them, the cries torn out of them at every bump and hollow in the road. Perhaps they'd switched off. Perhaps they didn't hear the cries any more than they noticed the flicker and rumble of guns. It's the hardest thing in the world to go on being aware of somebody else's pain. He couldn't do it, so he was in no position to criticize others who couldn't either.

Two miles up the road to hell. No point blaming those women because they couldn't imagine it. He could hardly realize it himself, sitting there by the window, stirring his coffee, bubbling with excitement about his room, the work he intended to do there, and the new idea that was beginning to take root in his mind.

On the other side of the glass, a woman was walking along the pavement with her child, a toddler. Every few steps she stopped and waited for him to catch up. He was tired, he kept pulling at his ears and whimpering, but he wouldn't let his mother pick him up, he's a big boy now, too big to be carried. He dances on the spot with rage, not knowing what he wants. Exasperated, his mother scoops him up and carries him off, the boy crying as if his heart will break.

Watching the small everyday drama, Paul thought, If it's safe for that woman and her child . . .

I've had an idea. Why don't you come out here? Oh, not to nurse—I know you'd hate that—but just for a few days. The town's full of women and children, it's never been shelled, I really can't see there'd be any risk, and you'd be interested. It mightn't be possible to get here, though. We're in the forbidden zone. Which sounds awfully dramatic, but really just means civilians (other than residents) aren't allowed, except on approved business. For women, approved business means nursing. (Though there is one other profession that's welcomed, or at least tolerated. I expect you can guess what it is.) It's the wives and mothers they want to keep out. Too big a reminder of other responsibilities: *heavy work needing to be done on the farm, roofs leaking, boys running wild, etc.*

Don't reject the idea out of hand. I know it sounds preposterous, but I do think you'd enjoy it. You could stay in my room. Please, please, consider it. You probably won't be able to manage it—in fact the more I think about it the less likely it seems—but at least give it a try. Honestly, I look out of the window now and the place is full of women and children and they're in no danger at all.

There must be masses of other things to tell you, but I can't think of any of them now. I can only think about you coming here and I want to get this in the post as fast as possible. Obviously, I'd have to keep working, but I could swap shifts if necessary so we'd have every evening together, and I could arrange to take my day off while you were here. So we would see quite a lot of each other. And on your terms, of course. I hope you don't feel there's any pressure. I can always sleep in the hut. Do please say yes.

Ever your Paul.

22

Lewis impinged on him more and more. His breathing, his habit of humming while he shaved, the way he tapped the razor on the edge of the bowl . . . Every second of the time they spent in the hut, Paul was aware of him as a physical presence. He even caught himself watching Lewis while he slept, and the longer he stared the odder Lewis seemed. That blotched skin, it didn't look human. Once, as Paul bent over him, Lewis's eyes opened unexpectedly. They were pale blue, with flecks of another color, brown or green. For Christ's sake, even his eyes were freckled.

Paul arrived on duty to find a patient just being brought back from theater. He'd had his left leg amputated three days ago but then further surgery had been required to try to eradicate gangrene. The stump had to be irrigated with hydrogen peroxide. Not the pleasantest of jobs. Gloved, gowned, and masked, Paul concentrated on trying to work fast. He couldn't bring himself to say any of the soothing anodyne things people did say, It'll soon be over. It wouldn't "soon be over" and even when it was there would only be a few short hours before the next dressing. Once the man arched his back, but he made no sound. Not a groan did he utter from beginning to end.

As he took off his mask Paul became aware of Burton standing beside him, still in scrubs though he must have finished for the night. He was pulling at his chest and arm hair, something he often did, either a constant irritable tugging or sometimes a fastidious fixing of the hair between index and middle finger like a barber lining it up for the scissors. Somewhere inside Burton was a hairless prepubescent boy who'd never got over the shock.

"Well done," he said.

The words jarred. The patient wiped sweat off his upper lip, his only small concession to the pain. There was never enough morphine. It was a disgrace what these men had to endure without anesthetic, and this one was going to die anyway.

They walked to the end of the ward together. Over a mug of cocoa, Burton seemed inclined to talk. You often found that on night duty, people opened up in a way they wouldn't dream of doing by day and there was less awareness of rank. With the wards darkened and night pressing in around the huts, people clustered round whatever light they could find.

"What we really need to do is operate sooner. Very few of them, you know, are on the operating table within twenty-four hours—that's what we need to look at. You can pour hydrogen peroxide and carbolic into the wound till you're blue in the face, but if the infection's well established you're not going to shift it that way. Browne was saying, in the Boer War he'd seen men with terrible injuries—sometimes they'd lain out in the veldt for days with no medical attention whatsoever and yet they survived. But that was on sand. You know, everybody talks about machine guns and shells, but it's not bullets and shrapnel that are killing the men in there. It's the *soil*."

"So what can you do?"

"What can *I* do?"

"No, generally."

"Turn the Casualty Clearing Stations into theaters. At the moment they just patch them up to get them here, but that's no use. You've got to do the surgery *there*. Excise the wound. And if a shell lands on your head while you're doing it, too bloody bad. As to what *I* can do . . . Oh, God knows. Get out of here."

"Why?"

Burton looked surprised. "It's not much fun, you know, day after day doing amputations, when you know they could have been avoided."

"So what would you do?"

"Research, I suppose. There's got to be something we can do that's better than pouring hydrogen peroxide into a wound. Or I could join the army, but then I risk getting stuck in a base hospital. They might think I'm too old for the front line."

"And the whole point is to get to the front?"

"Oh, yes. A base hospital would drive me mad." He looked into his mug as if he suspected it of emptying itself. "Ah, well, better be getting back."

Paul was unsettled by this conversation, and not merely because applying hydrogen peroxide to an infected wound now seemed pointless as well as unpleasant. Burton was thinking about the war and how he could best make a contribution. He saw alternatives. Paul had been plodding along like a donkey for weeks. Now and then something would catch his eye and he'd reach for a drawing pad, but that was as natural and unreflective as breathing. He hadn't allowed himself to think how long his present way of life would go on.

The next two hours were busy. He went round the ward, dispensing sleeping powders, fetching bedpans, straightening sheets, taking round the bedtime cocoa. The patients drank their cocoa and one by one slipped into a drugged sleep. The guns were loud, rocking the water in the glasses by each bed.

At last the ward settled down. Paul's eyelids were drooping. The change from day to night duty was always hard until the body adjusted. He filled in the hourly record, summoned Sister Roper to give a morphine injection, changed the sheets on a bed where a patient had vomited coming out of the anesthetic, and then sat for a while with his head in his hands, his mind simultaneously blank and busy.

When he looked up, Lewis was sitting by one of the beds. At first he thought he must be hallucinating: Lewis ought to be asleep in the hut, but, no, there he was. It would have been natural to go and ask him what he wanted, but something made Paul hold back. He recognized the patient now. It was the suicide, the one who'd fought them all the way to the operating table and when he recovered faced a firing squad. Now and then his head jerked and he shouted out. The other patients, dragged out of their heavy, drugged sleep, yelled at him to shut up.

What on earth did Lewis think he was doing? What could he hope to achieve, without even a language in common? Still he sat there. An hour, two hours. Eventually Paul made tea and took it across to him. He started to say, "You know you shouldn't be here, don't you?" but then stopped. Lewis was drenched in sweat. Not the light sweat that follows exercise, but a drenching that darkened his shirt and made it stick to his chest. His skin was white under the golden-brown freckles. Even his eyes looked paler than usual.

"I think he'll sleep now," he said, taking the cup.

◾

Over the next few nights Paul became steadily more aware of Lewis's obsession with the suicide, whose name was Goujet though nobody ever used it. Lewis would arrive at the beginning of the night shift and sit with him, and again at the end. Nobody else paid Goujet any attention. The truth was his presence depressed them. The patients resented him because he was noisy and demanding and because he had tried to escape from circumstances that they had also found unbearable, and gone on bearing. The staff resented having to nurse somebody back to health in order for him to be shot. Obviously this might be the fate of many of the patients, but only on the battlefield. It was the firing squad that made the irony of their efforts inescapable.

Goujet lay with one eye closed and the other, blind eye wide open. As the hours passed this eye seemed to shrink deeper into its socket, to become small, white, and shrunken. The sun in winter looked like that, seen low in the sky over frosty fields. It was hard to walk past the bed and not meet this eye that stared out oblivious to your presence. In his rare moments of clear consciousness he seemed full of hate, though he never said anything, not even beyond the few mangled words he spat at them whenever they tried to get him to eat. He wouldn't take food. If he accepted water it was only a couple of sips, and then he'd turn his head away.

Lewis would sit beside him, clasping his wrist. At first Goujet struggled to free himself, but then abandoned the attempt, though more from weakness, Paul thought, than because he found the contact acceptable. Something had to happen to stop this. If he'd noticed this, then Sisters Byrd and Cope would certainly have noticed it too.

One day as he was going off duty, Paul was asked to go to Sister Byrd's room. This room was really no more than a little cubbyhole off the boiler room, but she'd made it comfortable. She had her tea, her cocoa, a tin of biscuits, a kettle, and a blue-and-white mug with a painting of Edinburgh Castle on the side. Paul waited. He guessed what was coming and resented it. Was he Lewis's keeper? Evidently he was. Somehow or other this had been decided, though whether by accident—because the only vacant bed happened to be in his hut—or because Sister Byrd thought she discerned in him a particular talent for lowering new arrivals gently into scalding water, he didn't know. He only knew nobody had consulted him.

"Come in, Paul." She had a deceptively gentle Scottish accent that made him think of pale spring sunshine on gray granite terraces. "Sit down."

She poured hot water from the kettle onto the cocoa in their mugs.

She was . . . what, fifty? Something like that. A professional nurse with several decades of experience in civilian hospitals, unlike many of the other nurses who were really lady volunteers with minimal qualifications. She wore her professional status like an external corset. Unbending, efficient, detached, halfway to being a monster, perhaps, but she got the job done.

She sat down facing him. "How do you think Lewis is settling in?"

"All right, I think. It's early days."

"Yes," she agreed, a little too quickly. "I hope he's not getting overinvolved?"

He waited.

"With the man who tried to kill himself."

"I don't know."

"He sits with him a lot, doesn't he?"

"Yes, I believe he does."

"You know I've had to tell him to go off duty once or
twice. And he comes in on his day off."

"He's young. He'll get over it."

"It's so easy to let the work here grind you down. If he
goes on like this he'll be no use to anybody in a month's time. I
was hoping you might have a word with him, and . . . I don't
know. Get him away from the hospital. I don't want to see
him on the wards on his day off. Get him out, show him the
country."

He wanted to say, Why should I spend my days off nurse-
maiding Lewis? But then he remembered a number of occasions
after he'd first arrived when Hickson, for example, had
knocked on the door of the hut and almost dragged him into
town. "All right. I'll see what I can do."

He went back to the ward and found Lewis sitting by
Goujet's bed again. "Come on," Paul said, touching him on the
shoulder. "He'll still be here tonight."

Sister Byrd approved of Paul because she mistook his surface composure for real detachment. In fact he was every bit as
moved by Goujet's predicament as Lewis, but hid it better. It
would be better for everybody, he thought, if Goujet died. But
at the start of Paul's next night duty, Goujet looked, if any-

thing, stronger. His color was better, and he was waving his arms at the orderlies as they walked past. Close to, though, he didn't look so good. His skin felt hot and dry, and the mangled words didn't seem to be directed at an audience.

By two in the morning he was running a high fever. He kept making movements in the air with his right hand, brushing something away perhaps. At last, going across to him for the umpteenth time, Paul realized he was trying to convey that he wanted to write. He couldn't make himself understood in any other way. Part of his tongue and the roof of his mouth had gone.

"Paper? You want to write?" Paul made scribbling movements in the air.

Goujet nodded. Paper, Paul thought, looking round. They had the record sheets they filled in hour by hour, but nothing else. Over in the hut, he had whole pads of the stuff.

"Can you spare me a minute?" he asked Hickson. "I just want to go back to the hut and get something."

He walked out into the night. Always this shock of cool air on the skin, the moist smell of earth and wet grass. The moon was full, riding high and magnificent in a clear sky. From the road came the roar of motor lorries going to the front, and further off, in the distance, the bickering of artillery.

The open door sent an oblong of moonlight across the beds and the jumble of papers on his side of the table. He grabbed a writing pad and pencil, paused in the doorway to light a cigarette, and set off across the waste ground to the shed at a half run. The air was fresh and crisp. The puddle that lay in the hollow ground by the ambulances' turning circle had a gray film of petrol across it, like a cataract. He stopped to draw breath. An incongruous moment, standing there in the darkness, bracing himself to go back onto the ward, thinking like a painter. Deep breaths, one, two, three. A final drag on the cigarette and he pushed the door open.

Goujet stared at the writing pad and pencil in apparent bewilderment, so perhaps it wasn't what he wanted and the waving of his hand in the air meant something else entirely. Paul left the pad by his bed and, by the time he'd reached the end of the row, Goujet had reached for it and begun to write. He didn't seem to be keeping to the lines, but then the poor devil could hardly see. Paul brushed the incident aside, turning his attention to another patient who'd just been brought in from theater.

The new patient woke everybody with his screams. Sister had her hands full trying to settle him. What had been a relatively quiet shift became busy. Paul and Hickson attended to the other patients as best they could. As Paul passed his bed, Goujet offered him a sheet of paper. There were no words on it and no drawings either, it was meaningless scribble as far as he could see. But he smiled and nodded. "*Merci.*"

It happened again, and again, at intervals as the night wore on.

"*Merci.*"

"*Merci.*"

"*Merci.*"

Mercy, he started to translate it after a while. Precious little of that round here, he thought, looking at the body of a young man who hadn't recovered consciousness, and wouldn't last the night.

Up and down. Up and down.

Goujet became more insistent as the night wore on, more obviously deranged. As far as you could tell. But it's difficult to know whether somebody's mad or not if he can't speak. What he wanted, and he made this very clear, was for Paul to take the paper from him and keep it. By the end of the shift, the pockets of Paul's tunic and breeches were stuffed full of folded pages, every one of them marked by lines and lines of scribble. Only when the pad had been used up did Goujet lie back, apparently satisfied.

Lewis didn't appear that morning. No doubt Sister Byrd had talked to him. His absence was rather disconcerting. Paul had grown used to seeing him there.

Going off duty, he stood for a moment in the doorway, smelling the dawn wind. Two miles away, no more noticeable than the beating of his heart, the guns thudded: the usual early-morning intensification of fire. He took the sheets of paper from his pocket, bunched them together and tore them into tiny pieces. Released onto the wind, they whirled high above his head then slowly, bit by bit, drifted down till they lay on the bare ground. A driver was bending down, turning the crank handle of his ambulance. Soon, within a minute or two, the big wheels would force the scraps of paper deep into the mud, but before that could happen Paul had already turned away.

23

ELINOR STOOD IN THE STERN OF THE FERRY, looking out over bile-green water streaked with foam. It was growing dark. Soon she'd have to give in and go below deck like everybody else, but meanwhile she was enjoying the mixture of spray and drizzle blowing into her face.

The forbidden zone.

It was by no means certain they'd let her in, though she'd done everything in her power to make her story credible. Under her coat she wore a nurse's uniform, borrowed from Ruthie, who worked in a hospital now. Ruthie, who disapproved of this trip, who'd called it selfish and trivial and irresponsible. Ruthie, who'd given up painting and thought everybody else should do the same, but loved her too much to deny her anything. She'd used Ruthie—and not for the first time. She ought to stop doing it, and of course she would; but not yet. In her handbag, she had letters typed on hospital paper taken from her father's desk, recommending her to the chief surgeon at Paul's hospital. Oh, she'd worked hard to get everything right. Appearance, too. This old-maidish felt hat, a scrubbed and shining face, short-clipped fingernails, long skirt, sensible lace-up shoes. They ought to let her in. *She* believed her story.

A sailor walked past and stared at her. A young woman traveling alone, unchaperoned, would always attract attention and she couldn't afford to do that. She ought to go down below deck and find herself a group of nurses to tag along with. Cautiously, she went down the narrow stairs into the passage with its wet footprints and puddles of water, and then, bracing herself against the rolling of the ship, edged along the wall till she reached the ladies' cabin.

A fug of warm bodies greeted her, that female smell of talcum powder and blood. It always reminded her of the time when, as a little girl, nine or ten years old perhaps, she'd opened the drawer of Rachel's dressing table and found a pile of blood-stained rags waiting to go into the wash. Mother had been furious with Rachel for leaving them where Elinor could find them. "It might have been Toby!" she'd shouted, her voice edging up into hysteria. Elinor had looked from one to the other and tried to work out what the fuss was about.

Stepping inside the cabin, she closed the door quietly behind her. Most of the ladies had already become lumps under blankets, but a few were still undressing, placing hats carefully into hatboxes, covering them with tissue paper, lining shoes up neatly side by side. In the center of the room a girl with straggly dark hair was feeding her baby, a wizened little creature whose hand clawed at her breast.

The nurses in the far corner were still wide awake and chattering. All very young and fresh and pink looking. Volunteers, she thought, not professionals. Professional nurses didn't look like that. She found herself a couch close to them and sat down. No point undressing properly—they were due to dock before dawn—but she took off her hat, coat, and boots and wrapped herself in the blanket provided. Pulling it tight up to her chin, she peered over it at her fellow passengers and knew at once that she wouldn't be able to sleep. The lumpy figures in the sepia light; a woman's face sagging with exhaustion as she twisted and turned on her folded-up coat; the chattering, inno-cent, ruthless girls screeching like jays; and the woman at the center of the cabin who seemed to melt into her child, as if she were the wax that fed its guttering flame. There was just enough light to see. She propped the sketchpad against her knee and worked steadily for an hour, screening the page so that any-body glancing casually across at her would think she was writ-ing a letter. Only when she felt she'd exhausted the possibilities did she put the pad away.

Still sleep wouldn't come. She thought about Paul and what might be going to happen. In London she'd come close to sleeping with him, but in the end she'd drawn back. It seemed such a ridiculous way to take such a decision, because the night was warm and dry and wherever you looked there were cou-ples twined round each other, some of them actually making love on the grass. So easy to let herself be swept along, but it would have felt as if the war had taken the decision for her. So in the end, no, she'd pulled back and they'd gone to their single beds alone.

But her imagination had been busy ever since.

Her only worry was that she hadn't told Kit she was com-ing and he was stationed at a hospital just five miles outside the town. But Paul hadn't seen Kit in all the weeks he'd been there, so it wasn't very likely she'd bump into him. She couldn't consult Paul about it because Paul didn't know she was still writing to Kit. Neither of them knew how close she was to the other. If only she could bring herself to tell the truth, it was always better in the end, but short term, the lies were so convenient. Toby said she'd begun by lying to Mother, because that was the only way she could have a life of her own, but now she lied reflexly, pointlessly, to absolutely everybody. Including herself.

She closed her eyes. The smell of tar and talcum powder in the hot dark was making her queasy. The ship shifted and rose beneath her. *Oh God, don't let me be sick* was her last conscious thought before she slept.

Next morning she woke with a crick in her neck. She forced herself to sit up on the edge of the shiny leather couch; her mouth tasted foul, her eyelids seemed to be glued together. It was like a hangover, though she'd had nothing the night before except a small cup of black coffee. She grabbed her wash bag and joined the queue for the bathroom, standing in line behind two middle-aged women who were complaining loudly about the behavior of the nurses last night. When she finally got a place at the basins her face looked small and white and sick. She washed in cold water, brushed her teeth, combed her hair, straightened her clothes as best she could, and was ready to go ashore.

Back in the ladies' cabin, they were all completing their packing, stuffing articles of clothing into bulging bags and checking under the benches for lost possessions. That curious, dislocated atmosphere you get in traveling when a small fragile community fragments. Elinor got away as fast as she could and stood looking out over the harbor, where a light breeze pimpled the surface of the water.

Once on shore she began to feel better, though even on the short crossing her feet seemed to have forgotten where the ground was. She discovered that the nurses too were bound for the railway station and, since there was a spare seat in the second cab, she was invited to join them. A small, ginger-haired girl with red-rimmed eyes asked which hospital she was going to and she gave the name of Paul's hospital. It seemed to mean no more to them than it did to her, but they accepted it without comment and that encouraged her. Several of them had brothers who'd joined up, one or two of them sweethearts, and so of course they had to do their bit too. It was all represented as duty and patriotism, but even after an almost sleepless night, their eyes were still shining with excitement. Elinor produced a neatly matching story. Yes, she had a brother who'd joined up, and yes, a sweetheart too. Oddly enough it was Kit's face that flashed into her mind at this point, though he hadn't joined up exactly and he certainly wasn't a sweetheart. Before all this, she'd been an art student, she said, but of course now . . .

Everybody agreed. Yes, of course, now.

Elinor was left wondering why, when her story was accurate in almost every respect, it should be so far from the truth. The difference, she decided, was that these girls needed the war and she didn't. The freedom they were experiencing on this trip to Belgium she experienced every morning as she walked into the Slade. Though some people might say—and Ruthie was one of them—that she was simply too selfish to set aside her personal concerns and make some contribution to the common cause. Well, yes. She was selfish. She needed to be. She intended to summon up as much selfishness as she possibly could.

At the station they all went for a coffee together. The café was a long narrow room with dingy lino on the floor. A phlegmatic-looking woman stood behind a counter flanked by glass shelves lined with curly sandwiches. One of the nurses tried out her French; the woman replied in English with a look of dull contempt. Elinor got her coffee and croissants and was walking carefully back to their table when the door burst open and the room filled with soldiers.

Instantly they took possession of the place, laughing and joking and punching each other playfully in the chest. They were ushered to the tables, where they caught the eye of the little waitress and flirted with her, winking, nudging, egging each other on. So much prime male beef, so much muscle under their uniforms, thighs like tree trunks lolling apart, so much fresh sweat, so many open red-lipped mouths. The whole world belonged to them because they were on their way to die.

Elinor kept her nose in her coffee cup as much as possible, looking, she knew, old-maidish in her felt hat and shapeless coat. She hated the way the women in the queue deferred, accepting that now they must wait longer to be served. She forced a croissant down with gulps of hot coffee and was glad to get on the train.

For the last part of the journey she had a lump of fear in her throat, though the worst that could happen was that she would be refused entry. Nobody was likely to think she was a spy and bang her up in jail, and even if they did, a call to the British Consulate would surely put things right. Only, she dreaded having to face her father, whose comments on this reckless and—as he would see it—self-indulgent excursion she could easily imagine.

As if to spite her, the train crawled along, sometimes stopping altogether. Rain-drenched fields. Reflections of gray-white cloud drifting slowly across flooded furrows. She tried to imagine this land churned up by wheels and horses' hooves and marching feet, but she couldn't. And why should I? she thought, hardening again, when this was the reality. Grass, trees, pools full of reflected sky, somewhere in the distance a curlew calling. This is what will be left when all the armies have fought and bled and marched away.

The nurses had gone quiet. Even their high spirits couldn't be sustained indefinitely, and perhaps, like Elinor, they'd started to feel nervous. Finally, the train crawled into the station, burped apologetically once or twice, like a drunken husband arriving home late, and fell silent. There was a moment when nobody said or did anything, then the red-haired girl jumped to her feet and got her bag from the overhead rack.

On the platform the soldiers, no longer laughing, shouldered their kit bags and marched off. The civilians left behind looked fragmented and shabby after the uniforms and the disciplined vigorous movement. A porter told them to go into the waiting room, where an officer sat behind a table checking papers.

Elinor positioned herself towards the rear of the line of nurses, making sure, though, that she wasn't the last. Her mouth was dry, but she could see that the officer was bored doing this routine, unglamorous job and perhaps a little soporific too after a good lunch. A coil of expensive blue smoke rose into the air above his head. His color was high. He looked as if he liked wine and cigars and women. Boredom and resentment might make him aggressive, but not when there were young women to be flirted with and impressed. She saw him pull his stomach in as soon as he noticed them, and had to stifle a giggle, though it was more from fear than amusement. He kept the first girl—a bank manager's daughter from Bradford—chatting. Her blushing face and schoolgirl French did make her entrancing. The second girl got much the same treatment, but then a third, a fourth . . . He looked at the row behind, asked the first girl if they were all together, and when she nodded he stood up and waved them through. Looking back, Elinor saw him settling down again, disconsolately, to face an old man, a married couple, and two middle-aged sisters laden with suitcases.

Paul was waiting just inside the arch that led out of the station onto the open muddy street. Whenever she'd tried to imagine this scene he'd always been wearing the long black coat he'd worn last winter at the Slade, but of course he was in uniform, breeches, puttees, tunic, peaked cap, with a Red Cross armband on his right arm. He was looking away from her so that she saw his face in profile, and felt, for a moment, quite detached. A response to his own stillness, his own detachment.

He looked Egyptian, she thought, and not just because of his olive skin. Something about the nose and the heavy-lidded, slanting, dark eyes. It was a face made to be seen in profile, and the straight shoulders and narrow waist reinforced the impression. Perhaps that was why, when, lying in bed at night, she tried to think of him, he was always looking away. Surely you ought to be able to remember a close friend smiling, looking straight into your eyes? But she never could, and she didn't know whether this detachment came from him or from her.

"Paul?"

He turned, then, and his face flashed open in a smile that

made him immediately look ordinary. She started towards him, but he shook his head, holding up a card he carried with her name on it. In the story they'd concocted, he was merely somebody from the hospital sent to meet a young woman he didn't know. She drew back, scanned the crowd, eventually allowed herself to notice him standing there, walk forward, greet him and shake him warmly by the hand.

"There you are." He took her bag. "This way. I've got a cab waiting."

He took her arm as they crossed the road, but no more than a light pressure on her elbow.

"We could walk, but I thought with the bag . . . And you must be tired?"

A quick sideways glance. He seemed shy with her, but then she'd hardly looked at him, except at his profile in the station. Her mind was full of what was to come. Or not. Somehow the theoretical possibility she'd been entertaining that they would spend a few days together as friends had vanished. They'd met as lovers, though awkward, insecure, self-doubting lovers.

Since she couldn't look at him, she felt she ought to at least raise her eyes and take in the town, but that too seemed to be beyond her. All she could see were muddy boots and swishing skirts and shopping baskets dangling from meaty arms.

Out of the corner of her eye cab wheels appeared. He opened the door and the step tilted as she got in. He gave the address to the driver and walked round to the other side, his weight balancing the vehicle as he sat down beside her. The driver clicked his tongue, lashed the bony horse, and they lurched forward. Paul had been leaning out to close his door when the cab started, and the movement threw him back heavily against the leather seat, and he slid into her. He tried to push himself away. She was afraid they were about to have a stilted conversation about her journey, but then they looked at each other—his eye whites were startling in the gloom of the cab's interior—and they were kissing, jolted against each other, teeth jarring, losing the other's mouth and finding it again. She was afraid to stop because then she'd have to look at him and see a stranger. At last they separated, and it was a stranger, white-faced, breathless, black-eyed, Paul as she'd never seen him. She clutched his hand with slippery fingers and they smiled at each other; a brief respite from terror.

"I'll have to go back to the hospital. Just for a few hours. You'll be all right?"

She nodded. "Yes."

Trying to calm herself, she turned and looked out of the window. They were rattling along a cobbled road, tall white houses on either side, their walls dazzling in the late-afternoon sun. Soldiers kept passing on either side. For a time the cab ran along by the side of a canal with tethered barges and tall spindly trees that had begun to strip for winter, their bright yellow leaves twirling down to lie on the brown, smooth, reflecting surface of the water. She took it all in, indelibly; she'd remember those leaves in ten, twenty, forty years' time, though if she'd been asked fifteen minutes later to describe them she couldn't have done so.

"I think you'll like the room," Paul said. "It's a good room to paint in."

She nodded, though painting was so obviously not what he had in mind that she wanted to laugh, and had to turn aside to hide a smile.

At last they stopped. Paul got out, helped her down, and

paid the driver. She found herself staring at a narrow doorway in a tall narrow house. Paul knocked and a few seconds later the door was opened by a woman in a blue apron with bare arms as muscular as a man's and a cloud of fine dark hair lightly streaked with gray. This was Madame Drouet. She greeted Paul with obvious delight, Elinor with considerably more reserve, then led the way upstairs, her broad backside swaying massively from side to side under a dark blue skirt. A caryatid's backside, Elinor thought—not that you ever saw such a thing—built to hold up the world.

Her room—their room?—was right at the top of the house. The doors to the others stood open and the rooms seemed to be storerooms, as far as she could tell. She glimpsed a mattress propped against the wall, and a doll's house with two green bay trees painted on either side of the front door. Madame Drouet stopped, turned the stable latch, and opened the door onto a white-painted room that was full of light. Elinor went straight to the window. Far below was a narrow back garden, but she was looking out over angled roofs and attic windows. Turning back into the room, she saw a big bed—a bed that seemed to be getting bigger by the minute—a chair with a rush seat, a marble-topped table with a blue-and-white bowl and jug, and a wardrobe with a tarnished mirror set into the door.

"It's lovely," she said, in English.

Paul translated, but it wasn't necessary. Madame Drouet's face had already cracked into a smile. "I hope you will be very happy here."

As she spoke a shaft of sunlight reached the brass knobs on the bed, and they winked, knowingly, at Elinor. She had a vague, but vivid, sense that the room was more than a room, that it contained her future. Madame Drouet was still smiling.

She likes it that we're not married, Elinor thought. She likes the idea of illicit sex on the top floor of her house, or perhaps she likes the idea of *Paul* having illicit sex in her house. Madame Drouet closed the door, still smiling, and, like the Cheshire Cat, seemed to leave her smile hanging in the air after the rest of her had gone.

As soon as they were alone, they kissed again, trembling and laughing, trying to recapture the impersonal passion that had gripped them in the cab, but not quite managing it.

"I have to go, I'm afraid," Paul said, taking out his watch as he spoke. "I'm late."

First the Cheshire Cat, now the White Rabbit, Elinor thought. She pinched the skin on her left wrist, hoping the pain would restore the material world, but she continued to feel that the afternoon had become unexpectedly bizarre, and that she hardly recognized the self who was standing there.

They kissed. He went. She followed him to the end of the corridor and watched his head and shoulders descending the stairs, leaving her behind, going off about his business of which she knew nothing.

Back in the room she sat on the bed and tested it. The clanging of springs was so noisy she felt everybody in the house must hear, but that was nonsense of course. The room next door was used only for storage. She heaved her bag onto the bed and began unpacking. The wardrobe was so shallow she had to push the hangers sideways to get the door to close, but the wood smelled of something dry and sweet. Then she was at a loss. She stood at the window looking out over the roofs, as the sinking sun cast angular shadows that had not been there when she first looked out only half an hour ago. At one point she got up and fetched her sketchbook, but she couldn't settle, couldn't *see* anything. Her eye glided over surfaces, taking nothing in. Perhaps she should try to get some sleep, but then, looking down into the garden, she felt a blaze of energy. There'd be time enough to sleep when she was dead.

Quickly she poured water into the bowl, washed, ran a comb through her hair, grabbed a sketchbook, and went out into the street.

24

ELINOR FOUND A CAFÉ IN THE MAIN SQUARE, where she sat for an hour, lingering over her coffee and watching passersby in the market. Three men at the next table were waiting impatiently to be served. At last Madame appeared, a tall, heavy, dark-haired woman with premature creases in her upper lip, perhaps from the cigarettes she constantly and surreptitiously smoked or perhaps from her habit of clamping notes and even coins between her teeth while she negotiated the till, a shark of a machine that seemed determined to have her fingers off.

This was a small town. In Elinor's imagination it had swollen to the size of London or Paris, a vast anonymous city where you could move from place to place and never bump into anybody you knew. Now the town had shrunk to its real dimensions she expected to see Kit at any moment, and what would she find to say to him? How could she explain her presence here when her last letter had been full of what was happening at the Slade with not a whisper of any projected trip to Belgium? He would be hurt, and rightly so. She waited until the shadows started to lengthen. Then she walked rapidly back along the little side street she'd discovered, reaching the house just as the white bowl of the street began to fill with darkness, from the pavement upwards, like somebody pouring tea into a cup.

She lay down on the bed and, although she felt she wouldn't be able to sleep—too much whirring round inside her head—in fact she dropped off almost at once and when she woke again it was dark. She changed into the only dress she'd brought with her and had just finished brushing her hair when somebody tapped on the door. "Come in," she called, thinking it would be Madame Drouet, but no, it was Paul, still in uniform, looking tired and excited and unsure of himself in a way that made her stomach melt.

They looked at each other, aware of the angled roofs framed by the window and the moon staring in at them. The rumpled bed looked huge and white.

Paul laughed. "Come on, let's go and eat. You must be famished."

They went into town a different way, walking side by side, not touching, though she would have liked to take his arm. Just as they entered the square, they had to pause to let a crowd of nurses and men in wheelchairs cross the road. Drained, Elinor thought, as if somebody had pulled the plug and let their lifeblood run away. One man had bandages round his ears, with two red stains on the white gauze. She'd been telling Paul about her little trip to the café in the square. He'd said, "That's where I go to write letters. You were probably sitting at the same table," but after the wounded were wheeled past they walked on in silence till they reached the restaurant.

They ordered beef in red wine with potatoes and beans and a carafe of red wine. Paul could hardly wait to pour it out.

He drank two glasses quickly, like lemonade on a hot day, caught her watching him, and said, "Sorry! I'm not human till I've had a couple of drinks." But then, immediately, he poured himself another. The sight of his Adam's apple jerking as he gulped the wine down was shocking, not like the Paul she knew at all. She was afraid he was going to sit there and get drunk, but no, with the third glass the rate of drinking slowed. After the food arrived, he drank very little. He looked better too, not so white.

"You haven't changed at all," he said.

You have, she thought. There were lines around his mouth and eyes that hadn't been there the last time she saw him, but he'd gained weight.

"You look a lot better."

"I feel better."

"No cough?"

"No-o."

She shrugged. "I was worried, that's all. When they said about your mother and TB."

"My mother?" For a second he looked blank. "No, she didn't have TB. That's on my father's side."

She tried asking him questions about his work at the hospital, but he obviously didn't want to talk about that. Soon she was chattering on about her life in London, presenting it to him as more lighthearted, more like the life they used to share, than it really was. Trying to be honest, she mentioned Toby's rows with her father about enlisting, which for a time had made every weekend painful, and about Catherine's problems. There'd been riots, would you believe, in Deptford. Bricks through windows, houses set on fire, women and children joining in, not just the men, and the police watching.

"What about your work?" he asked.

"Oh, I keep going. I had three paintings accepted for the New English Gallery."

"Three?"

"Yes, I was surprised." She held up a hand to stop him re-filling her glass. "What about you?"

"What about me?"

"Are you finding time to do any work?"

A brief smile, noting that what he did at the hospital apparently didn't count as work. "A bit."

She waited for him to go on, sensing that he both did and didn't want to talk about this. "Sketches mainly. It hasn't really been possible to paint, though of course now I've got the room it might be different."

"It's a lovely room."

"Yes, I've been going there on my days off."

She finished eating and pushed her plate away. "What do you draw?"

"Oh, people at the hospital. Patients." His tone hardened. "That's what I *see*. Though I don't know what the point of it is. Nobody's going to hang that sort of thing in a gallery."

"Why would you want them to?"

"Because it's there. *They're* there, the people, the men. And it's not right their suffering should just be swept out of sight."

"I'd have thought it was even less right to put it on the wall of a public gallery. Can't you imagine it? People peering at other people's suffering and saying, 'Oh my *dear*, how perfectly *dreadful*'—and then moving onto the next picture. It would just be a freak show. An arty freak show."

Silence. They'd become surprisingly intense and were wondering whether to go on with the conversation or stop now before it became too confrontational.

"Anyway," she said, "I thought you didn't do people. Do you remember Tonks saying some of your nudes didn't look human?"

"That wouldn't necessarily be a disadvantage here."

"You can't use people like that."

"I'm not using anybody."

Silence again, louder this time.

"What's your solution, then? Ignore it?"

"Yes," she said. "Totally. The truth is, it's been imposed on us from the outside. You would never have chosen it and probably the men in the hospital wouldn't either. It's unchosen, it's passive, and I don't think that's a proper subject for art."

"So, what is?"

She lifted her head. "The things we choose to love."

"Hmm. No, I'll think about it. I didn't really mean us to argue, you know."

"It's better than the attitude you get at home. Most people seem to think art should stop for the duration. Inherently trivial. Like buying a new hat."

"They should have met one of our patients. You'd have liked him. He was an apache."

"An Indian?"

"Not that kind. He was a criminal. The French have special regiments for criminals to . . . I don't know, pay their debt to society, I suppose. They're supposed to be very good on the battlefield—born killers—but not so good at sticking it out between times. But the point about him was, he was covered in tattoos. Not his face and hands but literally everywhere else, every inch. And they were good. They were art. He'd used his own skin as the canvas, that's all. Now, that man was probably born in the gutter, knocked from pillar to post. . . . But he didn't think art was irrelevant. Or trivial. He suffered for it."

"Ornamenting himself. Is it the same thing?"

"In his case, yes, I think it was. Oh, and by the way, he didn't need ornament. He was extraordinarily beautiful."

Something deep inside Elinor pricked up its ears. *Beautiful* was not a word prewar Paul could ever have brought himself to use about another man. He was changing, in all kinds of ways, probably. They both were.

"Right, then," he said, raising his hand to summon the waitress. "Coffee. Would you like something to go with it?"

She shook her head. He was pleating the edge of the table-cloth, smoothing it out, pleating it again. "My mother didn't have TB," he said at last. "She killed herself."

"Oh, Paul, I'm sorry, I had no idea." She stared around the café as if there were help in waiters and chattering diners. "How old were you?"

"Fourteen. She was in a lunatic asylum for the last two years, in and out before that." He made himself stop fiddling with the cloth. "I don't think about it much."

"Don't you?"

"No. Well, a bit, I suppose, when the anniversary comes round, but it's got all mixed up in my head anyway. I think I remember the first time they took her away, I remember seeing the van drive away with her inside it, but I know I can't have seen that, because I was sent away from the house so I wouldn't see."

"That must have been awful."

"The worse thing is, I think part of me was relieved when she died because it meant I didn't have to go on visiting that place."

There was nothing she could say to comfort him. She reached across the table and folded his hands in hers.

They came out to find the whole street lit up by a magnificent full moon, which looked down on the town and seemed to deride its blue-painted streetlamps. Even the shiny road surface reflected a blurred white light back at the sky. Elinor looked up and saw how slack bellied and stretch marked it was, really, a mad old woman who'd decided to follow them home for reasons no sane person could guess at.

There were no people on the streets and the only sound was a mutter of guns in the distance and closer at hand the rumble of vehicles going up to the front.

"Let's walk a bit, shall we?" he said.

She knew he was trying to change the mood of the evening, to effect the transformation from friends to lovers before they got back to the house. Above all to erase the memory of his mother's suicide. She wanted to ask more but she daren't. She felt he'd given her a key and done so very deliberately, but she'd no time to think about it. He put his arm around her shoulders, and they walked on. A misshapen blotch of darkness, they must have seemed from the outside. Part of Elinor had detached itself and was now sitting on a rooftop somewhere watching them cross the square. She seemed to see the whole town spread out below her.

"It thinks it's safe, doesn't it?" she said. "I mean, the town thinks it's safe. It's really quite a smug little place."

"Well, it *is* safe. Safe as you can be with a war going on up the road."

"I like it. It doesn't seem to care about religion or the state or anything much except itself."

"Making money."

"No, I mean like Dutch painting, you know? It loves its own life. This life. It doesn't need anything outside to give it meaning. And the armies can march all over it, and it doesn't care."

They walked on, feeling their hips jostle as they tried to match their strides. "Do you miss me?" he asked.

"Do *you* miss *me*?"

"Yes, but it's different for me, because I've never been with you here, so there isn't a gap. And I don't get much time to think."

"No, in other words."

"I wouldn't have asked you to come."

"Why did you?"

"I needed you. A bit selfish, I suppose."

"Oh, you're allowed a little bit. You're doing more than most."

She shivered and he pulled her closer to him. "Come on, let's go back."

He had a key. She hadn't been expecting that, and it made everything easier. Stumbling along the top corridor, they saw a line of orange light underneath the door, and opened it to find that a fire had been lit in the tiny grate. Flames and their shadows chased each other all over the walls.

He reached for the switch. She said, urgently, "*No.*" They undressed in the circle of light, throwing their clothes into two dark heaps on the floor. He got into bed first, with a theatrical chattering of teeth, burrowing down into the cold sheets and pulling back the covers on her side. She felt unshelled, goose pimply, anything but seductive, but in bed they shuffled closer together and pulled the covers up to their faces until only their cold noses stuck out over the top. The firelight had got into his eyes.

It was different from that time in London, the last evening they spent together before he went to Belgium, when they'd come so close to making love. Then, she'd been excited by the sight of her own breasts against a man's chest, rather than by anything Paul did. Tonight, she lost herself. She looked up once and saw him watching her. When he climaxed, he hid his face in her neck and then slid sideways onto the pillow, gripping the cloth between his teeth, snorting and pulling and tearing. In those last few seconds, he couldn't have been aware of who he was with. Perhaps it was the shyness of their first time, which he might feel as much as she did, though he'd shown no other sign. But no, she thought, she'd discovered something about Paul that she hadn't known before and couldn't have found out any other way. Lovemaking for him would always be communion with a private god.

Then, almost immediately, the perception was lost. They were laughing with triumph, pushing the bedclothes back, not cold now, not cold at all, trampling the counterpane down to the foot of the bed, admiring the shadows the firelight cast on the hills and valleys of their bodies.

Then he talked for the first time about the hospital. She lay on his chest and felt the vibration his voice made, not listening; not wanting to know. One word kept recurring: Lewis this, Lewis that, Lewis the other.

"Am I going to meet this Lewis?"

He seemed surprised. "Yes, I suppose so. Yes, why not?"

This is where his life was now. She remembered how he'd smiled as she talked about her life in London, the painting, the exhibitions, the Café Royal, the Slade—like somebody looking through the windows of a doll's house.

"I'm sorry if I've gone on a bit. It's just there's nobody to talk to here."

"Lewis?" she said, her tone now frankly ironical.

"You don't talk about the hospital when you come off duty." He lay and thought, started to say something, ended by laughing. "Do you know, at the end of a shift we sometimes just sit in silence?"

"You could always paint."

"What, a man peeing out of the hole where his penis used to be? Oh, yes, a great demand for that."

"No, other things. Landscapes. The things you used to paint."

"No, it's all a mess, I don't know what to do with it. Anyway, we'd better get some sleep."

He rolled over and kissed her, and they made love again, more gently, lingering, taking time. Only at the end did he turn his face away. Afterwards, they lay back to back, their spines touching, like a butterfly, she thought. Their spines were its body, their arms and legs its wings. She could feel his hands all over her now, even when he wasn't touching her, as if they'd left a permanent imprint on her skin. She was thinking about this, trying to find the words to express it, but it was too much trouble to open her mouth, and an instant later she must have drifted off to sleep, because when she opened her eyes again the fire was out and gray rainy light was leaking under the skimped curtains, finding the little puddles of clothes they'd left on the floor.

She turned over and found him still asleep. He'd turned to face her so the butterfly they'd made together was already broken, before she moved. She lay and listened to his breathing, a little whistle at the end of every breath. His arm was flung across his face—he hid himself, even in sleep—and it came to her that he didn't love her at all. The conviction was absolute for about one moment, then began to soften with the strengthening light.

He woke abruptly, going from sleep to complete wakefulness in a second, like an animal alert for danger. Almost at once he swung himself out of bed. Perhaps he thought he was late for the hospital, though after he looked at his watch he came back and kissed her. She watched him dress, donning the unfamiliar uniform that clearly, to him, had become a second skin. Her hip joints ached, her lips felt bruised, she was blinking and dazed, her whole body felt different, and there he stood dressed for work. He'd opened the window wide and a stream of cold air came in.

"I'll see you tonight," he said, bending over for a final, abstracted kiss, and then he was gone.

There had to be a reason why she always remembered him in profile. Certainly, if she ever did try to paint him, he'd be turned away, searching for something—or somebody—but not expecting to find whatever it was. The loss had been long ago, and now only the posture, the expression, remained. What she loved most about him was the quality of detachment that pre-vented his ever really loving her.

She was nowhere near as unhappy as this thought should have made her feel. In fact she wasn't unhappy at all. He'd hardly reached the end of the street when she jumped out of bed and started to get dressed, eager for the day that lay ahead.

25

SHE WASN'T LONELY, THOUGH SHE HARDLY SPOKE
to a soul all day. This was what she liked: being alone in a
strange city; walking by the canal, smelling dank water, dead
leaves, and grass; staring at people in the streets and at lunch-
time pushing open the door of a little café, and finding nobody
there except a woman with auburn hair who smiled at her
but didn't speak. Kit was constantly in her mind, the dread of
meeting him, of having to explain, so finding this almost empty
café was a relief. After lunch, she sat in the park and sketched,
watching, out of the corner of her eye, a group of schoolgirls in
blue uniforms, who sat on the next bench and twittered together, as unself-conscious as the birds who gathered round
them in expectation of crumbs. By the time they'd gone, long
blue shadows were creeping across the grass, and it was time to
go home.

Back in the room, though, she felt insubstantial, the result
of eating scarcely anything and speaking to nobody all day. She
put her sketches away in a folder, then settled down to draw the
rooftops from her window, but it was getting too dark and soon
she had to stop. She was thinking about Paul all the time, but

she felt peaceful, now, not inclined to pick and tear at the relationship as she'd wanted to do when she first woke up.

Round about the time she expected Paul to arrive, she heard a quick, heavy footstep on the stairs and jumped up to greet him, but it was Madame Drouet. There was a young man downstairs, she said, with a distinctly disapproving air. Oh, Elinor said. She couldn't think who it could be, but immediately her mind filled with the dread that Kit had somehow found out where she was and had turned up like an outraged husband to demand an explanation. Apart from Kit she knew nobody here, but then she remembered Lewis. Yes. But why hadn't Paul come with him? She ran a brush through her hair and went downstairs, smoothing her skirt nervously as she reached the last few steps. She had no idea what to expect, certainly not this extraordinary-looking youth with hair that seemed about to take off.

"Good evening," he said.

Oh dear. He sounded as shy as she felt, or worse.

"You must be Lewis."

"Yes, that's right. Paul had to go into theater so he asked me to take you to the restaurant."

"All right. Wait a minute, I'll get my hat."

She ran all the way upstairs and all the way down again, wondering what on earth she would find to talk to him about until Paul arrived.

"Is Lewis your first name or your second?" she asked as they set off.

"Second. My first name's Richard, but nobody ever uses it. Well, except at home."

"But Paul is always Paul."

"Yes, he is, isn't he?"

"I used to use my surname at college sometimes."

"I've never heard of girls doing that." He glanced sideways at her, curious. "Why did you?"

"Oh, I don't know. I suppose it was a way of saying, Take us seriously. It's hard, you know, for girls to be taken seriously as artists. We don't do it so much now."

They walked a little way in silence.. "What's keeping Paul?"

"He had to go into theater. We had a rush on. Did he tell you they've made him a dresser now?"

She couldn't remember. "That's special, is it?"

"You have to be pretty good."

She caught the note of hero worship in his voice, the way Andrew sounded, sometimes, when he talked about Toby.

"So what do you do exactly? If you're a dresser?"

"You bandage them up after they come out of theater. Some of the wounds are . . . quite difficult."

"I'll bet."

He looked startled, then laughed. "Paul's not pleased, because he thinks now they won't let him drive an ambulance."

"Which is what he volunteered for."

"Yes."

"And you? What do you want to do?"

He was striding ahead. She had to trot to keep up with him.

"The same, I suppose. I know it's wrong, because you ought to be prepared to do whatever needs doing most, but, no, I've got to admit, I'd rather drive an ambulance."

That speech, which should have sounded priggish, but didn't, because his enthusiasm and energy kept bursting through, confirmed her liking for him. More than liking, perhaps. Attraction. He was attractive, in spite of his freckly skin and staring hair. He didn't look human, not entirely human. Ariel. That's who he was. She smiled as she sat down at the café table and looked across at him. Ariel and Miranda.

She suggested a carafe of red wine while they waited. He hardly seemed to know what to do and kept looking at the door hoping salvation in the shape of Paul might suddenly appear. When the wine had been brought to the table and poured, she asked, "Do you think you'll get your ambulance?"

"I don't know. We keep nudging them."

We. Evidently this had become a joint project.

"Nurses are coming out all the time now. Proper nurses, so you never know, we might be lucky. Anyway." He raised his glass. "To happier times."

He was happy now, and because of the times, not in spite of them.

"Didn't you ever think of enlisting?"

He flushed, perhaps suspecting her of being about to produce a white feather. Little did he know.

"No, I'm a Friend. It wasn't an option."

"A Friend?"

"A Quaker. We oppose all wars."

"Because Jesus said so?"

"Yes—and because the inner light leads us in that direction. I know, that probably strikes you as—"

"Doesn't strike me as anything, particularly. I don't think I have the right to judge other people's decisions. I'm a woman. Nobody's asking me to fight."

"And you don't want to . . . nurse?"

"Good God, no."

"So what do you do?"

"Ignore it—as far as I can."

"And how far is that?"

"Not very far, because there's Paul, and there's my brother who's joined the army. *And* I've got a German friend whose father's just been interned. But I keep working. Painting," she explained, to cut off the question.

"Landscapes, Paul says."

"Quakers pray in silence, don't they?"

She couldn't have done that, not that she prayed much at all. But to lose the vaulted aisles, the stained glass, the music, the words of the Book of Common Prayer and put nothing in its place except silence and other people's faces and tummy rumbles. God, no.

"Yes, we have a meeting at the hospital every Sunday morning. Paul joins us now and then."

So, added to the image of Paul expertly winding bandages around amputated stumps, she had to try to imagine him sitting in a hut in silence, surrounded by earnest, well-meaning—but surely rather dull?—men. Women too, presumably—all excellent people, no doubt. But *Paul?*

At that moment, as if summoned by her incredulity, Paul appeared in the doorway and began threading his way between the tables. As he bent to kiss her, she smelled the cool night air on his cheek, overlaying, without hiding, the hospital smell of disinfectant and blood. He nodded to Lewis, picked up the carafe, and caught the waiter's eye, before sitting down. Silently she passed her own almost full glass across to him. He looked slightly embarrassed, but took it nevertheless.

"Cheers," he said, toasting them both, but nothing could hide his need for that first glass.

She went on talking to Lewis, aware all the time of Paul,

of the color coming back into his face. She could see Lewis was concerned. We've a lot in common, she thought. We're both in love with Paul. Three months ago, she wouldn't have thought to use those words.

A waitress, with a white cloth tied round her waist, came up to the table. She was invisible to them, standing there with a pad and pencil in her hand, but then, when Paul looked up to give the order, she said, "I haven't seen you here for a long time."

"No." He'd flushed slightly. "I've been busy."

"And you too, Monsieur Lewis. You have been too much occupied, I think?"

Lewis agreed that he had been too much occupied. After she went, there was an awkward pause, and then Lewis and Paul both rushed in to break it, frustrating each other's efforts. Elinor stared down into her glass, realized she didn't care—she ought to care, but she didn't—and then she started to smile, and then to laugh.

Paul stared at her in amazement. "What's funny?" He sounded irritable, resentful even.

"Nothing. I'm just happy to be here."

They ate some spicy sausages with potatoes. Paul looked even more tired than he had the night before and contributed little. Elinor talked about the things she'd seen and done that day, the places she'd sketched, and they asked about home, about London. Had it changed much? No. The searchlights were beautiful, there was a huge gun on Hampstead Heath, all the lamps were painted blue. The worst thing was the gutter press—always going on about "the enemy within." Lewis asked about the Slade, what was it like now? A convent, she said. A nunnery. A herd of sheep with Tonks the only ram, but she kept faltering into silence.

Paul burst out that when he looked back on those days now he thought they'd all been barking mad.

"No," she said. "*This* is mad."

"Well, all right." He was tapping his fingers on the table. God, he was bad tempered. "Perhaps not mad, but like children. Spoiled, self-indulgent, selfish children."

"And this is better? Young men in wheelchairs. Or dead."

"At least it's not contemptible."

"And we were?"

"Weren't we?"

She shook her head. Lewis tried to change the subject, and from then on she concentrated entirely on him, asking him about his schooldays—not long past—and his ambitions for the future. He wanted to play the piano, he said, professionally, but he didn't know if he was good enough. If he couldn't do that, he'd teach.

"Music?"

"Oh, yes—I don't know about anything else."

It had been a warm day—perhaps the last day of the long Indian summer. It couldn't go on much longer, they were into November now—and the café was airless. She seemed to be breathing in the same breath over and over again. And the candles didn't help.

When the rumbling started, she thought: thunder. Good. She'd always loved storms. She imagined them lying on the bed with the curtains open, blue flashes lighting up their bodies; and they wouldn't need to talk, and perhaps that was just as well. Then she became uneasy. Paul and Lewis were staring at each other, not alarmed, just puzzled.

"That was close," Lewis said.

Then the candles guttered and the whole room shook and from the look on people's faces she realized it wasn't thunder.

Paul had gone white. "It's a stray. Has to be."

But even as he spoke there was another crash and everything on the table did a little jump into the air. The lightbulb was swinging at the end of its flex, sending shadows from side to side. All the people in the room seemed to be clinging to the clapper of a bell. The electric light flickered again, only it was more than a flicker now. A long, fierce, edge-of-darkness buzzing and then the lights went out. The candles, which were really no more than ornaments, wobbled but kept going, giving just enough light to show people's faces and hands. What Elinor remembered afterwards was the inertia. Nobody moved. They couldn't believe it had happened; they didn't want to abandon their nice meals and their bottles of wine, and so they all just sat there, staring at each other, until another thud, closer, brought with it the sound of breaking glass.

Scraping chairs, screams, panic. Paul grabbed her and dragged her towards the door. Lewis was just behind them, treading on their heels. Outside in the dark people were running all in different directions, but Paul stood on the pavement with his hand gripping her upper arm. She wanted to run too, though there was no point running from danger that struck randomly from the air.

"I'd better get back," Lewis said.

"Yes," Paul said. "You go."

Lewis felt for her hand. "I'll see you again."

She nodded, stammered something, and then he was gone, running like a stag down the center of the road. Paul put his arm around her and they walked back, slowly, to the house. At intervals, the ground shuddered under their feet. The streets were ravines of darkness now, all the lights extinguished, only in the sky was a whirl of sparks flying upwards and an orange glow lighting the underbelly of the clouds.

Another explosion. Paul took her hand. "Come on. Not far now."

As soon as they turned the corner and saw the house they started to run, though running made her more afraid. She stood, gasping for breath, while Paul fitted the key in the lock. The back of his hand was meaty red with the light from the sky. They got inside and switched on the light, but nothing happened.

"Madame?" Paul called. They waited but there was no answer. "She'll have gone to her mother's."

The walls and floors seemed to be trembling all the time now, not just when a shell landed. They went down to the kitchen. You had to go down a flight of stairs to get to it; once there they looked for another door leading down to the cellar, but the one Elinor tried opened onto a cupboard full of deck chairs and old coats.

"There'll be candles," Paul said, opening the cupboard under the sink and beginning to rummage about among floor-cloths and scrubbing brushes, but he didn't find any. Elinor opened the curtains and the full moon shone in. Another shell burst, and the rocking chair in the corner started to rock as if to comfort itself. The grinding of its rockers on the stone floor was worse than the bombs, and she went across to it and held it still.

"Under the table," Paul said.

"No, I want my passport."

"That can wait."

"No it can't, I want it now."

"All right, but you'll have to be quick."

Though when they got to the top of the house he was the first to go across and stand at the window. It was far worse than she'd thought. At street level you couldn't see the extent of the devastation. Up here, the clock tower was encircled by fires and seemed to float above the city, borne aloft on billowing clouds of smoke.

Because this window was level with the roofs, they could follow the shells as they came in. Three hundred yards away a house burst open, like a ripe pod, as if the pressure came from within. She felt Paul beside her.

"I ought to go back to the hospital. If it's hit . . ."

She didn't ask him not to leave her, and in the end he didn't go, though she could feel him disliking her for standing between him and his duty. That's why it's called the forbidden zone. That's why they didn't want wives and girlfriends here.

She found her passport and money and they crept downstairs again and sheltered under the kitchen table. From time to time the floor shook. Paul built a barricade of chairs intended to protect them from flying glass. At first every explosion made her heart jump, though she made no sound, not because she was brave but because she'd found out the hard way that her own cries frightened her. It was easier to be stoical, to force her clenched fingers to uncurl. They talked about their childhoods, the good parts, the woods and fields, the excitement of learning to paint, and then he talked more about his mother. The years of her illness when he hadn't known from day to day which face she would turn towards him.

"Eventually she stuck a pair of scissors in my neck. That's when Dad decided we couldn't manage with her at home anymore."

Through her fear of the repeated shock waves shaking the

table Elinor reached out and took his hand. "Make love to me."
She didn't know what else to say.

"I'm not sure I can. I'm frightened too, you know."

But there was no problem. Afterwards, leaning on Paul's
shoulder, she managed to get some sleep, and woke with a neck
so stiff she could barely move. The room was lit with dirty-
dishwater light and the shelling seemed to have stopped. They
drank cup after cup of hot, strong coffee until her veins buzzed,
and then walked out into a street covered with plaster dust, like
gray snow. A thin mist of dust hung on the air; they'd walked
only a few yards and their heads and shoulders were white.
It got into your throat. Paul was coughing really badly. She
looked around. Buildings still burned, the flames licking black-
ened timbers. Some of the house fronts had been ripped off and
all the little private things laid bare: wallpaper, counterpanes,
chamber pots, sofas, a crucifix hanging askew above a bed, a little girl's doll. It was indecent. In one living room everything
had been smashed except for the china ornaments on the
mantelpiece, which sat there, bizarrely untouched. A huge
puddle of water lay in a dip in the road where the fire engines
had worked all night to damp down the smoldering timbers. As
she watched, rings of rain began to pockmark the surface. She
saw it in the puddle before she felt it on the back of her neck. It
seemed important somehow to notice and remember that. Important and meaningless.

In a daze they began to walk towards the square. In the
center were several bundles covered with rugs or blankets. At
first she thought some families bombed out of their homes had
rescued their possessions and covered them to keep them dry.
She was almost standing over the bundles before she saw the
feet sticking out of one covering, a hand out of another. Further

on were other people lined up but not yet covered: a woman with a little dog in her arms, three other women, two men, and then, lying on the cobbles, a child. She thought how strange it was, to lie on the cold ground looking up at the sky with rain falling into your eyes, and not blink or turn your head away.

Paul's voice in her ear. "Come on, now. Come away."

She hadn't know she was shaking till he touched her. Now she looked up into his face. His eyelids were crusted with white dust. In the middle of it all, a red, wet mouth making sounds. "We've got to get you to the station before it starts again."

"It mightn't."

"Why would they stop?"

So they ran back along the cratered road. She looked down one of the side streets and saw water from a burst main jetting fifteen, twenty feet into the air and a gang of boys daring each other to run through it. Their dark figures leaping about against the plume of water were full of joy.

She was packed in minutes. They hardly spoke. Paul tried to help, but two people packing one bag doesn't work, so he went and stood with his back to her, staring out of the window. She thought about her mother and father. Until she saw the child lying dead in the square she hadn't given them a thought. Now she thought of nothing else.

When she'd checked that she'd got everything, she joined Paul by the window. One of the houses that had been hit last night had a green silk bedspread lolling out of its upper window. It looked . . . sluttish.

"Well," Paul said, turning to face her. "That's that, then. We'd better go."

Paul carried the suitcase, striding ahead so fast she had to run to keep up with him. The station was packed. Ruthless suddenly, nothing like the man she thought she knew, he elbowed his way through the crowds. They stood near the edge of the platform, looking up and down the line, not knowing when, or if, a train would arrive. Many of the other people looked like refugees, weighed down with as many possessions as they could carry.

"Write as soon as you can," Paul said.

She could see him itching to get back to the hospital. "Look, why don't you go? I'll be all right."

"No, you won't. This is going to be a real scrum."

It was. As soon as the train appeared the crowd surged forward. If it hadn't been for Paul, she'd have ended up on the line. As it was she lost a shoe. The guards shouted and blew whistles and yelled at people to keep back, but they were clawing at the sides of the train before it stopped. Paul got on and hauled her up behind him, then had to fight to get off again. She was hemmed in on all sides, her suitcase, or somebody else's, cutting into her calf. She wasn't sure her feet were on the ground, even, and she couldn't see anything except backs and heads and necks. Whistles blew, doors slammed. At the last moment she twisted her head and saw him standing there, one hand raised, and then somebody moved and a shoulder hid him from her sight.

26

Paul to Elinor

The hospital itself wasn't bombed, though we have a huge crater a hundred yards away to show how close we came. There's talk of evacuating us to somewhere further back, but we underlings play no part in such decisions. Lewis and I have both put in for ambulance driving again, and, since we're supposed to be getting an influx of professional nurses soon, we may succeed. I don't want to go further back. All the pressure is to go the other way, to be part of it, though I'm sure I shall hate it.

They brought a child in last week, a little boy, ten years old perhaps. It's not supposed to happen, but the ambulance driver who'd been flagged down at the side of the road by the parents just dumped him here and drove off before anybody could argue. He'd lost both arms. The stumps were curiously like wings. When he tried to move them he looked like a fledgling trying to fly. Even with the morphine he was in terrible pain. His mother visited—she runs a café on the outskirts of the town—I've been there once or twice—but they were busy doing repairs so they could open again, so she wasn't here often. One night I was on my way to change his dressings. I pulled aside the screen and found her there, bending over him. She turned round when

she heard me, and I apologized and went away. I meant to give them a
few minutes alone and then go back, but something else cropped up so
it was over an hour before I got back. His mother had gone. He was
lying there, alone, with his eyes closed, and at first I thought he was
asleep, but then I noticed his chest wasn't moving and when I touched
his skin he was growing cold. Everybody said, What a merciful release.
Sister Naylor cried. She'd have liked to put flowers in his hands, I
think, only of course he had no hands to put them in. Mr. Burton,
who'd done the operation, was called and like everybody else said,
Perhaps it's just as well. But then, when we were alone—I'd got the
job of laying him out—Burton pushed up the child's lids and said,
"Look, petechiae." (They're little red spots—hemorrhages—in the
whites of the eye.) I didn't understand. He said, "She smothered him."

It's strange, isn't it? You go on and on, or I do rather, seeing God
knows what horrors and learning not to care or anyway not to care
more than you need to do the job, and then something happens that
gets right under your skin. I can't forget them, the boy and his mother,
the look on her face when she turned round and saw me standing there.
She had a pillow in her hands. I didn't realize. What would I have
done if I had?

If I don't get a transfer to ambulance work soon, I think I may
have to take some leave.

Elinor to Paul
I wish you would take leave. It would be lovely to see you here
and just sit in Lockhart's having a coffee or go for a meal or back home
for toasted crumpets by the fire and . . . Anything to be together again.
I thought seeing you out there would make you feel closer, but it seems
to have had the opposite effect. It feels as if you're in the belly of the
whale and I'm out here on dry land. Just. The war impinges a little

more each day. The papers are full of atrocity stories, they seem designed to whip up feeling against Germans living here. Catherine feels it very badly.

I missed classes last week. I had to go to stay with my sister. The new baby arrived five days ago, a boy. Mother was in the bedroom trying to take over from the midwife, and then things were going so slowly the doctor had to be called. I walked up and down the corridor outside, standing in for the absent father who's doing important work in the War Office and couldn't be spared. Eventually Rachel's cries stopped and I heard the chink of instruments so I thought the doctor must have decided it had gone on long enough. It certainly had— thirty-six hours!—and then there was a cry, a wail rather, and relief all round. I went in to see the baby who had forceps marks on either side of his head, as if he'd been mauled by an animal. Oh Paul, his skin. You know how a poppy looks when you peel the outer green casing back too early? It looked like that: red, moist, creased, and then, gradually, it started to fill out. Even a few hours made a difference. Rachel looked shocked. She wasn't at all the blooming contented mother I'd been expecting. She said labor was the best-kept secret in the world, though when I think of some of the noises coming through the bedroom door, I don't think it can be all that well kept.

At least then we thought, it's over. But it wasn't. A few hours later the doctor had to be called back, Rachel was losing so much blood. In fact she collapsed just as he arrived. I think when he walked through the door he thought she was dead. They had to raise the foot of the bed to try to slow the bleeding down. We sat up with her all night and gradually she became a little stronger. Now she can sit up though only for ten minutes at a time. She has to eat raw liver twice a day. I can't bear to watch her. I go out of the room. You can hear her crying and choking as she tries to force it down.

But the baby's lovely. I watch the nurse bathe him. When he's held out over the water there's a moment when he goes perfectly still. Then the water touches him, and his chin wobbles and he makes little convulsive movements with his arms and sucks his breath in. Of course everybody oohs and ahs, but there's something terrible about the little naked scrap dangling over the abyss.

It's been an extremely educational week. I think the role of eccentric maiden aunt will suit me very well. Though I suppose it's a bit late for the maiden part. I do miss you, Paul.

Did I tell you I've almost decided to move? Yes, I know, again. So: more decorating, more buckets of glutinous muck, and no Ruthie to help this time. Doesn't approve of me anymore. She's volunteered to go out to France and is waiting to hear so can't be bothered with silly empty-headed people who go on painting while Rome burns. I've got to get out of here. Downstairs there are Belgian refugees, grumbling like mad about the food and the weather—which is awful. The rain it raineth every day.

How is it over there? I don't know what to say about the little boy. How horrible. I hope they let you drive an ambulance soon if that's what you want, but I'd be even more pleased if you came home on leave.

Toby went off to Scarborough last week on some sort of course, but he had a weekend at home first and saw the new baby. He's expecting to be sent out early next year. We went for a long walk around all our special places and talked about the future with great determination. After it was over and he was gone I realized my cheeks ached and I couldn't think why and then I realized it was because I'd been forcing myself to smile for hours and hours.

Barbara—I don't know if you remember her, she used to go around a lot with Marjorie Bradshaw?—just came in to say she's been taken on by the Omega Workshops, starting after Christmas. Three mornings' work for thirty shillings a week. She doesn't mind designing cushions and decorating teapots. I suppose it might be quite fun really, though some people are awfully snooty about it. Prostituting one's talent, would you believe? They should try teaching flower painting to the young ladies of Kensington. Not that that's an option anymore. I think I might do it too. It leaves you plenty of time to do your own work, and the Slade's awfully grim at the moment. Tonks sweeping up and down the corridors like the pillar of fire by night.

Mother's gone back to her bandaging again. Toby's in the army. Dad's busy with his head-injuries unit. Tim's in the War Office. Rachel says the baby's her war work. Ruthie's off to France. So you see how things are, Paul. Everybody doing important war work, except me. I alone preserve an iron frivolity.

Paul to Elinor

You're not serious about leaving the Slade, are you? Do take time to think about it. Painting teapots may keep the wolf from the door but it won't do anything to establish you as an artist. On the other hand you know the situation better than me, and I suppose we all have to stop being students sometime. Anyway, I'll buy your teapots, honey— if you do leave. And your cushions.

The rain that rains on you also rains on us, and it makes things devilish difficult. All the paths between the huts are lined with duckboards now and even so we sink. The mud bubbles up through the slats. I've taken to getting right away on my days off, can't stand the place, can't work (draw, I mean, the other sort of work I do in a trance). I managed to get an ambulance driver to take me up to the front line, promising if he was full on the way back I'd walk. He's called Guy and he's a Canadian, very dark skin, furrowed cheeks, he looks too old to be here, but here he is. And taciturn in the extreme, which suited me. I didn't want to talk, I wanted to look.

The first part of the road I was familiar with, because I've walked along it before, but after that there's open country. Very strange, mad feeling as you go further out, away from the town, because there are fields and farmhouses and it all looks normal until you see that the farmhouse has a hole in the roof and the corn's still standing in the fields, beaten flat of course in lots of places, but in others, where it's more sheltered, still standing. I remembered a cornfield I walked through last summer, how restless it was. How it whispered all the time though there was hardly any breeze, and I thought about the farmer who planted this field last spring, with no idea he wouldn't be there to harvest it. And then after that a stretch of normal countryside: tall, spindly trees, willows—some with yellow leaves still clinging to their branches, bending to meet their reflections in the canals. Everything end-of-year and stagnant, but beautiful too in its own way.

The road was clogged with limbers and motor vehicles and men marching towards the front. They look like a machine: all the boots moving as one, shoulders bristling with rifles, arms swinging, everything pointing forwards. And on the other side of the road, men stumbling back, trying to keep time, half dead from exhaustion and with this incredible stench hanging over them. You get whiffs of it when you cut the clothes off wounded men, but out there, in the mass, it's as solid as a wall. And they all look so gray, faces twitching, young men who've been turned into old men. It's a great contrast, stark and terrible, because they're the same men, really. It's an irrigation system, full buckets going one way, empty buckets the other. Only it's not water the buckets carry.

Further on the road dipped down then leveled out again and that was where the sense of strangeness began. What I didn't know— though it's obvious enough when you think about it—is that companies in a column of marching men take synchronized breaks, so, at a given moment, all the men fall out and sit by the roadside, blending into the muddy ground. So for a time the road looks empty. I'm not explaining this very well, but I saw it happen and it made the hairs on the back of my neck stand up. I don't quite know why. It's the feeling of an empty, desolate landscape that isn't empty at all, but teeming with men.

We were crawling along most of the time, edging past columns of men in wet, gleaming capes and helmets, like mechanical mushrooms. Now and then somebody looks up, and you get the sense of an individual human mind among the bundles of soaked misery. All this is in semidarkness of course. Close to the front people move only after dark, with dawn and dusk the most dangerous times. That's when the heaviest bombardments are. Nothing dramatic happened to us though. It rained all the way there and all the way back—I didn't have to walk.

This will sound heartless, and perhaps it is, but close to the front line where the land on either side of the road is ruined—pockmarked, blighted, craters filled with foul water, splintered trees, hedges and fields gouged out—I realized I felt the horror of that landscape almost more than I feel for the dying. It's a dreadful thing to say, I know—a flaw in me—but the human body decays and dies in some more or less disgusting way whether there's a war or not, but the land we hold in trust.

Sorry! This has got awfully deep and I didn't mean it to, but it leads up to some good news at least. When I got back I found Lewis in the hut almost bouncing on the beds with excitement. The nurses—the fully qualified ones who, we were beginning to think, were as mythical as the nine muses—are on their way at last, so it can't be long now before we get our transfer. I want to be up there. I don't want to be stuck here in comparative safety doing a job that a woman could do equally well, and in the case of a qualified nurse, BETTER!

Elinor to Paul

I'm pleased for you, Paul, I really am—since it's what you seem to want. I wonder whether you know how hard it is to answer your letters? A week has gone by since I received your last, though I meant to sit down and reply at once. I know you say you want to hear about all my doings but I can't help feeling that my doings are terribly trivial compared with yours and that this may even be part of their attraction for you. It's like looking through the window of a doll's house, isn't it?

Anyway doll's house or not, here goes. I've been to tea with Lady Ottoline Morrell! I never thought I'd live to see the day. I met her at the Camden Street Gallery and she looked at me very intently for a long time and then she said in that vague way of hers, wafting a jeweled hand about above her head, You must come to tea sometime. Do come to tea.

I thought that was fairly meaningless really—no time, no date— and immediately forgot all about it, but yesterday morning I came downstairs and there was the invitation on the mat and so this afternoon I set off, wearing one red stocking and one blue as a reminder to myself not to be nervous though of course I was. Close to, in broad daylight, she really is quite extraordinary. We sat in a red room overlooking a walled garden and the rainy afternoon light fell full on her face, which was heavily rouged with purple shadow on the eyelids, and in a way she looks quite beautiful and in another almost grotesque. She's obviously decided that being ordinary is not an option for her and she's right. So although she's very tall—six foot if she's an inch—she wears thick cork soles that add on another two inches. Her dress was brightly colored green silk with an intricate web of gold embroidery— very beautiful, but for afternoon tea? My pathetic little gesture with

odd stockings was nowhere, I can tell you. She's not easy to talk to,
though she is interested in everything you say. You feel she's listening,
not just waiting for the chance to make some clever remark herself like
most of that Bloomsbury crowd. Only—now I'm going to carp and I
shouldn't—there isn't much humor, and it's all very intense. She
seems to be drawing your soul out of your body. It's a kind of
cannibalism. I felt I had nothing to offer her. Not enough meat on my
bones. We talked about the war. Oh my God, yes, the war, I'm so
heartily sick of it but it seems to be unavoidable even with people like
her who hate it as much as I do. She said she was totally opposed—a
point in her favor—but had decided that it was pointless trying to stop
it. I was trying not to laugh. The vanity of these people!—thinking
they can influence the fate of nations when it takes them all their time
to organize their own lives. But then she said she'd switched her
energies to trying to help the wives and families of German internees
who've been left with no income, dependent on charity handouts. Even
when the wife is English she can't get even the most menial work, not
even doorstep scrubbing, which is the lowest-paid work there is—or so
Lady O says. I sort of half promised I would go and hand out parcels
with her but all the time I was thinking about Catherine and how I
ought to have done more for her. She's a friend for goodness' sake and
that matters more than charity, or ought to, but when I got her letter
about her father being interned I was so excited about going to see you
I didn't do anything. I should have gone to see her then. Made time. It
was wrong of me not to. Lady O meanwhile was trying to move the
conversation onto a more personal plane. She wants something from
you—not in any crude material way—something emotional. Or
intellectual perhaps, but she must have guessed there was no point
expecting anything like that from me! I told her about Catherine and
how worried I was about Toby and it was all true, every word of it
was true, so why did it sound so false? But these were just bits of

gristle, not really juicy flesh. So then I bethought me of my trip to see you, and I told her about that—she's the first person I've told— which is wrong, because what is Lady O to me, or I to her? I haven't told Rachel. I haven't told Mother. But I did tell her and she was ecstatic. It became quite embarrassing and I've no doubt she'll repeat the story with embellishments all over London and I shall acquire a reputation for—I don't know what—recklessness, romantic passion— something.

But I enjoyed meeting her. In the end I wasn't nervous or intimidated at all. And yet I came away with a bad taste in my mouth in spite of her lovely cream cakes and her real genuine unaffected kindness. It all seemed so false somehow but the falsity was not in her but in me.

When I got back, I started decorating. I'd intended to put it off because it's so time-consuming. I was going to live with the Victorian wallpaper—huge green roses that look like cabbages—perhaps they are cabbages—but I can't live with it, Paul, I simply can't. It all has to come off and then I might be able to work again. So you must think of me wielding that horrible triangular scraper thing that hurts your hands, moving along the paper row by row, murdering cabbages. I'm sure you're much more usefully employed.

27

He knew he'd cut himself, the minute he did it. He felt a sharp pain as the scalpel sliced through his glove, but there wasn't much he could do about it. He was cutting the dressing from a twitching stump of amputated leg at the time, and needed both hands, one to cut, one to keep the leg still. Gangrene had set in and the discarded dressing was yellow with pus.

As soon as he'd finished, he scrubbed his hands, the peeled-off gloves lying by the side of the sink like sloughed-off skin. Blood flowed from the cut. It was at the top of his right index finger, not big, but deep. A quotation was teasing the fringes of his mind. What was it? *Not so wide as a church door, nor so deep as a well, but t'will serve.* Morbid bugger. He scrubbed his chilblained hands till the flesh stung, stuck a wad of cotton wool over the cut, and hoped for the best.

The following day was his day off. When he reached the end of his shift he decided to walk into town and stay overnight in the room in order to be able to start work at dawn. He was nearing the end of a painting and so excited he couldn't bear to be away from it. Even woke up in the middle of the night and lay thinking about it, unable to get back to sleep. It was a tricky time, though. At the end of his last painting session, a week ago now, it crossed his mind that it might be finished. At any event, he was aware of the danger of doing too much. This was when somebody else's eye would have been invaluable. Elinor's, or better still, Tonks's, though what Tonks would have made of it he hardly dared think.

At last he was free to go. His cut finger was throbbing, but it had been painful for the last few days because of the chilblains, so that was nothing new. He felt tired and sweaty, but he felt like that at the end of every shift. Unusually, he changed out of his uniform before going out and the cool touch of clean cotton on his skin soothed him and persuaded him that he didn't feel too bad after all. Nothing that a good night's sleep wouldn't cure. He always slept more deeply in the room than in the hut, though he'd long since become accustomed to Lewis's presence and even welcomed it. Something about the proximity of the wards and the theater kept him on permanent alert. He woke if a mouse ran over the floor.

The walk into town in the fresh clear air, stars pricking overhead, revived him. He turned the key in the familiar lock, brimming with excitement and hope. The room was not so powerfully full of Elinor's presence as it had been even a week ago. Now it was the figure on the canvas he hurried up the stairs to meet, but once in the room he didn't go immediately to the easel. Instead, he sat down on the edge of the bed, unconsciously cradling his right hand in the left. When he became aware of what he was doing he made a conscious effort to separate the hands. He was treating it like a real injury and that was ridiculous. Children playing in a playground get worse cuts than that every day.

The easel had a cloth draped over it. Ideally, he shouldn't look at the painting at all tonight. The gaslight flickered, its bluish tinge changing every color and tone in the room. No, no, it would be a complete waste of time. But the painting seemed to call to him. At last he could stand it no longer. He jumped up and pulled off the cloth.

My God. It looked as if it had been painted by somebody else. That was his first thought. It had an authority that he didn't associate with his stumbling, uncertain, inadequate self. It seemed to stand alone. Really, to have nothing much to do with him.

He'd painted the worst aspect of his duties as an orderly: infusing hydrogen peroxide or carbolic acid into a gangrenous wound. Though the figure by the bed, carrying out this unpleasant task, was by no means a self-portrait. Indeed, it was so wrapped up in rubber and white cloth: gown, apron, cap, mask, gloves—ah, yes, the all-important gloves—that it had no individual features. Its anonymity, alone, made it appear threatening. No ministering angel, this. A white-swaddled mummy intent on causing pain. The patient was nothing: merely a blob of tortured nerves.

It shook him. He stood back from it, looked, looked away, back again. It must be the gaslight that was so transforming his view of it. And he was no nearer knowing if it was finished, though at the moment he felt he wouldn't dare do anything else.

Cover it up. Once it was safely back behind the cloth, he relaxed a little, even began to wonder if he were not flattering himself a little. Perhaps it was his own feverish state that accounted for the painting's impact. He raised a hand to his brow and wiped the sweat away. Probably he should have an early night, but the thought of lying in that bed, alone, with only the painting for company, was not attractive. He'd do better to go out and get some food. Not to any of the usual places, though. He wasn't fit for company tonight.

The night air restored him. By the time he reached the café he was feeling almost normal again. It was very strange how this thing came in waves. He sat down and ordered a carafe of red wine, feeling almost elated, but no sooner had he drunk the first glass than he was starting to sweat again. The café that had seemed so welcoming when he pushed open the door now looked yellow, with dark dancing shapes all over the walls. Nothing was the right size. The barmaid's face loomed and receded, all bulbous nose and fish eyes like a face seen in the back of a spoon. There was a ringing in his ears and the French being spoken at tables all around him had suddenly become incomprehensible. A man with a drooping mustache and eyes to match asked him a question. Was this chair taken? Was that it? Paul stared blankly back at him, unable to attach meaning to the words.

There was a cellar underneath the bar, no doubt opened up since the bombardment to give customers somewhere to shelter should the worst happen again. He'd go down there. It might be quieter there. Draining his glass, he picked up the carafe and stumbled down the stairs.

It was slightly quieter and there were alcoves where you were secluded from the general crush. He made his way towards one of them, thinking it was empty, but then, there at the back, in the shadows, he saw a smudge of white face. He was turning away, not wanting to intrude on the solitude of somebody who'd clearly chosen to drink alone, when something about the breadth of the man's shoulders, the pudgy, truculent features staring up at him, as if daring him to occupy one of the vacant chairs, struck a chord. Kit Neville.

Simultaneously, Neville's expression changed and he jumped to his feet. They shook hands and then, finding that inadequate, pulled each other into a bear hug. So much back slapping and smiling and hand pumping, and all of it sincere, and yet they'd made no attempt in the last two months to seek each other out, though the hospitals where they worked could not have been more than five miles apart. Ten, at most, Paul reminded himself, sitting down.

"Well," said Neville.

After greeting each other like long-lost brothers, there was an immediate awkwardness of not finding anything to say.

"How are you?" Paul asked.

"Oh, pretty well. The old rheumatiz is playing up a bit." He probed his left shoulder as if for confirmation. "And you?"

"All right. Have you been doing any painting?"

"Not much. I've got masses of drawings, though. I've got to get back home and do some serious work."

"Are you still at the same hospital?"

"No, they've put me in charge of the German wounded at another hospital. Like a fool, I admitted to speaking German."

"What's that like?"

"Not bad. Some of the younger ones come in fighting mad, but I generally manage to get them on my side. I help them to write home. Oh, and I met one who used to be a waiter at the Russell Square Hotel. He was working there when I used to drink there, so he must have poured me many a glass of whiskey, though I can't say I remember him. But he speaks good English, so I've more or less recruited him onto the staff. It'll be a blow when he has to leave."

"I thought you were going into ambulance driving?"

"Bloody shoulder put paid to that. I only lasted a week. The steering's so heavy you wouldn't believe. When you come off shift you don't feel you've been driving. Feels like you've gone fifteen rounds with an all-in wrestler. By the way, that's strictly between the two of us, you understand?"

Paul was puzzled until he realized that nursing enemy soldiers, however necessary, and even admirable, the work might be, didn't fit in very well with Neville's desire to present himself as a daring war artist risking his life daily on the front line.

"You won't tell anybody?"

"No, of course not."

"You see, the thing is, I was a rotten ambulance driver, but I seem to be pretty good with the wounded, only . . ."

"I won't say anything."

How strange to find that Neville possessed the qualities needed in a good orderly, and how typical of him to be ashamed of them. He seemed to be under enormous pressure. Even in this short exchange it was possible to tell that he was drunk. Oh, not incapable—far from it, he had an immense capacity—but his speech was just beginning to be slurred. Certainly, his inhibitions were gone. He belched several times loudly and made no attempt to apologize or cover his mouth. Since the carafe in front of him was still almost full, it was evidently not the first. He was staring at Paul, almost aggressively. Pale fish eyes, caught in a net of red veins.

Neville raised his glass in a toast.

"What are we drinking to?" Paul asked.

"Elinor."

Immediately, Paul felt a strong sense of her presence sitting in the empty chair between them.

"Do you hear from her at all?"

"Yes, now and then. Do you?"

He knew Neville didn't. Elinor had said they'd lost touch.

"Now and then. And Catherine keeps me in touch with what's going on."

"How is Catherine?"

"Bloody awful, I should think. How would you feel if your father was locked up?

"I thought you and she were . . . ?"

"No point, old chap. Can't decide anything like that while this bloody war's dragging on. So, you hear from Elinor, do you?"

Did he know she'd been here? He couldn't know, unless she'd told him and she wouldn't do that. Though she might have confided in Catherine and Catherine might well have mentioned it to Kit. The more he thought about it, the more probable it seemed. But then Elinor had said she'd told nobody except Ruthie. She'd also said she didn't write to Kit. God, what a muddle, and he was being dragged into it. Even not mentioning her visit was a lie. Well, stop that.

"Yes, I do. She writes quite frequently."

They stared at each other, the earlier effusion of friendship forgotten. Paul knew there was something in this situation he was failing to grasp, and that made him uneasy. It didn't help that his head was full of cotton wool. He couldn't think.

Suddenly Kit laughed, a great wheezing belly laugh that

turned into a cough and came embarrassingly close to tears. God, he was drunk.

"Shall I tell you something?" Neville said.

"About Elinor? I think I'd rather you didn't. If it's something she wants me to know I expect she'll tell me herself."

He was afraid of being told she'd slept with Neville. Neville was just about drunk enough to say it.

"For Elinor men come in twos. Always did. Right back when I first knew her at the Slade, it was two brothers then, can't for the life of me remember their names, anyway, doesn't matter. Point is, she wouldn't fancy either of us if it wasn't for the other."

"I don't think that's true."

"I know it is. Those brothers she ran around with, playing one off against the other, she didn't give a damn for either of them. That's it, you see." He was leaning forward, blinking those muculent eyes of his. "I don't think Elinor actually loves anybody. Her brother, of course, but that's different. And Catherine."

Paul made a sudden jerky movement, scraping his glass across the table.

"Yes, Catherine," Neville said.

Leaning across the table like that, he looked like something Brueghel might have painted. He was enjoying his little feast of drunken malice, but how much pain there was underneath. Clown he might be, but he was a talented clown, and his love for Elinor was real. Now, with an enormous effort, he raised his glass to the empty chair. "Elinor. Our Lady of Triangles."

Paul's thoughts were scattered across the table like spilled pins, every one of them sharp enough to hurt. He needed to get away from Neville as fast as possible, and since Neville was sinking rapidly into a morose stupor it wasn't difficult to disengage. Paul left him sitting there, scarcely capable of raising a hand to wave farewell.

Outside a sleety rain was falling. He raised his face to it, enjoying the cold splashes on his skin. The town was in almost total darkness. The streets were chasms where nothing moved but a cat slinking along the gutter. He was feeling so ill now he wondered if he should return to the hospital, but the room was so much closer and he wanted to lie down. The thought of walking all that way in the cold wet night was more than he could bear. He turned his coat collar up, thrust his hands deep into his pockets, and strode on through the dark. His footsteps ringing out across the cobbles proclaimed his loneliness. If only Elinor were there waiting for him, but she was miles and miles away, never further than tonight. Triangles, what nonsense, Neville was jealous, that was all.

A light still burned in Madame Drouet's living room, but it was too late to put his head round the door and say good night. He trudged upstairs until he reached the room where his draped painting waited on the easel. He mustn't look at it. Not now, not tonight. He was too afraid of finding out that it was rubbish, that he'd been deluding himself in thinking there was something there. Meeting Neville had done him no good. Quite apart from his slur on Elinor, Neville had thrust him back to those evenings in the Café Royal, where Neville was famous and he was an unknown art student, and an unsuccessful one at that.

Sitting on the bed, he took off his shoes and socks. He meant to undress completely, but he was feeling weaker by the minute and ended by crawling under the eiderdown still half

dressed. With an effort he turned off the light. The easel immediately took a step closer. He turned over onto his right side to
avoid seeing it, but that made him feel even more uneasy. It was
ridiculous of course, but he felt the need to keep an eye on it. In
some mysterious way it had become menacing. Like the faces
he'd seen in the wallpaper when he was a small boy confined to
bed with pneumonia. He shivered, thinking of deep, cold, dirty
water, but then gradually his eyes closed. For a long time he
hovered on the edge of sleep, dimly aware that the shrouded
mummy in his painting had stepped out of the frame and was
standing by his bed.

28

Richard Lewis to Elinor Brooke

I'm afraid I have rather bad news. You must be wondering why you've had no reply to your last letter. Please don't be alarmed. Paul is ill but is being well looked after. What happened was that he accidentally cut through his glove while dressing a badly infected wound. He washed his hands as soon as he noticed the cut, but the trouble is he's got chilblains rather badly at the moment—we all have—and although they itch like mad they also make your fingers feel quite numb and so he didn't notice immediately. (They also make you rather clumsy, which is how the accident came to happen, I suppose.) Infected fingers aren't unusual. All our hands are in a real mess. But Paul developed a high temperature and has had to spend several days in bed, the last two of them on the ward, so he's having the unusual experience of seeing the ward from both sides. Everybody's making a tremendous fuss of him, so he's thoroughly spoiled. Whenever one of the other orderlies has a spare moment they go and sit with him. They are a thoroughly decent set of chaps. I don't think you could find better anywhere.

I have very happy memories of the evening the three of us spent together, even though it did come to a rather dramatic end. I hope you're keeping well and once again don't be too concerned. Paul is in good hands and I'm sure he will soon be on the mend. Which will be a relief to all of us since he makes a far better orderly than he does a patient!

Elinor Brooke to Richard Lewis

Thank you for letting me know about Paul. It was a great shock to get the news, though I was beginning to suspect he was ill because I hadn't had a letter from him for almost a week. He is such a reliable correspondent despite being so busy (whereas I am a rather bad one, despite leading what some might call an idle life). Give him my love and best wishes for a speedy recovery.

I too have very happy memories of that evening in Ypres, though it seems a long time ago now. Perhaps one day we can all meet again in more peaceful circumstances. I would like that.

Paul to Elinor

I expect by now you've had Lewis's letter. He's been very kind to me throughout, fussing over me like a mother. (Not that mine ever did, but you know what I mean.) Before I was transferred to the ward he was always racing back to the hut to make sure I was all right. What a stupid accident. And such a small cut too. I went off duty and into town quite cheerfully, feeling no ill effects. The following day was my day off and I wanted to spend the night in the room so I could start painting as soon as it was light.

There was a particular painting I wanted to finish. It shows a gowned, masked, capped, gloved (ah, yes!) figure, standing by the bed of a man with gangrene, getting ready to do one of those awful hydrogen-peroxide dressings. The face is of a particular patient whose wound I used to dress—now dead, poor chap. I should have left it till morning when my mind would have been clearer, but, no, I had to get it out and look at it by gaslight, and the longer I looked the more menacing the figure became. Though it's clearly a nurse or a doctor so I don't know where the sense of horror came from. I couldn't make up my mind whether it needed more work or not, so in the end I put it away and went out for a drink.

By now the cut was throbbing, but after a few glasses of wine it felt better. I was drinking in a cellar—several of the cafés that were hit during the bombardment have opened again, but many of them use their cellars.

I was drinking on my own, but then I happened to bump into Neville. I suppose it's surprising it hasn't happened sooner. After all, we've never been more than five miles apart. We raised a glass to your good self, had a little chat about this and that—he's nursing German prisoners, did you know?—and parted. A few minutes later, back in the room, I could hardly believe he'd been there at all. The whole meeting seemed like some hallucination from the past.

By morning I was really quite ill and, after trying and failing to work on the painting, I gave up and went back to the hospital, where I was promptly put to bed by Lewis. The hours drifted past in a blur after that, except that the throbbing in the finger increased. By the middle of the night it really hurt and next day, after breakfast, Lewis summoned Sister Byrd who summoned Mr. Burton and I was transferred to the ward. All the patients who were well enough to take an interest thought it a huge joke. And there I lay and sweated and mithered. Every so often I caught a glimpse of my finger, which was swollen out of all recognition and didn't seem to belong to me. By this time it was stiff, hard, pink, shiny, and drooling pus from a cut near the tip. I thought I'd caught the infection from the brush while painting the gangrenous patient who died. I also at one point thought I was dying, but it didn't seem to matter very much.

And then the lancing of the wound, lavish dressings of antiseptic paste—there's a new one out, Sister Byrd swears by it—and gradually my temperature started to come down. I came round to find myself shivering in cold wet sheets with Lewis sitting by my bed.

It's been quite an experience. The odd thing is that though I know now that it was cutting myself while dressing an infected wound that caused all the trouble, part of me still believes I caught it from the brush. The true belief and the delusion sit quite happily side by side.

Today Lewis took me to the room to see the painting—which is finished. If I'd worked on it any more I'd have ruined it. It's the best thing I've ever done and yet I don't like it. It reeks of some kind of Faustian pact. No, that's ridiculous—and pompous. I'm not expressing myself very well. I need to see you face-to-face to tell you what I mean. Oh, yes, desperately, desperately, I need to see you face-to-face. But it's not possible. Write soon, my dearest love. Ever your Paul.

29

Paul to Elinor

Ambulances at last. I've left the hospital. So has Lewis; we're
here together in a ruined village in what used to be the school. All the
houses are in ruins, but the school is untouched except for a hole in the
roof. I've realized something about ruins. When it first happens
they're shocked, like patients coming out of theater, then gradually they
start to get over it, they don't mind so much and acquire a raffish,
anarchic air, flowers and weeds sprouting from improbable places like
trimmings on a hat. We've raided the houses to make the school
comfortable—chairs, beds, sofas, even rugs. We are very comfortable
indeed and you needn't worry about me. We have good supplies of
wood for the stove. In fact the smell of woodsmoke and tobacco is so
powerful it reminds me of the life class at the Slade. When I'm sitting
dozing in an armchair in the middle of the afternoon, I half expect
Tonks to walk in. Is that really the best you can do? He grows in
my memory. Isn't that strange?

      "Dozing in an armchair in the middle of the afternoon?" I hear
you say. Yes! We work at night and even then not every night. I'm
amazed how much easier this is than working in the hospital. We do
twenty-four hours on, twenty-four hours off, but in quiet times the

hours off can extend to days. (Equally, of course, in a bad patch we're
on duty all the time.) There's much more time for drawing than there
used to be. I'm doing a lot—I daren't think how many drawings I've
got—but there's also cards and football. We kick a ball around every
morning to keep ourselves fit. Then after breakfast we work on the
ambulances, who are a bevy of extremely demanding ladies, I can tell
you. I'm not much use at that, I can do the basic emergency repairs but
nothing complicated. Fortunately there are two chaps here who can
strip an engine down and reassemble it in record time.

Yesterday we had our first snow. As evening was falling, we
walked out into it. All the heaps of rubble and the furniture that had
been blown or dragged into the street were coated with snow and the
cobbles in the road glittered. I slept long and deep, as people do in
snow, but now it's begun to melt. We're all sorry to see it go. Nobody
here minds the cold, even in the trenches, because you can cope with it.
It's this endless, drenching rain we don't like.

Life here is so uneventful I really can't think of much to write
about. It's not at all what I expected, and not what I wanted either.
But there's certainly no need to worry about me. I am perfectly,
disgracefully safe.

Elinor to Paul
Yes, I know. No letter for a long time. Yours has been lying on
the table beside my bed reproaching me for I don't know how long. It's
so hard to imagine where you are. I can put you in that little room
overlooking the roofs and in the restaurant we went to together, but I
know you're not there now. I liked your description of the ruins though.
I wonder where the people have gone?

I've been working hard day after day, so hard my head feels
bashed in. When I can't stand it any longer I go up to the Heath and

watch people swimming, which they still do even in the middle of winter. Pallid creatures, some of them decidedly plump, and they splash and harrumph about like porpoises and their skin turns mottled blue and red and we're supposed to find it beautiful but it isn't. And then you see the wounded men in their blue uniforms being pushed along the paths in wheelchairs. They seem to congregate in the Vale of Health as if the clean air might make their stumps sprout. And back at the Slade where I spent so many happy girlish hours being patted on the back—oh, platonically of course—by Tonks and winning prizes and scholarships and all that sort of rubbish, some portly madam is even now mounting the dais and a new class of young ladies prepares to contemplate the Human Form Divine and I think—

But that's the problem, Paul. Always was. I don't think, I only see.

I expect all this is really about Ottoline and her friends. She kisses me now whenever we meet and introduces me and shows me off and I spend most of my time feeling inferior—rightly, for so I am— and trotting out my little tale about being in Ypres during the bombardment, a tale which has grown so stale in the telling that even I no longer believe it happened.

But I have been working, Paul, and I think at last I've done something good. In the ladies' cabin on the night crossing there was a woman breast-feeding her child and her whole body seemed to be a wax candle feeding the child's flame. It made an enormous impression on me. Anyway it's the first thing I've ever done that doesn't reek of Sladery and winning prizes and wanting to be praised.

I do miss you so much, but it gets harder and harder to keep you in my mind. You're like a ghost almost, fading in the light of dawn. Sometimes I close my eyes and try to summon up your face and I can't see you anymore. Then at other times I hear your voice so clearly I turn round expecting to see you standing there, and every time it happens there's the same pang of loss. Can't you send me a sketch of where you are? It would help me a lot if I could picture you somewhere definite, not just have letters dropping in from outer space.

Paul to Elinor

A sketch of where I am might help you, young woman, but it would very likely get me shot! I don't think our letters get censored very often, but it does happen. We have to hand them in with the envelopes open. Still, I do see what you mean. I was quite shocked when you said you were thinking of moving and leaving the Slade. A large part of my survival strategy is going back (in my mind, obviously!) to known places and finding you there. Anyway, a sketch would be difficult—to say the least!—so I'll have to do the best I can with words.

The most important place isn't a place at all. The bus. You saw ambulances like her in the square—red crosses, canvas sides. She takes five stretcher cases or ten walking wounded—and that's about all the good you can say of her. She regularly stalls and her crank handle could break a man's wrist. So picture me then in darkness and driving rain, up to my knees in mud and slush, pleading with her to start first time. All the time going round and round in my head there's a couple of lines of verse.

A red cross knight forever kneel'd
To the lady on his shield

I can't remember where it comes from and it's driving me mad. The only way I can chase it out of my head is to sing very loudly. One night I was bellowing "God Save the King" at the top of my voice when a column of French soldiers marched past. They obviously thought they should keep their end up and broke into "La Marseillaise."

Watching ambulances lumber round the turning circle at the hospital I used to think they were huge, but inside the cabin's rather cramped. The stretchers are level with the back of the driver's seat so the groans and cries go right into your ears. Sometimes they seem to be inside your own head. You can hear pleas for water but you can't answer them, only drive hell for leather down dark, rutted, congested roads. I never get used to the screams that are jolted out of people when I get it wrong and bump into a shell hole. Sometimes they die on the way to hospital. That's hard. I'm surprised how difficult it is. I thought because I didn't have time to get to know them I wouldn't mind so much. Instead I feel personally responsible in a way I never did on the ward, where you were always part of a team. One morning driving back to base just before dawn I found myself crying, and yet nothing worse had happened on that trip than on any other. Big fat baby tears trickling down my cheeks. I didn't even feel particularly upset. It seemed to be something my body had decided to do without consulting me.

The other place is a place—our common room, which is where I'm writing this. It's comfortable and warm, in spite of, or because of, the rain that pelts down outside. There's an oil lamp on the desk and Lewis is writing one of his endless letters home. Do you know he writes to his mother every day? I can't imagine what he finds to say. The wood stove is blazing away, and there's a card game going on at the next table. We're on duty but no calls have come in yet, though the guns have started up, louder than usual, I think, so perhaps there's something brewing. Every time the gun near us goes off, Lewis's inkwell gives a little jump. This table was taken out of a schoolroom and has boys' initials carved all over it. Some of the carving's so deep it must have taken ages to do. Dates too. I wonder where they are now, those boys? So this is where I am, thinking of you (as always). And now somebody's come in with a tray of cocoa. The door opens, and the wind lifts the thin carpet and sends dead leaves rattling across the floor, but inside we're warm. Full of hot cocoa and fingers crossed for a quiet night. Good night, my love. I can't say I wish you were here, and I can't really, except at the most superficial level, wish I were there, but I do wish with all my heart that we were together in some place where the war couldn't find us.

Elinor to Paul

I suppose my headline news is that I've sold two paintings. The mother and baby from the ferry crossing, and another one I did of some schoolgirls in a park. Based on one of the drawings I did when I came to see you. Dad took one look at the mother and child and roared with laughter. He says if my idea of motherhood ever catches on there'll be no need for Marie Stopes. I got five pounds each! Of course I can't think what to spend it on. Not that I don't need masses of things, but it's my first painting money so I feel I should buy something special with it, but nothing seems special enough.

Speaking of places, picture me in an Islington workhouse. There, that's a challenge, isn't it? The day before yesterday Catherine's mother said she was too ill to go on the fortnightly visit to Catherine's father, so Catherine was faced with going on her own. "I'm dreading it," she said, so of course I offered to go with her. We sat on the top of the bus in a slight drizzle, our knees safely tucked away under the rain apron. Catherine said what a relief it was to be back in London where nobody knew them. I was determined to make her laugh or smile at least and I did, several times, but then we got close and she went quiet.

It was only a short walk from the bus stop to the workhouse. Oh God, Paul, what a place. I thought of all the people over the years who'd dreaded going in through that door, how it must have seemed like the end of everything and been the end of everything, and it's exactly the same now. We were kept waiting a long time. A long time. Perhaps unavoidably, but I don't know—there was a whiff of little-minded people with a lot of power. Catherine had brought a cake with greaseproof paper wrapped round it and she sat cradling it like a baby. The room was packed. Children, wives, mothers, no men of course—no boys over the age of fourteen. When the big doors opened Catherine went in alone. I sat there and tried to take it in. Ugh, the smell. Gravy, sweaty socks, drains, oh, and on top of it all, Condy's Fluid. What would we do without it? I heard a woman sobbing and tried to look round the door. I was afraid it was Catherine, but it wasn't. People were exchanging gifts. Some of the internees had made wooden toys for their children. One elderly couple simply sat and looked at each other across the table, holding hands, not speaking.

The visit lasted an hour. I started sketching and one of the guards came up and told me to stop. Of course I asked why and he didn't have an answer, but I still had to stop. Then at last Catherine came back holding a letter rack her father had made for her mother. She was crying and laughing at once. "I don't know what use he thinks this is going to be," she said. "Nobody writes to us anymore."

I can't get it out of my mind. The papers are full of it, all the time now—the enemy within. The enemy within is Catherine's father, a dentist, for God's sake, who never hurt anybody (well, you know what I mean!), and he's locked up "for the duration of hostilities" without a trial or anything. If this is the kind of thing that can happen, what are we fighting for?

Paul to Elinor

If you ever again hear me complain about things being too quiet will you please hit me over the head with a large blunt instrument—a book or a doorstop or a sculptor's mallet would do. Last night I was

leaving a CCS—a Casualty Clearing Station—when I heard a
screech followed by a crash. The man ahead of me fell and lay
spread-eagled on the ground. Another shell landed, sending debris
cascading across the roof; then another. This particular station's in the
cellar of a ruined farmhouse. A cloud of dust billowed up into the air.
I was rooted to the spot. When I tried to run I found my knees had
turned to jelly. A very strange sensation because my mind was quite
calm. At the entrance to the station, I ran full tilt into one of the other
drivers trying to get out. One of the barns at the back of the building
had been demolished, but the clearing station itself was still intact, full
of wounded men stumbling about, hair and eyelids crusted with plaster
dust. Poor devils, that was the last thing they needed. But the surgeons
went on operating, though the lights swung from side to side and the
shadows rocked.

Elinor to Paul

I asked Lady O if I could bring Catherine to her Thursday night
party and of course she said yes. Catherine came round to my place
first and we got dressed up and set off to walk to Bedford Square.
Streets rather quiet. It's the full moon and London's expecting to be
bombed. You can feel it everywhere, the tension, the watchfulness, the
excitement. The few people who venture out after dark keep looking up
at the full moon—and so the war makes werewolves of us all.

We arrived at the house and were shown into the drawing room
where a man was playing a pianola, and Lady Ottoline was standing
over a huge box in the middle of the floor holding up a purple feather
boa. "Who wants this?" she boomed, and handed it to a tall etiolated
man with a straggly beard who wrapped it around his neck and
immediately started to dance a minuet —though the music was nothing
like that. Gradually others joined in. Ottoline, looking rather splendid

and baroque, kissed me and greeted Catherine very kindly. Catherine blushed and stammered and when Ottoline had moved on looked astounded. "I did warn you," I said. I got a gypsy shawl from the box and Catherine a fan, and we started to dance a tarantella. When I stopped to get my breath I was seized by a man who looked like a highly intelligent teddy bear and spoke with dry, devouring passion about how the war must stop, now, at once, this instant, keeping his gaze fixed on my bosom the while, until Ottoline swept him up and onto the dance floor where any fool could see he didn't belong, only then, to my astonishment he began to jump up and down, his face shining with that solemn joy you see on the faces of children when the Christmas candles are lit.

Towards the end of the evening, when everybody was worn out from the dancing, a woman with short black hair sang. I looked up and saw Ottoline standing just inside the door listening with one big white hand held to her throat and her pearls looped round her fingers. I find her very moving. She's like a giraffe that's fallen among jackals and stalks about with that improbable head level with the treetops and a pale swaying underbelly within reach of so many teeth and claws. She was caught up in the music as we all were but even her being caught up was different from anybody else's. Then the dark-haired girl sang a song that I sort of half knew.

> Cold blows the wind to my true love
> And gently falls the rain.
> I never had but one true love
> In cold grave he was lain.

I knew as soon as she started I was going to cry and I started edging towards the door. I don't think anybody saw me go. It was raining outside so I went upstairs and hid in a bedroom and only came down again when the singing stopped. I stood on the bottom step looking into the drawing room and saw the red walls and the chandelier lit and all the heads bobbing up and down and a great stamping of feet—on bare boards because all the carpets had been rolled back—and Ottoline with her red hair flying loose from its pins and streaming across her face. I thought, either they're sane and the rest of the world's gone mad or . . . ? It was silly and splendid and I didn't know if I was part of it or not, or even if I wanted to be. I thought about the dead people lying on the cobbles. The dead child. I think about them all the time, but crying won't bring them back.

I'm losing you, Paul. Or myself, I don't know. I'm tired and this is a stupid letter. I suppose I ought to focus on the good things. Catherine enjoyed herself. She's sure of a welcome there and that isn't true anywhere else now. I think perhaps I should just go to bed and hope it all looks better in the morning. Write soon. Ever your own Elinor.

30

LEWIS HAD FALLEN ASLEEP WITH HIS HEAD ON the table. A stump of candle guttered only an inch away from his slackened mouth. The French batteries behind the school had started up the dawn bombardment and the table juddered beneath his distorted cheek. Once, a louder crash than usual made him grunt. He raised his head, stared around him, sank back into sleep.

Five minutes later the first call came. They ran towards the camouflaged shed where the ambulances were parked. Paul cranked the handle, survived its first vicious kick, and climbed into the cabin. Soon he was bumping gently across the uneven ground. Peering through the muddy windscreen at the road ahead, he thought, for a second, of Elinor, before the reality of his surroundings grabbed him. Snow stippled fields. Here and there, a blurred moon stared up from frozen puddles at the side of the road. He kept the ambulance in low gear, laboring up the hill. As he got closer to the front, it needed all his attention to steer round pits and craters in the road. The road was crowded now with motor lorries, columns of marching men, horse-drawn limbers taking the rations up. At the crossroads, which had been subjected to repeated heavy bombardment, a shattered crucifix stood in the middle of desolation, the figure of Christ reduced to one hand hanging from a nail. He hated that hand: it offended him that such a banal image should have so much power.

But he hardly existed now as a person who could hate anything. He was a column of blood, bone, and nerves encased in a sheath of cold, sweaty skin. His hands kept slipping on the wheel. When at last he dropped down from the cab and began to walk towards the clearing station his legs again threatened to give way under him.

The CCS was in the cellar of a ruined farmhouse. You went down a flight of narrow steps—so narrow you had to plant your feet sideways—into a whitewashed room lit by oil lamps. At the far end a surgeon worked in a makeshift theater, patching men up for the journey back. On benches ranged along the wall the walking wounded waited. They'd had iodine sloshed into their wounds and been bandaged, but all were in shock, blue some of them, jaws wobbling, hands shaking. Paul shared out his cigarettes.

"What about me?" the surgeon called plaintively from behind his mask. "Don't I get one?"

He was bent low over the table, now and then pausing to drop handfuls of flesh into a bucket by his feet. Paul went across, pulled the surgeon's mask down, and stuck a lighted cigarette between his lips. The tip glowed red as he inhaled. "Thanks. I've been dying for that."

As he spoke, he straightened up and groaned—he must have been hunched over that table for hours.

Paul risked a glance at the patient, an abdominal. He thought of all the shell holes between here and the base hospital and felt like groaning himself.

He took one stretcher case, the rest walking wounded. Now they were on the move, going away from the front, the lightly wounded became positively cheerful, laughing, joking, clenching their teeth against the pain only to burst into laughter again a minute later. A canteen was passed from mouth to mouth and it certainly didn't contain water. But then the stretcher case recovered consciousness and from then on every jolt of the wheels on the shelled road produced a scream. He was begging for water. Paul shouted at the others not to give him any and they grumbled assent, obviously offended at being taken for idiots. Paul crouched forward in his seat, hunched over the wheel, peering through the windscreen at what little the fitful moon revealed of the road ahead. He felt useless. Nothing he could do in the way of nursing care was more likely to save the man's life than just getting him back to base as fast as possible. But in places the road was almost impassable. The bombardment had been heavy and accurate. At one place he came upon a tangle of broken wagon wheels and dead horses where a limber had been hit. He pulled to the side and slowed to a crawl. He'd just drawn level when one of the apparently dead horses reared its head and screamed. Frightened though he was, he'd have got down and put the poor beast out of its misery, but ambulance drivers didn't carry revolvers. Screwing up his face, he drove on.

Once past the horse he began to relax—he was almost at the end of the worst stretch of road—but then, no more than ten, twenty yards further on, he saw a dark shape ahead. As he slowed down, it was joined by a second, and then a third. Men, some of them badly wounded, crawling out of the ditches that lined the road. He stopped and wound down his window. He couldn't understand the words but it was obvious what they wanted. They had no faces, only flaking mud masks with white circles round the eyes and red wet mouths struggling to speak. When words failed, they pointed to their wounds.

He raised two fingers. "*Deux.*"

That was more than he ought to take, but he couldn't just drive past. Jumping down from the cab, he walked round to the back of the ambulance, feeling them behind him jostling and treading on his heels. These were the drivers of the horses he'd just passed.

"*Deux,*" he said again, but they all pressed forward, clutching at him, showing their wounds. He opened the door, jumped inside, and said, pointing at random, "You and you." Another scrambled in before he could get the doors shut. Then he struggled through the others, the ones he couldn't take, back to the driver's cabin. He'd call the relay station as soon as he got to the hospital. An ambulance would go out to pick up the rest.

But they couldn't know that and one or two of them mightn't last. As he drove off, the wheels churning in slush, he hardly dared look into the rearview mirror, where, framed in that small space, a group of mud men dwindled into the distance, staring after the ambulance, which took away with it, as they must believe, their best chance of life.

31

Paul to Elinor

After all the excitements of last week we seem to be in another
quiet patch. I managed to get back to the town for two nights and
spent them painting and lying in the bed in our little room thinking
of you. I try to convince myself there's a ghost of your scent on the
pillows though I know it isn't true. You seem ghostlike to me now.
I've lost the sense of your voice, the way you move. I always see you
sitting still somewhere, more especially in the window at the Slade.
Do you remember how you used to sit there waiting for Tonks to
come out and sign your exhibition entry forms? I walked past you
once, but you were too deep in your thoughts to look up and notice
me. I see you like that now, framed by the arch of the window, very
tiny and far away.

Because it's so quiet we've been given another job: transporting
the dead (which The Hague Convention does allow; it doesn't allow the
transport of military personnel who are alive and all in one piece, even
if they've collapsed with exhaustion). We didn't mind too much
because we thought we'd be dealing with the recent dead, but it seems
this particular Casualty Clearing Station had a backlog of corpses. It
wasn't clear why. Men who die at a CCS are generally buried as close

to it as possible. They're surrounded by these little dark crosses that always look like birds' footprints to me, though I mentioned that to Lewis and he couldn't see it at all.

Anyway there they were piled up in a corner of a yard under a black tarpaulin cover weighted down with bricks. We put on surgical masks and gloves and just got on with it, though it was depressing, to say the least. You go into a trance, it's the only way, then suddenly I looked down and realized that one of the men at the bottom of the heap was wearing British army uniform. The others were all French. He must have got separated from his unit or perhaps this ground was fought over by the British in the first few weeks of the war. He'd been there a long time. In fact he was so badly decomposed that when we tried to lift him he came apart in our hands.

Somebody loved him once. And still does, that's the devil of it.

What a gloomy letter! I always feel I have no right to burden you like this, but these things happen and if I didn't write about them I don't know what else I'd find to say. On a more cheerful note (and high time, too, you may think!) we've finished that job now and we can start putting it behind us. This morning we treated ourselves to a bath and a shave in town and came out into the raw air afterwards pink as shrimps with tight, raw, shiny faces. Now it's afternoon and we're going to kick a football round the field behind the school for an hour or so and then have supper.

Lewis has just come in to get me. He sends his affectionate greetings and asks to be remembered to you. Do you know he told me the other day he's never been afraid? He wasn't boasting either. As you know, he's not exactly the boasting type. I'm afraid all the time, though it doesn't seem to make much difference to what I do. Write soon. Even your handwriting on an empty envelope might help to convince me that there's still a girl called Elinor Brooke.

Ever your own, Paul.

Elinor to Paul

What does "ever your own" mean, Paul, if you don't believe the person you're saying it to exists? I haven't stopped living just because you can't imagine me. I go on living. I move on. I don't spend much time sitting in the window outside Tonks's room, or anywhere else for that matter. I work, Paul. I work as I've never worked before. I always feel apologetic when I say that because I know your time for work is limited, and you must find it almost impossible to concentrate even when you do find time, but I can't help that. If painting matters you have to give your life to it and that's what I'm doing. Not quite to the exclusion of everything else, I do get out now and then, but every day's spent working. Most of the time I don't even remember to eat.

One of the reasons this letter's late is that I've been hesitating over whether to tell you something. I saw Teresa again. She got my new address from somebody at the Slade and just turned up on the doorstep. She looks well, asked after you; her husband was called up in the first days of the war—he was a reservist—and nobody's heard from him for two months now so she's beginning to think he's dead. I couldn't make out what she felt about it, I don't think she knew herself. I hope this doesn't upset you. But if I'm so unreal you can hardly picture me, Teresa must be even more so. Just another of those funny little figures at the wrong end of your telescope.

Apart from that there's very little news. Catherine's making me a dress. It's a way of slipping her a few shillings without making her feel she's accepting charity. Father has raised my allowance (just when I don't need it). Of course he's not supporting Toby at medical school now. Toby came home to see the baby who's going to be called William. His father pretends to be indifferent to him but is secretly pleased, I think.

I'm sorry you had such a dreadful job to do. I don't know much about what's going on out there because I don't read the newspapers anymore. Like you, I find it hard to cross the desert that divides us. It feels like standing on top of a mountain sending semaphore signals across the abyss. But don't, whatever you do, stop writing. Although I felt quite angry when I read your letter, I do very often think about you—in that long black coat you used to wear.

Write soon. This war destroys so much, don't let it destroy us as well. Elinor.

32

WRITE SOON, SHE SAID. BUT IT BECAME HARDER and harder to write at all.

Dear Miss Brooke (I reserve this formal style of address for young ladies I haven't heard from lately/for a long time),

Damn. He'd meant that as a joke, but on the page it sounded bitter. True, though. She didn't write often now, and when she did her letters were full of people he hadn't met and places he hadn't been to. She went on living, he was buried alive. That's how it felt. He sometimes thought he might as well be one of those poor chaps under the tarpaulin. No doubt their girls had "moved on" too.

Pushing the writing pad away, he sat for a moment with his head in his hands. When he next looked up, he saw a woman watching him. He'd noticed her earlier, sitting at a table in the corner, eating croissants, edging a crumb delicately into her mouth with her ring finger as she looked out onto the street. It had long since been cleared of rubble, though there were boarded-up buildings at intervals along the terrace like black teeth in a smile. She looked up at the sky, wondering, perhaps, if they were to have more snow, and the movement revealed the creased, white fullness of her throat. He liked the slight sagging of her skin that revealed the orbits of her eyes more clearly and the downturn of inbuilt sadness at the corners of her mouth that vanished when she caught him looking at her and smiled.

He got up and asked if he could sit at her table. Did she mind? She looked round at the empty café, smiled back at him, a little doubtfully, and said, No, of course not. Of course she didn't mind. She was wondering whether he knew what she was. He could see her wondering and deciding not to care, to take the moment for what it was. Her name was Madeleine, she said. Behind the bar, a lugubrious middle-aged waiter flicked a dirty dishcloth at the counter and looked at them with contempt, assuming the young Englishman was too naïve to know he was making a fool of himself. She aroused hostility, Paul could see that. When the waiter brought her more coffee, he set the cup down on the table so carelessly the coffee slopped into the saucer. Paul asked for another, and got it. His French was improving, though his new vocabulary, acquired while nursing badly wounded men, varied between the clinical and the obscene. Her English was good, but she wasn't confident in using it, so they talked haltingly at first, making a joke of their difficulties, laughing a lot. She was carefree, and became more so as the minutes passed, forgetting who she was and what she did, as he, too, was forgetting who he was and what he did.

When at last she got up to go, he said, "Can I see you again?"

Immediately she frowned, and he was dismayed, thinking he'd misjudged the situation.

"I'm here most mornings."

"I was thinking an evening, perhaps?"

"No, I'm not free then."

After that he made a habit of meeting her on his days off. Once, to the waiter's undisguised amusement, he brought her flowers. They flirted, talked about Paris, Brussels, cafés, holidays, food, wine—never anything connected to the present. She mentioned a husband once, but he didn't pursue it. And then, one evening, walking through the town after a day spent painting, he saw her going into a house beside the café, looking heavier, older, her flesh sagging like dough. As she turned the key in the lock, she glanced up and must have seen him, but she gave no sign of recognition.

It changed everything, that sight of her, though he didn't know why. It wasn't as if he'd been under any illusion about what she did. On his next day off, he slipped down the back street but, instead of going into the café, knocked on the side door. It was opened by Madame's husband, a drooping, tadpole-shaped man.

Paul was ushered into the parlor, a room of such stifling respectability he immediately wanted to laugh. A glass case full of artificial flowers, a picture of the Virgin—oh, for God's sake!—a fan of red crepe paper in the empty grate. The paper was peppered with soot, the only dirt allowed in the room, which was otherwise spotless. Dust motes sifted in a shaft of sunlight. The room smelled of beeswax and Condy's Fluid, or whatever the Belgian equivalent of Condy's Fluid might be.

Paul sat on the pink sofa and contemplated Madame's knickknacks. He was already regretting his visit. Inertia, rather than sexual need, kept him pinned to the cushions. Like a big, fat, juicy insect, he thought. As they all were, the men who sat here, listening to the floorboards creak in the room above. In the café he'd always been repelled by the sight of men sneaking off to the house next door. He'd wanted no part of it. Now he didn't know why he was here, except that it had less to do with Elinor, the coldness of her letters, than with the man in British army uniform he'd found lying under a heap of French dead. Something was needed to sluice that memory away. Drink didn't do it. Painting didn't do it.

When, eventually, he was led upstairs and found her lying on the bed in a room that seemed to be all pink and shiny, like intestines, he couldn't think of anything to say.

"Come in," she said, weariness trapped behind her smile. "I wondered when you'd come."

After counting notes at the dressing table, he undressed, washed, and climbed on top of her, smelling her powder and the sweetness of stale urine in the pot under the bed. The sex was much as he'd expected. Afterwards, he pressed his face against the creases in her neck and closed his eyes. She tolerated his weight for a second, then heaved him off. There was a queue, he understood. However tactfully things were managed, there was a queue. He fumbled into his clothes as fast as he could and clattered downstairs, out onto the slushy street, feeling as if he'd committed a small, unimportant murder.

33

THE CLOCK OPPOSITE THE DOOR SHOWED TWENTY minutes to midnight. They'd been on duty six hours, though so far only one ambulance team had been called out.

"Shall we go and play cards?" Lewis said, nodding towards a group in the corner.

"No, I don't think I will, thanks. I've got a bit of a sore throat. You go."

Paul spent the next two hours huddled under a blanket in a chair by the wood stove. From time to time he dozed, only to jerk awake as rain spattered against the one intact window. The beds had been pulled together in the center of the room. The sacking that draped the broken windows kept the worst of the rain out, but you still woke cramped with cold to find the upper blanket damp. Every time he surfaced, his sore throat felt worse. Despite his proximity to the stove, he was shivering. He'd had a dream of falling into cold, rat-infested water and he knew it was connected with his discovery of the British officer. His visit to the prostitute—as he now thought of her—seemed merely to have driven the chill of that moment deeper into his bones.

It was still dark when the call came. He was going to be driving with Lewis. One of the advantages of relatively quiet nights was that you had the luxury of a second driver. Walking out to the ambulance, they were cold, yawning, stiff from sleep in cramped positions. Their breath whitened the air. Lewis was stamping his feet and clapping his hands against his shoulders, like a ham actor portraying the idea of extreme cold. Paul was fingering the swollen glands in his neck, though he made himself stop when he saw Lewis watching him.

"Are you all right?"

"Fine. No, actually, I'm cold, tired, and pissed off beyond belief."

"Normal, then?"

As they turned into the village's main street, they saw scribbles of black and yellow smoke low in the sky. The darkness had begun to thin. Dawn was the most dangerous time to be on the road. When they reached the main road they had to wait to let a column of motor lorries go past. Once on the road they made slow progress. Motor lorries and ambulances were slowed to walking pace because the road was clogged with horse-drawn limbers taking the morning rations up to the line. A column of men who'd been relieved were trudging towards them. Lewis wound down the window, and a powerful yellow stench came into the cabin. Helmets bobbed beneath the window, the faces beneath them drained and almost expressionless. Once they were past, Lewis should be able to overtake the limbers. At last the way was clear and they pulled out. Ahead of them the column of motor lorries was moving slowly in a cloud of spray.

"I'll never get past," Lewis said. "I'm going to slot in behind them."

Paul nodded. You weren't supposed to join convoys of military vehicles, but sometimes it was the only way to make progress. Another column of men marched past and then the lorries accelerated, the rear vehicle sending up a sheet of water that sloshed onto the ambulance windscreen.

The road wound uphill from this point on. As they neared the crossroads, the pits in the road became deeper and the pace of the convoy slowed. At the top of the slight crest the motor lorries stopped. Lewis muttered under his breath as the ambulance's sluggish brakes let them slide almost into the rear lorry's tail. Lewis jumped down to see what was happening. He walked a little way along the column, peered into the darkness, came back shaking his head.

Paul was leaning out of the open door. "What's wrong?"

"Don't know. Can't see."

A column of black smoke hung over the road ahead. Men jumped down from the lorries, but none of them seemed particularly concerned, more glad of a chance to stretch their legs.

"I'll see if anybody knows what's happening," Lewis said, and disappeared round the corner of the lorry in front. Paul could hear him asking the driver what was going on. He got down himself, his legs numb and threatening to collapse under him. He'd had nothing to eat and was buzzing from too much coffee on an empty stomach, that exhausted, stale, irritable alertness. He took a deep breath to freshen himself and simultaneously there came a long whistling roar so close it seemed to be caused by the movement of his chest.

When he was next aware of himself he was staggering around in smoke with the screams of wounded men all around him. The motor lorries ahead of him were on fire. From somewhere men came running and started trying to pull men out of the burning vehicles, but there were too many of them in a crowded space. He could hear an officer shouting at them to get back. Lewis. He started pushing forward against straining, jostling backs. Men were milling around the stricken vehicles, beaten back by the flames. His leg felt different. He put his hand down and brought it back up covered in blood but there was no pain and he walked on. At one point he collapsed against the side of a lorry only to find himself being dragged away by the same young officer he'd heard shouting at people to get back. He found himself being hauled down the side of the road into a declivity, wrenched so hard he stumbled and fell and rolled the rest of the way. Immediately he was up on his knees and crawling forward. The officer tried to hold him back. "Fuck off!" His voice sounded strange and he realized he'd gone deaf, which must be why everything was muffled, the shouting and cries, the explosion of petrol tanks, the crump of shells bursting further up the road, the slosh of boots through mud, all smothered, adding to the unreality of shock and fear.

He went round, assessing the damage of some of the men lying screaming on the ground, quickly selecting those who stood the best chance of life. It was easier to keep calm now he was doing what he knew how to do. One man was lying on the ground cradling his intestines in his arms as tenderly as a woman nursing a sick child. Another was trapped inside a burning lorry. Sheathed in flame his face appeared at the shattered windscreen screaming for help. Paul grabbed an officer's arm and pointed. "For Christ's sake, shoot the poor sod." He had no way of knowing if it happened or not, he was already moving forward again. The smell made him gag, but his mind was clear. At last he saw Lewis, sitting by the side of the road. His cap had fallen off and Paul recognized him by the wet-wheat color of his hair. "I'm blind," he kept saying to anyone who would hear. He was unaware of Paul's presence until he felt the touch of his hand. "No, you're not." There was a wound at the front of his head, not serious though blood was streaming out of it, and another in the lower abdomen. No apparent damage to the eyes, but he daren't risk exploring and disturbing any shell fragments that might be lodged in there. He hauled him to his feet and half carried him back to the ambulance. He was turning to go back and collect more wounded, when he stumbled and fell. His left leg wouldn't work. A moment later hard hands lifted him by the armpits and seemed to want to put him into the ambulance. "No." He fought them— deaf, mad, blind, covered in blood he didn't know was his own—until they pushed him onto a stretcher and strapped him down.

The doors banged shut. The ambulance started to grind and bump along, sweeping round in a sharp turn, then accelerating away. He could feel the movements as if he were driving. A row of wounded men sat beside the stretchers, their jaws juddering with shock. He stared up at the stretcher above him and saw a patch of blood, spreading.

"Lewis?"

Muttered words, then a groan as the ambulance bounced along. Despite the pain in his leg, Paul didn't believe he was injured. Bloody fools, tying him down like this.

"Lewis?"

The red stain was spreading. Still the groans and gabbled words went on. "Mum," he heard. And again, "Mum?" Then silence. Groping above his head, he found Lewis's hand and touched it. It was still warm. He thought he felt an answering pressure before the fingers went slack.

He was in the Salle d'Attente. He had a vague memory of being lifted out of the ambulance, talking too much, waving his arms, spit flying. He couldn't understand why they were putting him into bed when there were so many patients to be attended to. They seemed to want him to get undressed, and when he wouldn't they cut his uniform off. His left thigh was covered in blood.

"It's nothing," he said, but still they kept pushing him down and all the orderlies were there, their familiar faces strange as he looked up at them from the bed. They were cutting his breeches off, easing bloody cloth away from the wound as so often he'd done to other people, uncovering just such a mess as this one on his left thigh. He stared at it, bewildered, and his bewilderment increased his deafness so when Burton (was it Burton?) leaned over and spoke to him his lips moved but he made no sound, opening and shutting his mouth like a goldfish. Cool fingertips on his thigh searched for soil in the wound and then the fish lips swelled and filled his whole vision and he slipped over the edge into unconsciousness and the whistling roar of the exploding shell which seemed to be lodged inside his skull followed him down into the dark.

34

LONDON WAS DRAB, FULL OF MUD-COLORED PEO-
ple. As the night closed in and the streetlamps were lit, their
blue-painted globes seemed not so much to shed light as to make
darkness visible. Nelson on his column looked out over a city
that had moved closer to its origins, a settlement on an estuary
whose fragile lights kept at bay a vast darkness.

Walking down Regent Street to the Café Royal, Paul stumbled and almost fell. It had been a long day, his knee was starting to trouble him. He hated the atmosphere in London now, it
was so different from last August. Then there had been crowds,
heat, dust, cheering, the burnt smell of London foliage in late
summer. Now there were these trampling shadows with their
blue-tinged skin. Oh, and everywhere, the posters. One in particular pursued him from street to street. A jackbooted German
officer trod on a dead woman's bare breasts, while behind them
a village burnt. Beside the picture was a letter from a serving
British soldier.

*We have got three girls in the trenches with us, who came for
protection. One has no clothes on, having been outraged by the*

Germans. . . . Another poor girl has just come in having had both her breasts cut off. Luckily I caught the Uhlan officer in the act and with a rifle shot at 300 yards killed him. And now she is with us but poor girl I am afraid she will die. She is very pretty and only about 19 and only has her skirt on.

Nothing Paul had heard or seen in Belgium suggested that this scenario was probable or even possible, but then, it's difficult to persuade young men to lay down their lives to preserve the balance of power in Europe. Some other cause had to be found, more firmly rooted in biological instinct. Pretty young girls with their blouses ripped off did the trick nicely. God, the cynicism of it.

Not a bad painting, though. In fact all the posters he'd seen were good. Elinor might complain that painting was being dismissed as irrelevant, but it seemed to him that the exact opposite was true. Painting, or at least its near relation—printmaking—had been recruited.

He should have asked Tonks what he thought about the posters. Tonks was the only person he'd seen so far, and there, too, he'd thought Elinor was wrong. Her portrait of a Tonks unswervingly dedicated to the teaching of art while the war crashed and rumbled round his ears didn't hold up for a second. Tonks had gone back to medicine, and now spent more time working in a hospital than he did at the Slade.

"What else could I do?" he said. "I'm a surgeon, for God's sake. I have to do something."

The sight of Tonks bending over his paintings—the familiar question mark of his curved spine—could still inspire fear in Paul. He waited for the whip crack of contempt, but it never came. Instead, Tonks put his hand over his eyes. "I'll see what I can do."

"There's this too."

Tonks took the drawing to the window. It was of a young man who had had the whole of his lower jaw blown off by a shell. It was several minutes before Tonks turned to face Paul again. "I don't see how you could ever show that anywhere."

"No, I know. But I wanted you to see it."

Tonks mentioned names and promised letters of introduction. He would do everything he could to help, but his time was limited. He was expecting to go to France himself soon. When, at the end of the corridor, Paul looked back, Tonks was still standing at the doorway to his room, watching him go. Perhaps from the window too, though Paul didn't look up, merely smiled at the men in their wheelchairs and hurried past.

A few minutes later, in Russell Square, great rosy-cheeked, rawboned lads charged and twisted bayonets. He stopped to watch. Afterwards they lay on the grass, their strong young limbs sprawling, smoking Woodbines and crooning sentimental songs. "Row, row, row." Oh, and "Itchy Coo." Over and over again. He could cheerfully have bayoneted the man who wrote that.

Nighttime was best. London in the dark still had an excitement, a glamour, that it had entirely lost by day. The cold and gloom made the Café Royal seem fragile, a bubble floating on a black river. At first he thought nothing had changed, but then he looked again more closely and realized everything had. Burnt-butter smears of khaki darkened the red and gold. Young men everywhere: carefully cultivated mustaches over mouths not yet thinned into certainty, breeches and puttees self-consciously worn. Out there, the war stank of blood and gangrene; here, it smelled of new clothes.

Kit Neville was there. It was strange after their last meeting in Ypres to see him here, in his element, beaming, rubicund, gleaming with success. He seized Paul and bore him off to a quiet table by the far wall. As soon as they were sitting down he summoned the waiter and, without consulting Paul, ordered two large whiskeys.

"You're back, then?"

"Ye-es."

"Sorry, I know, obvious." Neville seemed to be wanting to say something that couldn't be said here or, perhaps, anywhere. "How are you finding it?"

"Strange. I don't seem to be able to slot back in."

"No, nor me."

Nobody could have looked more at home.

"Congratulations. Everybody's talking about your paintings."

"Hmm." Several more gulps of whiskey went down. "You know what I think? What I really think?"

"No, what do you think?"

"I think that once the bloody war's over nobody's going to want to look at anything I paint."

Paul started to produce some reassuring pap.

"No, listen, it's a Faustian pact. I get all this attention for a few months, however long the bloody thing lasts, but once it's over—*finish*. Nobody wants to look at a nightmare once they've woken up."

How typical of Neville to find grounds for self-pity amidst the blaze of success. Paul couldn't think of anything to say, so ordered two more large whiskeys instead.

"Seen Elinor?" Neville asked, carefully casual.

"No, I've only just got here."

"You know she's in with that Bloomsbury crowd?"

"I know she goes to Lady Ottoline's parties. Do you?"

"Good Lord, no. You have to be a full-blown conchie to get in there. They don't like my stuff, that's for sure. Or me."

Their drinks arrived. Neville swished his whiskey round and round the glass, but judiciously, careful to spill none. "You must have seen something of Elinor?"

"She came to see me in hospital."

"Oh, yes, of course, you were wounded, weren't you?" Was that a twinge of envy? "How is it?"

Paul pulled a face.

"Still. Keeps you out of it, I suppose."

"Depends how much movement I get back. The knee's quite stiff at the moment, but they seem to think it'll improve."

"Ah, well, early days. Have you managed to do any painting?"

"I have, yes, quite a bit."

"More cornfields?"

"In winter?"

"Well, I don't know, do I? Mangel-wurzel-picking, perhaps?"

Paul repressed a smile. "No, nothing like that."

A few minutes later Neville caught somebody else's eye and moved off. Twisting round in his chair, Paul watched as he was welcomed into the circle around Augustus John. Oh, he was flourishing, was Neville, the great war artist. Paul thought of his own paintings and the determination to get his own exhibition together grew stronger. He'd painted them with such a curious cold intensity—in some cases knowing that a particular painting could never be put on public display—and yet here he was scrabbling around for contacts, envying Neville his success.

He finished his whiskey and went outside, walking up

and down the street until his mind felt clearer. His relationship
with Neville was strange because he couldn't call it friendship
and yet Neville was one of the most significant figures in his
life. That remark about the Faustian pact had echoed his own
feelings in a way that nobody else could. He'd lain in bed in
Belgium looking at the swollen hand that didn't seem to belong
to him and thought exactly that.

It was twenty minutes before he returned to the café. And
there she was, her shining cap of hair reflected in the mirror behind her. She looked older but not as tired as most people did
at the end of this long winter. Quite the contrary, in fact. She
glowed. The lights caught the gloss in her hair, the sheen of her
eyelids, the full, red pouting mouth. She hadn't seen him. He
watched her for a while talking to the men on either side of her,
teasing, flirting, playing one off against the other, then suddenly
sitting back against the red plush seat, self-exiled, bored, thin
arms folded across her chest. He walked across and kissed her.
She was expecting him—they'd arranged to meet here—and
yet her lips were slack with surprise.

Recovering, she said, "Oh, come on, Angus, move along.
I want to talk to Paul."

The seating was rearranged and he sat down beside her.
Her whole body was turned towards him, screening the other
men out with her shoulder, but the eyes that looked up at him
were wary. The feeling of hope that had flared in him when he
first saw her began to fade.

"I haven't seen you for quite a while," she said.

Getting in first, he couldn't help thinking.

"I don't move in the same exalted circles as you do."

"Where are you staying?"

"Gower Street."

"Ah, the old stamping ground."

"Just across the road."

"Are you sure that's a good idea? On a quiet morning you'll be able to hear Tonks shouting, 'I suppose you think you can draw?' "

He smiled. "I saw him this morning. I went to show him some stuff I've done."

"And . . . ?"

He raised his shoulders.

"Did he like it?"

"I don't know about 'like.' He's going to put me in touch with some people. With a view to getting an exhibition together."

"Paul, that's fantastic."

She leaned across and kissed him. There was no doubting her sincerity.

"Have you seen Nev's show?" she asked.

"No, I've heard about it. Have you?"

"It was amazing. Totally new, somehow, though obviously he's building on what he did before. It's as if he was born for this." She smiled. "Do you know, as I was leaving there were these two old codgers wandering about shaking their heads and I heard one of them say, 'It's not much like cricket, is it?' "

"It's terrifying people still think like that." He felt her withdraw and said quickly, "I'm pleased for Neville."

"So am I."

A pause. She was looking round the room. "Are you working?"

"Yes, I am. I thought at first I wouldn't be able to, but once I started I couldn't stop."

"Landscapes?"

"No. Well, some, but not the sort you mean. The hospital and the road."

She put her hand on his arm. "Don't let's talk about the war, Paul. *Please?* It gets into everything."

"Well, yes, of course it does."

Her expression hardened. "If you let it."

"Oh, I see. Not mentioned in Bedford Square?"

"Sometimes. Not often. Mainly we talk about art."

"*Ah.*"

"Don't let's quarrel, Paul."

"I've no intention of quarreling." He shifted restlessly in his seat. "Do we have to stay here?"

"No, I'm quite happy to move on. It was just a place to meet."

She stood up and said good-bye to the two young men.

"Who are they?" he asked, as they left.

"No idea." She pulled a face. "Hangers-on."

They hardly spoke on the journey in the cab. Under cover of the silence, a bead of tension formed and grew. He was aware of the shape of her shoulders under her coat. Remembered seeing them too, the bones standing out from the skin. Her collarbones in particular looked poised for flight. He could picture it all exactly, down to the bluish shadow between her breasts. He leaned towards her—her hair smelled of scent and smoke—and tried to kiss her, but she moved away.

Her rooms were on the top floor. Slanted, beamed ceilings; stonewashed walls; red, rust, and brown rugs on the floor.

"This is lovely," he said.

She pulled the curtains closed before switching on the lamps. "Will you light the fire? I'll put the kettle on."

The fire was already laid. He put a match to the paper, then sat back on his heels, watching the flames lick and flicker round the sticks. The paper turned orange first, then brown. Black holes formed, glowing red at the edges, and little fluttering helpless wings that whirled away up the chimney on a shower of sparks. There. That ought to go.

While she was busy in the kitchen he wandered through into the other room and found a painting on the easel. It was a view of the hill behind her parents' farmhouse, covered in deep snow.

"Finished?" he asked, hearing her come into the room behind him.

"Nearly."

"Don't do too much more to it, will you? It's perfect as it is."

"You know we had snow the week before Christmas? I was at home looking after Mother, so in the afternoons when she was asleep I painted."

"How is she?"

"Up and down. Worse since Toby left."

The kettle whistled. She disappeared to make the cocoa. When she came back with the tray, he cleared a space on the table by the fire and said, "I did do one painting you'd approve of. A canal with poplars."

"At least you're working."

"Are you really content to let it all pass you by?"

"The war? Yes."

"Why?"

"I don't think it matters very much. I don't think it's important."

Silence. She looked slightly uncomfortable.

"Of course it matters, in one way, it matters that people are dying. I just don't think that's what art should be about. It's like painting a train crash. Of course it's dreadful, but it's not . . ." She was groping for words, which had never come easily to her. "It's not *you*, is it? An accident's something that happens *to* you. It's not you, not in the same way people you love are. Or places you love. It's not *chosen*."

"You think we choose the people we love?"

She shook her head.

"Toby's out there now, isn't he?"

"Yes. He left about a month ago."

"Is he at the front?"

"I don't know."

"Well, suppose something happened to him? I'm sorry, but, you know, suppose he was killed, would you still say the war doesn't fundamentally matter?"

"Yes, then more than ever."

"I don't believe you."

"The last thing I'd want to do is paint any part of what killed him. I'd go home, I'd paint the places we knew and loved when we were growing up together. I'd paint what made him, not what destroyed him."

"Well," he said, taken aback by her ferocity. "Let's hope it never comes to that."

"I'm so frightened for him."

"But you still don't want to know what's happening?"

"I do know, as much as he can tell me. He writes every week. What about you? Will you go back?"

"If I can. I'll do something."

"I won't. Daddy keeps dropping hints about nursing, but I won't do it. That's how it is, you see, even for a woman." She laughed and shook her head. "We all have to give in to the great bully."

They sat in silence. The firelight crept over her face and throat. She was blossoming. It hurt him to see her, though it would have hurt him far more to see her thin and pale with grief.

"How are you really?" she asked. "The truth."

"I don't know. All right."

"Only all right?"

"Lewis is dead."

She bowed her head. "Yes, I know."

"I only realized how fond—" The truth. "I only realized how much I loved him when it was too late."

She looked startled. "I suppose men do become very attached to each other in those circumstances."

"No, it wasn't like that. I'd have loved him anywhere." He laughed. "Don't worry, I haven't been converted. I shan't be jumping on any of your new friends."

"I can think of one or two who'd be delighted if you did."

He lay back in the chair, his injured leg stretched out in front of him. "You know in Ypres you said I didn't love you?"

"I didn't."

"I'm sure you did."

"No. I thought it."

"Anyway, it isn't true. There's not an hour goes by I don't think about you." He looked directly at her. "I think we should get married."

He didn't know what he'd expected. Certainly not this cool, considering stare. "Why?"

"Oh, lots of reasons." He was smiling now, getting ready

to pretend he hadn't been serious. "We could share a studio. Save rent."

She shook her head.

"No, listen, that's not a bad idea."

"It wouldn't work."

"Why wouldn't it?"

"You'd need somebody to take care of you while you were working."

"Not true."

"You don't mean it. You're at a low ebb at the moment, so you're clutching at straws, but as soon as you felt better you'd wonder what on earth had possessed you. You don't love me."

"I do, you know."

"As a friend."

"No, as a woman."

"No."

Exasperated, he said, "You seem remarkably determined not to be loved."

"I don't think you can love a woman."

That shocked him. "That's very sad, if it's true."

"You don't trust us."

"No, I'm not sure I do. Mind you, I don't trust men either, so I don't know where that gets us." He sat thinking. "And I probably wouldn't be faithful to you."

He saw the recoil on her face. For all her contempt for the conventions she didn't like that.

"No, I know you wouldn't."

"I suppose we could always have an open marriage."

"You mean you sleeping with anybody you fancy and me sitting at home pretending not to mind? No thanks."

"Anyway," he went on, after a pause, "I can't ask you to marry me, my knee won't bend."

Instantly she threw herself at his feet, gazing up at him with clasped hands and adoring eyes. "Darling Paul, please say you'll be mine."

"I am yours." He was serious. "Forever."

Her smile faded. "No, Paul."

"But it's true. Why shouldn't I say it?"

She got slowly to her feet. "So what are we going to do?"

"Go on as we were?"

"You mean go to bed."

That was what he meant. He looked up at her and smiled. "You're a disgrace."

"I've asked you to marry me. I can't do more."

"No, I suppose you can't."

They got undressed slowly, unself-consciously, like an old married couple, and lay side by side on the bed holding hands. It was a long time before he turned to her. Her eyes were huge in the half darkness. For Paul, every gesture, every caress, every kiss was heavy with pain. He felt they were saying good-bye.

Afterwards she was silent for so long he thought she'd gone to sleep, but then she turned to face him. "What are we going to do?"

"I don't know," he said. "I love you. But that doesn't seem to be enough. Wait to see what happens, I suppose."

"What do you think's going to happen?"

He shook his head. At the moment he thought they were two twigs being swept along on a fast current, now thrown together, now pulled apart. What happened next wouldn't depend on what either of them desired. Perhaps there was wisdom just in accepting that. He started to speak only to realize she'd fallen asleep with her head on his shoulder.

Towards dawn, the pain in his leg jolted him awake. He slipped out of bed and limped across to the window. It was snowing. He'd thought it might be: something about the silence and the quality of the light. Feeling a flicker of the excitement he would have felt as a child he pressed his face to the cold pane and watched the heavy flakes tumbling towards him, gray against the white sky. He thought of Lewis in his grave under a thin covering of snow. Of the ambulance crews coming to the end of a long night. Of Sister Byrd, slipping and slithering on the duckboards as she left the Salle d'Attente and walked back to the hut where she slept alone.

The sooner he was out there again the better, he thought. He didn't belong here.

God, it was cold. Chafing his upper arms, he went back to bed and slid between the sheets, snuggling into Elinor for warmth. After a while he stopped shivering and turned onto his back. The room was full of her quiet breathing. He looked up at the ceiling, as the light strengthened, waiting patiently for her to wake.

Acknowledgments

A number of biographies of artists who were at the Slade in the years before the First World War were useful in the preparation of this novel, providing, singly and together, a lively account of that remarkable generation:

First Friends by Ronald Blythe
Interior Landscapes: A Life of Paul Nash by James King
Mark Gertler by Sarah MacDougall
C. R. W. Nevinson: The Cult of Violence by Michael J. K. Walsh
Isaac Rosenberg, Poet and Painter by Jean Moorcroft Wilson

All these artists, and many others equally distinguished, studied under Henry Tonks. In 1916, Tonks, who had been a surgeon before he became an artist, went to work with Harold Gillies, who was then pioneering the techniques of modern plastic surgery on the faces of mutilated young men. Tonks's job was to make drawings of the patients before, during, and after surgery. In addition he embarked on a series of sixty-nine portraits of facially mutilated men which are among the most moving images to have come out of any war. They were not exhibited in his lifetime, nor for many years afterwards.

Henry Tonks: Art and Surgery by Emma Chambers pays tribute to the man and his work while raising a number of interesting and disturbing questions about the ways in which the wounds of war are represented—or, more often, hidden.

Several writers recorded their experiences of nursing wounded men:

A Diary Without Dates by Enid Bagnold
The Forbidden Zone by Mary Borden
Chronicle of Youth: Great War Diary 1913–1917 by Vera
      Brittain, edited by Alan Bishop
The Backwash of War by Ellen N. La Motte

Two books dealing with other aspects of the medical history of the war were particularly useful:

Gentlemen Volunteers by Arlen J. Hansen describes the work of
      American ambulance drivers at the front.
Doctors in the Great War by Ian R. Whitehead is an account of
      how the army medical services expanded to cope with
      unprecedented casualties until, by 1918, more than half
      the nation's doctors were on active service.

Several books give an insight into the atmosphere on the home front:

The Katherine Mansfield Notebooks, edited by Margaret Scott
Ottoline Morrell by Miranda Seymour

The Enemy in Our Midst: Germans in Britain During the First World War by Panikos Panayi

I would like to thank my agent, Gillon Aitken of Gillon Aitken Associates, and my editor, Simon Prosser at Hamish Hamilton. Above all, I am grateful to my husband, David Barker, for his unfailing love and support.